ASCENT

A YA DYSTOPIAN SPACE ADVENTURE (BOOK
ONE OF THE CRIMSON DUST CYCLE)

J.S. ARQUIN

WORDS ON THE WIND, LLC

Library of Congress Control Number: 2019920318

❀ Created with Vellum

This book is dedicated to my Grandfather, Howard Davis. For a lifetime of stories delivered to my doorstep.

WANT EXCLUSIVE DEALS AND A FREE PREQUEL STORY?

Sign up for J.S. Arquin's newsletter here:
www.arquinworlds.com

1

———

Five hours. That's how long I've got. Five hours until the final round of the Guardian tournament. Five hours to make quota and get to Wayfinders. Three years of searching for my sister, Ianna. A year of training and planning. A whole month of qualifying rounds. And it could all fall apart in five dust-sucking hours.

I chew my lip as I crawl through the deep dark, far from the blazing sun of the dust-covered surface. My depth gauge says I'm at 1,500 meters. A kilometer and a half beneath the surface. Every year we deep divers have to delve farther to find greicagins, the mines branching and spreading in our wake like a deranged ant farm.

I usually like it down here, alone with the silent rock and the lichen shining on the cave walls. It's cool and quiet and there's no Papa Grady threatening to cut me loose if I grow another centimeter, no gang thumpers pushing me off their patch of sand. The shellbabys are my only company, retreating from the light of my headlamp, sucking their pale segmented legs back into crevices like vid run in reverse.

I check the time again and grind my teeth. Spines. I haven't made quota in three days. Of all the dust-sucking times to hit a dry spell. If I don't find some greicagins today, my entire plan blows away on the wind. Papa Grady's thumpers will never let me out of camp without my quota. And if I'm stuck in camp, I can't get to Wayfinders to compete in the final round.

Then I feel it. My skin gets warm, tingling like tiny bugs are burrowing beneath the surface. There are greicagins around here.

I stop and turn in the dark, trying to figure out which direction the tingling is strongest.

There. I step forward and angle my headlamp down into the fissure. The warmth intensifies. Blue flashes in the darkness. Relief makes my knees wobble.

Three meters down the crack opens up, and a small constellation of crystals sparkles. Greicagins. I can see blue, green, red, and yellow gins studding the walls of a cavern, a dozen or more. Each one containing enough power to run a gravbike for a week. Enough gins for a week's worth of quotas. My ticket out of here.

I dive face-first into the crevice, pushing my backpack in front of me. My belly scrapes over the cold stone. It's a tight squeeze, and I have to keep my arms extended, pushing myself along with little thrusts of my toes. I hate to admit it, but Papa Grady's right. I am getting too big to be a deep diver.

I scoot forward, contorting my body through the tight fissure. My hips scrape rock and I shift them to the left, sucking in my stomach and twisting them around a small spur of rock. Suddenly they wedge, the spur digging painfully into my hipbone. I try to twist my hips back, but they won't move. I'm stuck.

This is the moment all deep divers dread. Alone in the dark, stuck thousands of meters below the surface.

When I don't show up at the end of shift, they might send a runner to find me. One of the runners could trace my string down into the depths. Find me before dehydration turns me into a dust-mummy.

But why would they? It'd be easier to pretend they couldn't find me. A real shame, but oh look now there's a deep diver job open and they're ready to fill it.

And what about Ianna? My sister is out there somewhere, alone, with no one to look out for her. They separated us after our parents died three years ago. I've been trying to find her ever since. But

Canyon City is too big for a little deep diver like me to search. There are too many places she could be hidden.

That's why I have to win the Guardian tournament. Once I become a Guardian, I'll be able to find Ianna for sure. If I die down here, who will help her?

I turn my head, trying to shine my headlamp back to see where I'm stuck. My torso is in the way though, and the walls are too close to see anything. Next I try to wiggle backward, pushing at the cold rock with my hands, flexing my feet. Nothing. I can't go forward and I can't go backward.

My heart is thumping in my ears, my breath puffing in little gasps. Sweat slicks my forehead. Spines. I can't die here. Not when I'm so close to getting out.

Panic windmills my thoughts around and around. It's all I can do to stop myself from screaming and thrashing.

Stop. Think. What are your assets?

Jmini. Of course. I'm such a Rockhead. I didn't patch together my own salvaged AI for nothing.

"Jmini," I gasp. "What do I do?"

His dry British accent crackles through my earcone, "Well, Twist. You need to stop crawling into cracks you're too big to pass through, obviously."

"That's great, Jmini. You're one of the smartest AIs in Canyon City, and all you can do in this situation is make fun of me? I'm so glad I rescued you from the scrap heap."

"You do make a rather easy target, Twist, given that you can't move. It would be disgraceful to miss the mark."

"Thanks. Do you have anything to add other than snark? Helpful suggestions would be great."

"You could try climbing stairs. I hear it's very slimming. Though I suppose that would make your bottom bigger, not smaller."

"Jmini!"

"All right, no need to shout, Twist. Have you got anything on your belt that might be catching?"

I cock my head, trying to picture my belt and all the little things hanging off of it.

"Yeah, I might."

I wiggle back and forth a bit, trying to figure out exactly where I'm sticking. Sure enough, it seems like the root of the problem is on my left hip. I've got a small pouch there filled with rock samples. I'm supposed to put the samples in my backpack, but I've got a bad habit of slipping them into my belt pouch because it's quicker than taking my backpack on and off every time I knock off a chip of rock. Now that bad habit has got me wedged tight.

The good news is, if I can pull some samples out of the pouch, I should be able to get myself unstuck. The bad news is my arms are stretched out in front of me, and getting either of my hands to my belt will be difficult, maybe impossible.

I contort my body and manage to get my right hand tucked down beside my ribs. As I wriggle my fingers toward my belt, I hear a noise. I freeze. Nothing good makes noise all the way down here.

I click off my headlamp and lay still in the dark, listening. Down here the darkness is absolute. So dark you can't see the end of your nose. I usually find it comforting. I like to kill my light and sit in the dark and the quiet, letting it surround me like a cocoon. Pretend I'm somewhere far, far away from Canyon City. Far from Greica.

Not now though. Now my imagination fills the dark with things. Rock Horrors and Outsiders and Papa Grady's thumpers. Now I want it to hide me, keep me safe.

I hear the noise again, a scuffling, scraping sound. I hold my breath, my heart thumping too loud in my ears.

Beyond the crevice, the clustered greicagins sparkle with their own inner light. Multi-colored pinpricks shimmering in the darkness. Even through my terror it's beautiful. A tiny underground universe.

Then a beam of light lances across the cavern, followed by a dark shape. The light turns toward me, burning into my pupils.

"There you are, Twist. I thought I'd lost you." The voice is familiar, and cautious hope surges through me.

"Mink! What are you doing down here"

Mink's a runner. One of the scrawny kids that carries messages up and down the mine shafts. He's maybe nine years old and has a centimeter of knife-cut hair and a ragged vest full of pockets. He shouldn't be down this deep, but I'm glad he is.

"Scoring, obviously." He sweeps his headlamp around the chamber, illuminating the glittering greicagins.

"That's my score, Mink. Don't even think about it."

He puts a chisel to the wall and knocks a red greicagin free with a pair of quick, ringing taps of a hammer. He tucks it away in a vest pocket.

"I don't see your name on it, Twist."

"I was here first, Mink. And runners don't make scores. I'm the deep diver, not you."

"That's where you're wrong, Twist." Another greicagin goes into his bag. "After today, I won't be a runner anymore. After this score, Papa Grady will have to make me a deep diver." His voice quivers with excitement.

"You can't have it, Mink. It's mine. I need that score." I work my fingers down my side, frantically trying to reach my belt.

He barely glances at me, intent on knocking another greicagin free.

"Doesn't look that way to me. Looks to me like your deep diving days are over."

The tips of my fingers finally brush my belt pouch. I try to pull open the flap on top, but the snap is down around the side, right in the spot where it's wedged. Dust storms. I grit my teeth and suck in my stomach, doing everything I can to pull my body away from the rock. I strain with every muscle, jamming my fingers into the space. Skin peels back against the rock, slicking my knuckles with blood. Just a little farther.

The snap comes free with an audible pop.

I collapse with relief, laying my cheek against the cool stone, panting.

When I look up, Mink has knocked five more greicagins free. There are only four left now, three yellows and a green.

"At least leave me two," I plead. "You've got more than enough."

Mink shines his light into my face again.

"Would you have shared with me if I asked?" I want to say yes, but the first lesson you learn in Papa Grady's camp is you've got to look out for yourself. He sees the answer on my face and raises the hammer again. "I didn't think so."

I try bribery. It's the only play I have left.

"I need this score so I can get out of camp tonight. I've qualified for the final round of the Guardian tournament. Leave me two greicagins and I'll tell Papa you can have my job when I'm gone." There it is. All my cards on the table.

He sucks in a breath, eyes glittering with desire.

"You'd give me your job?"

"I swear it on the spines, Mink. Blood swear."

He eyes me warily, wanting to believe me.

"Do you really think you can win the Guardian tournament? What position do you play?"

"Chaser."

"You any good?"

"Level twenty-two. Fastest chaser in Canyon City."

I'm not lying either. When I'm on a gravbike, I've got wings.

"Huh." I can tell he's impressed. He swings the light from me to the last greicagins and back. He jingles his pocket, weighing the gins within. "Tell you what. I'll leave you something, on one condition."

Hope balloons inside me, making it hard to breathe in the tight crevice.

"Anything you want, Mink. Just say the word."

"When you become a Guardian, swear you'll come back for me. Get me out of here."

"You want out of the mines?"

"Come on, Twist. In a couple of years I'll be too big to be a deep diver, and I'll never be strong enough to be a breaker. Papa Grady will cut me loose, and then what? If I'm lucky I'll get in with a gang, get some protection. If not…"

He doesn't need to say any more. I know as well as he does how hard it is to get into a gang, and how bad the alternatives can be.

I nod, then lick my lips and find my voice.

"Ok, Mink. It's a deal. When I become a Guardian I swear I'll come back for you."

He knocks two more greicagins free, than stands over the last one, chisel poised. His shoulders hunch, and I can see his lips moving in some silent debate with himself. For a horrible moment I think he's going to change his mind, knock the last greicagin free and leave me here, stuck in the dark.

Then he pulls away. Turns to leave.

"I'm counting on you, Twist. Don't let me down."

"Mink! Give me a hand getting out of here?"

His back goes rigid, then his headlamp swings back toward me. His lip is curled with scorn.

"You want me to believe you're going to be a Guardian, and you can't even get yourself out of a crevice? Forget it, Twist. Deal's off."

He taps the last greicagin free and walks away. I writhe and curse, time running out as I lay trapped. Imprisoned over a kilometer beneath the surface of Greica.

2

———

I t takes ten minutes of grunting, sweating, and straining to pry myself out of the crevice. Then I'm running after Mink, sucking the blood from my scraped knuckles.

I've got to catch him before he gets to Papa Grady. Those greicagins are my ticket to the qualifier. Without my quota, there's no way Papa lets me leave camp tonight.

I pound through the cave, scrambling through cracks quick as a shellbaby. I follow my line up, retracing the path I took to get here. Mink has to be following my line too. How else would he have found me? He must have seen my legs wedged in that crevice and skirted around, found an easier way into the cave with the greicagins.

I would have found the easier way too, if I wasn't so impatient. That's what acting first and thinking later does: leaves you stuck in a crevice while some spine-sucking little runner steals your score.

Mink's had time to get a good lead, so I push myself to make up ground, dancing across ancient cave-ins without breaking stride. Down here, far from the straight paths of the mine shafts, nobody moves faster than a deep diver. After years of navigating caves, I can find the quickest way across a scramble at a glance. My best chance to catch Mink is down here, off the map. If he gets to the mine shafts, my advantage will be gone.

I think I see a light in the distance, across a grand cathedral cave draped with stalactites. I redouble my speed, but when I get to the far side of the cave, there's no sign of him.

I'm thankful for my deep diver's endurance. Ascending and descending thousands of meters every day has made me strong and tough as waxed rope. I've been climbing fast for half an hour and I'm hardly even breathing hard.

I emerge into a lit mineshaft and cast my eyes up the tunnel. No sign of Mink. Despair sags across my shoulders. Mink's gone. The runners spend their days carrying messages up and down the tunnels. His legs are as strong as mine are. On a straight, clear path I'll never catch him.

Still, I keep running. It's all I can do. Keep moving and hope for a miracle.

The tunnel becomes populated with miners and carts as I approach the surface. Dirty faces and rusty wheels. By the time I reach the entrance shaft, I'm weaving through a crowd.

Heat punches me like a fist as I burst out onto the surface, squinting against the sun. The camp spreads before me, spilling away from the mineshaft like tossed flour. It's bounded by high canyon walls, striated curves of red and white. Dry wind spins dust devils across the canyon floor, tickling my nose with the scent of hot stone. The devils shimmer in the waves of heat.

Sandstone spires rise thousands of meters from the valley floor, fantastic shapes sculpted by dust storms and monsoon rains. The ghostly pink outline of Hera, the larger of Greica's two moons, looms in the sky behind them. Silver spouts from the water collectors drip down the spires like gigantic icicles.

In contrast to the natural beauty of the surface, the camp is a disaster. Patched tents and falling down buildings fill the caves that pock the bases of the spires. Barracks that are little more than broken down lean-tos. Rocky streets lined with trash. All of it covered in a thick layer of crimson dust, reeking of the piss and sweat of a thousand unwashed bodies.

Home sweet home.

I find Mink in Papa Grady's office. It's one of the few permanent structures in camp, baked mud-brick walls and a fiber-press roof. There's even a poured cement floor, embedded with broad, flat stones, which helps to keep the sand and the heat out.

Papa Grady is a broad-shouldered man in an unbuttoned white shirt and a straw hat. He's got a permanent squint and deep lines in his tanned face from years in the desert. A puckered scar underlines his left eye.

Papa Grady looks up from his desk as I burst in past Orrin, the thick-armed thumper who guards the door. My greicagins are scattered across the fiber-weave surface.

"Those are mine!" I burst out, sliding to a stop beside Mink.

"Are they?" There's a warning growl in Papa's voice, his eyes small and hard.

"I mean, it's my score. I found them," I correct, squirming beneath that gaze.

"Did you." It doesn't sound like a question, but I make myself answer anyway.

"Yes, Papa, I did. Mink stole them from me."

"That's a serious charge. Mink, is this true?"

"No, Papa. It's not. I harvested the gins myself."

"After you followed me to them!" I shout. "That was my score and you stole it!"

Papa Grady sits back in his chair and crosses his arms over his chest. He looks pointedly from me to Mink and back again.

"Seems to me you're bigger than Mink here. Care to explain how you let a little runner steal your score?"

Too late, I see the trap. But I've already put my foot in it, no choice but to press on.

"I was wriggling through a crevice, with my eye on the score. Only half a meter away. Mink found a back way into the cave and stole my gins while I was getting myself out of the crack."

"He had time to do all of that? It must have been some crevice."

"That's not the point! He shouldn't have been down there at all! He was following me!"

Papa Grady's eyes flick to Mink, "Is that true?"

"No, Papa. I was off shift and just doing some exploring on my own. I didn't even know Twist was there until I started chiseling out the greicagins."

"You lying little dust-licker!"

I launch myself at Mink, tackling him to the ground. I get in two good punches before Orrin catches the back of my belt and jerks me up off the boy. The belt cuts into my stomach. I dangle in his grasp, my toes kicking above the ground.

"Papa, those are my gins. That's my quota. I need a pass into town tonight!"

Papa laughs, an ugly, grinding sound.

"No, I don't think so, Twist. You've missed quota four days in a row now. I think it's time for some fresh blood in the deep diver ranks." Papa Grady tosses me an assignment badge. "I'm reassigning you to the scrap vats tomorrow."

My mouth fills with dust.

"But, Papa…"

I don't get any further before a casual heave from Orrin lands me face down in the dust outside the office door. I pick myself up, knees and palms scraped and smarting. I turn to march back in, but the big thumper plants himself across the doorway, arms crossed over his chest.

I sway on my feet, clutching my new assignment badge. My head is spinning, the desert a blur around me. The scrap vats are full of toxic fumes and chemicals. Everyone who works there is dead within a few years.

"Give me another chance, Papa!" I call out. "I'm the best deep diver in this camp!"

"You were the best deep diver," Orrin rumbles. "Now you're nothing."

"Papa!"

No response comes from within. Orrin glares at me, immovable as a boulder across the entrance.

"Better move before I have to move you."

I turn and flee across the camp, blinking back stinging tears.

I slow as I approach the perimeter fence. The spires of Canyon City loom in the distance beyond it, less than twenty minutes by foot. They might as well be up on Hera.

"Jmini, how much time until the final?"

"Two hours, forty-two minutes and thirty-three seconds."

I wipe my eyes with the back of my hand, then my fingers close over the crescent-shaped pendant hanging against the base of my throat. The day I got it is the last happy day I can remember.

It was Founders Day morning, and the air was cool, the way it always is on Greica when the sun hasn't crested the wall of the canyon yet. Ianna and I were sitting on a blue blanket in the dust, staking out our family's spot for the parade. Founders Day is the biggest holiday of the year in Canyon City, and Ianna always dragged me out of bed early to get a good spot.

I remember her brown hair curling behind her ears, and her threadbare ragdoll, Kati, lying on the blanket beside her. We were playing marbles to pass the time, flicking the little glass orbs into a circle with our thumbs. The tip of Ianna's tongue peeked between her lips as she concentrated on lining up a shot.

"Spines, Ianna! Stop cheating!" The end of her red polka-dot scarf had come unwound again, falling across the marbles, disturbing their position.

"I'm sorry! It was an accident!" She tucked the scarf back around her neck, scattering more marbles in the process.

"I don't know why I even play with you." I huffed, crossing my arms.

"Sorry, I'll put them all back just like they were."

I watched her gather the marbles and place them back inside the circle one by one. Ianna had an amazing memory for small details, and I watched her return each marble to the exact spot it had been before. My little sister was thin and clumsy and always messed up our games. Her ability to fix her mistakes was the only reason I let her play with me. Well, that and our dad made me.

On cue, a shadow fell across the blanket.

"How are my little shellbabies today?"

"Dad, don't call us that!" I looked up, scowling.

"Yeah, we're not babies anymore." Ianna crossed her arms, mimicking me. Nothing brought us together more quickly than resisting an adult.

Dad plunked himself down on crossed legs, unfazed. His dark hair fell over his brown eyes, and he absent-mindedly pushed it aside.

"You'll always be my babies. Look, I brought you something. Hold out your hands."

We obediently stretched out our palms, and he dropped two small chunks of metal onto them. I opened my fingers to find a pendant as long as my little finger, strung on a piece of thin wire. Three small copper circles shining within a crescent of twisted wire and metal.

Ianna held her pendant up.

"It's beautiful. It looks like a moon."

"Or a warpknife." I slashed the air with my pendant.

"Where did you get them?"

"I made them." My dad proudly fished his own pendant out from under his shirt. It matched ours exactly. "Happy Founders Day."

Ianna peered through the pendant.

"It's got three circles. One for each of us?"

"That's right, smart girl." My dad smiled and ruffled her hair.

The three of us. Our mom died when Ianna was born. I don't even really remember her. It's always been me, my dad, and Ianna.

The low thump of a drum boomed in the distance.

"The parade's starting!" Ianna jumped up and down, clapping her hands.

I rose to my feet beside her, caught by her enthusiasm. I stood on my toes and peered down the street, trying to catch a glimpse of the approaching parade. The pendant slipped into my pocket, instantly forgotten.

If dad was hurt by how quickly our attention moved on from the pendants, he didn't let it show. He just stood behind us and placed his big hands on our shoulders. I could feel the warmth of his palm as the band swung into view, their instruments flashing in the sun.

Ianna squealed with delight and grinned at me, her cheeks dimpling. I grinned back, and we both grinned up at dad. A perfect family trio.

A week later, our dad was dead. Killed in an Outsider attack.

After that they stuck me out here in Papa Grady's work camp, while Ianna got sent somewhere else. I was only thirteen, and she was eleven.

I should have never let them separate us. It's my fault, I'm the big brother.

I thought if I won the final tonight, everything would change. But nothing ever changes around here.

I stare up at the five-meter-high fence surrounding the camp. There's only one gate, and it's guarded by half a dozen thumpers. No way I'll ever get past them. So much for all of my planning. I'll never even make it to the final, let alone win the dust-sucking thing.

Jmini clears his throat.

"Light thickens, and the crow

Makes wing to th' rooky wood."

I scowl and glance up to where the sun sits atop the canyon wall. In half an hour it'll be dark.

"Now is not the time for poetry, Jmini."

"There is another way, you know."

"I can't go through the mines after dark, Jmini. The Horrors come out at night. It's suicide."

"Are the scrap vats any better?"

He's got a point. I won't last a year in the scrap vats. I'd rather go feral than report to that assignment. Even if I don't win the tournament tonight, I'll have to run away. Join a scavenger gang or … something.

No. I won't. I'm going to win the final round. I have to.

But to get there, I have to get past the Horrors.

I stop at my tent and grab my few possessions - my game gear, my lucky blue marble, my grey scarf and goggles - then I'm off and running again.

3

The mines are quiet as I creep along the base of the cliff. Hera has nearly set and there's no sign of the second moon, Eros, as the stars wink into view behind the deepening purple sunset. The breeze brushes the hairs on my arm with the cool of incoming evening. Shadows pool around the entrances to the mine shafts, thickening to an impenetrable sludge inside their yawning mouths.

I stand outside the entrance to the shaft closest to the perimeter fence. Everyone knows there are secret paths to Canyon City inside the mine. During the day Papa Grady's thumpers guard the entrance.

Nobody guards them now. Nobody has to. Nobody would be stupid enough to go inside the mines after dark.

"I guess you can call me Nobody," I mutter.

Jmini clears his throat before he speaks. He thinks it's polite to warn someone before speaking directly into their ear. He's not wrong, really.

"Would that be your familiar name or your surname?"

"It's the name you can carve into my tombstone."

I stare into the midnight darkness of the mineshaft. It's still and silent, but I know there are things inside. Rock Horrors and Sand

Horrors near the surface. Deep Horrors that live thousands of meters below. Other Horrors with no names. Horrors that will take your head off in an instant.

"How much time until the final?"

"One hour, fifty-eight minutes, thirteen seconds."

"Right." I suck in a shaking breath. "I guess it's now or never."

I step forward and am swallowed by the shadows.

The Horrors were here long before we were. When the Interplanetary Extraction Coalition's first ships landed, the Horrors were waiting for them with crystalline claws as long as a human's body. The scientists couldn't communicate with the dumb, savage beasts, and their diamond-hard carapaces were impervious to conventional weapons. Moving with startling speed on their insectile legs, the Horrors cut the first scientific exploration team to shreds. And the one after that. Despite the fantastic wealth the planet's greicagin horde offered, the IEC almost had to abandon their attempts to colonize Greica before they even got started.

Then they developed warpknives. Blades with molecule thin edges that could cut through anything, even the tough carapace of the Horrors. Put the warpknife wielders in suits of power armor, and the first Guardians were born. It took a few years, but the humans eventually managed to carve out Canyon City, the first settlement on Greica.

The Horrors have been trying to kill us ever since.

I snap on my headlamp as soon as I'm out of sight of the entrance. There's no point trying to hide in the dark. The Horrors can see in infrared, ultraviolet, and other spectrums of light we cannot. The dark won't hide me from their multi-faceted eyes.

Jmini whispers in my ear, his voice dark and dramatic.

"Beware the Jabberwock, my son. The jaws that bite, the claws that catch! Beware the Jubjub bird, and shun. The frumious Bandersnatch!"

"Jmini! You are not helping!"

"My apologies. I turn to poetry when I'm nervous."

I roll my eyes. I must have the only AI in the world with a thing for poetry.

I move as quickly as I dare, walking on my toes, trying to stay silent. I'm not sure how well the Horrors hear. I only know that if they see me, I'm dead.

Forty meters down the path starts to branch off, and at each split I choose the one that seems to go toward Canyon City. I have no idea where I'm going. I've never been down here before. This shaft was mined out long before I came to the camp. All I can do is keep moving and pray for luck.

My ears strain at the darkness, alert for any sound beyond the rasp of my breath and the quiet crunching of my feet over the dust. So far, all I hear is silence. I hope it stays that way.

At the next branch I get my first piece of luck. Scratched into one wall is a symbol: two lines inside a rough circle.

"What do you think it means, Jmini?" I subvocalize carefully, forming the words with my tongue inside my mouth, letting no sound escape my lips. After the long minutes of silence, Jmini's answer sounds loud in my earcone.

"I would guess that the symbol was carved by smugglers."

"That's what I think too. But what does it mean?"

"Clearly the symbol means you should either take or not take this particular branch."

"Thanks, Jmini. That makes it clear as crystal."

"Always happy to help." His voice lacks any trace of sarcasm. I sigh quietly. Sometimes AIs can be oblivious.

I search the walls for other symbols, but find nothing. I hesitate, unsure what to do, terrified of making the wrong choice. Sweat beads on my forehead. I can practically hear the seconds ticking by in my head. I don't have time for this.

Finally my brain kicks into gear and I remember to search the floor. Relief breezes through me as I see scuff marks in the dusty floor of the marked tunnel.

Thirty meters into this new tunnel, I hear a sound behind me. Like rusty nails scratching over a steel plate. My blood turns to ice.

I walk faster, still trying to stay as quiet as possible. Praying the Horror isn't on my trail.

Then I hear the sound again, closer this time. I can't afford to be quiet anymore. I throw caution to the wind and run.

Anyone else would be caught easily. But I'm a deep diver. Running through the dark is what I do.

But even as I dash down the passageway, I hear the sound behind me. Many feet skittering and tapping. Metal on glass.

And it's getting closer.

I push harder, flying across intersections without slowing, choosing passages at random. Driven by pure terror.

Spines. Why did I think this would be a good idea? I wish I never heard of the Guardian tournament. I wish I was back in Papa Grady's camp. Dust, I even wish I was in the scrap vats. Anything would be better than Horrors in the dark.

I round a corner and my heart leaps. Light. There's light in the distance.

I redouble my speed, feet pounding, air whooshing in and out of my lungs in great gulps.

I shoot from the mouth of the cave, out into the star-filled night.

Two hundred meters ahead of me, the wall of Canyon City towers, floodlights glaring off the face of the massive stone structure. Eros rises in the sky behind it, the small moon a thin blue reclining crescent. Guardians stand on top of the wall, silver armor gleaming in the light.

Relief hits me so hard, my knees wobble. I'm still alive. I'm going to make it.

Then an enormous shadow rushes out the darkness behind me.

I run faster than I've ever run in my life. I don't think my feet are even touching the ground as pound across the dust, screaming and waving my arms at the Guardians.

They see me.

The Guardians' silver armor shines as they come boiling out of the gate. Warpknives hum in their fists. Each warpknife is powered by a greicagin embedded in its hilt, and streaks of blue and red power run along the edges of the blades.

I dash past them, and they close ranks behind me. Not a second too soon.

Five Guardians face down the Rock Horror. It towers over them, five meters tall, scuttling like a crab on a half dozen segmented legs, multi-faceted eyes shining in the floodlights. It holds its crystalline pincers high, gleaming yellow with an internal light, each razor-sharp edge longer my legs. A red and black carapace covers its back.

The Rock Horror flashes forward and suddenly it's got its pincer locked around one of the Guardians, lifting them up into the air, crushing them in its grip. Someone in the crowd screams as the pincer closes, the serrated edge slicing right through the Guardian's torso, nearly cutting them in half.

One of the other Guardians lunges, their warpknife parting the black carapace. The pincer tumbles to the dust, crushed Guardian still in its grip. Mist rises from the severed stump.

The Rock Horror shrieks, a piercing cry that echoes off the walls of the canyon. I reel at the sound and fall to my knees, eyes watering, shards of agony stabbing through my head.

By the time I recover, it's over. The body of the Rock Horror lies motionless, chopped into gory pieces, shrouded in rising mist. I stare at the massive carcass, caught between disgust and fascination. I've never seen a Horror this close before. In death, it seems unreal, like something from a game.

So does the Guardian that got caught in the pincer, their chest plate torn apart like rotten meat. Then I see the sparking wires within and realize it's not a Guardian at all, but a HAMRdroid, one of the remote-controlled units the Guardians use when they don't have enough manpower on site.

The other Guardians ignore both the dead Horror and the downed droid, clapping each other on the shoulders as they sheath their warp-knives. They look right past me too, but I don't mind. I'm alive. That's all that matters.

I eye their warpknives hungrily. Every kid with a stick pretends it's a warpknife as soon as they're old enough to know what they are. Playing at being Captain Steel and Heda Dustorm.

I wonder if the warpknives can do all the things the stories say they can. I wonder if I'll get the chance to find out.

Of course, to get a warpknife I've got to become a Guardian. And to do that I've got to win the tournament.

If I fail, I don't even have a deep diver's job to go back to now. If I don't win the Guardian tournament, I'm bound for the scrap vats, the scablands, or a desperate life scavenging on the street.

And I'll probably never see my sister again.

No pressure.

I turn and stagger away from the carnage. Through the gates. Into Canyon City.

4

———

Canyon City is a honeycomb built inside the towering sandstone spires that jut up from the canyon floor. The streets are a maze of broken roads and alleys winding between them, filled with dusty, exhausted people.

The IEC brought my grandparents here as part of the first wave of prisoners on Greica. Conscripts sentenced to work off their debt to society. Their hands carved rooms out of Canyon City's first spires. They say you could pluck the greicagins right off the surface back then.

Unfortunately, my grandparents didn't live long enough to pay off their debt. My dad didn't either. And now, after three generations of rockheads combing the canyons, the days of easy scores are long gone. Now we have to tunnel a kilometer down to find anything.

Meanwhile, the debt we've inherited from our parents and grandparents grows with every passing year. We're never getting out of here. I know it, and everyone I pass knows it too. You can see it on their faces. The hopelessness. The unbearable weight of the knowledge that we'll never be free.

Above it all sits Sunrise, home of the IEC executives and the original Guardian families. It's a town built on top of a flat mesa nine stories tall, where the Sunrisers bask in the sun and look down on the rest of us.

If I become a Guardian will I get assigned a bunk in Sunrise?

I snort. Not dusting likely. Keep dreaming, Rockhead.

The evening wind spins devils of crimson dust around my legs. The wind is picking up and there's a wall of clouds building on the horizon. Sandstorm. Maybe a big one. Glad I'm not still out in my ragged tent in Papa's camp.

As I pull my scarf up over my nose and mouth to keep the dust out, a clock on the side of a spire catches my eye. My stomach lurches as I realize how late it's gotten. I start to run again.

Wayfinders is on the third floor of an enormous, table-top mesa full of shops. It's one of about a dozen bio-electronic salvage centers that double as low-grade net connection centers. The kids of Canyon City flock to them, spending their hard-won coin to hone their skills at the Game.

Stick sees me come in and immediately gravitates to my side. His dark eyes are wide with excitement.

"Are you ready for the final?"

I smile down at him and ruffle his close-cropped hair.

"Ready as I'll ever be."

Stick's a wiry little kid who's been following me around Wayfinders the past couple of months. He never talks about his home; I don't think he has one. I try to give him tips on the Game when I can. I remember what it was like to be a little kid with no one to look out for me too.

The Game is singular. There's only one Game. If you get good enough at it, you can compete in the qualifiers. If you win a qualifier, you move on to the next round. If you win enough rounds, like me, you qualify for the finals of the Guardian Tournament.

After that? Nobody knows. What happens after the Guardian Tournament is secret. All we know is that if you win the Tournament, you train to become a Guardian. And we all want to be Guardians.

We all want to be anything, really. Anything other than what we are.

I come to Wayfinders whenever I can get a pass out of Papa

Grady's camp. I bring in bio-electronics I salvage from the camp scrap heaps, and in return Fin, the old junk dealer who runs the place, lets me comb through the piles of old parts and use whatever I want. That's how I found Jmini, and all the rest of my gear. Soldered together chip by chip from other people's trash.

Fin is bent over his workbench behind the counter, magnifying lenses down over his eyes. A fringe of grey curls tufts out around his gleaming, age-spotted dome. Wispy white hairs straggle from his chin.

He's got a soft spot for kids that ask questions, and he taught me everything I know about bio-electronics. Since my dad died his shop has been my refuge from the gangs and pimps that rule the streets, and from Papa Grady. I owe him a lot.

"You're in a hurry today, Theo," he observes without looking up.

"The final of the Guardian Tournament's tonight," I explain. "And my name is Twist." I snatch my gear out of my bag, tangling the wires in my rush.

"Guardians. I can't believe you worship those apes, Theo." Fin ignores my correction, as usual. I can never get him to call me anything but my proper name. It drives me crazy. "They are nothing more than prison guards puffed up with self-importance."

"Yeah? What about the Rock Horrors? One almost killed me on my way in. You think we could protect ourselves with this junk?" I wave my hand, indicating the cluttered, dusty shelves that fill the shop.

"I'm sure we'd find a way. People always do."

"What about the Outsiders then? Who would fight them? Did you forget they killed my dad?" I tug at my gear impatiently, tangling it worse.

"Without the Guardians, there would be no Outsiders. You should study some history."

"Spines take this thing!" I shout, hurling the tangled mess to the floor.

"Patience, Theo. Deep breaths. Think before you act."

"Easy for you to say. You never get upset about anything," I mutter.

I pick my gear up off the floor and take a deep breath. It doesn't make me feel any calmer. I chew my lip as I trace the paths of the wires, trying to find some way out of the mess. It seems impossible.

"That's not true. I get upset all the time. I just don't let it rule me. I recognize that I'm getting upset and give myself time to cool down before I do something rash."

"I'm young, Fin. I've got hot blood. Maybe when I'm old and crusty I'll have cold blood like you. But right now it's not that easy."

I put one of my earcones through a loop on the wire, then unwind it around my goggles. I think I'm making progress.

Fin laughs. "Oh, I remember what it was like. Believe it or not, I was young once too."

"Yeah, yeah. And when you were a kid, you could pluck greicagins from the street. I've heard it before, Fin. I still don't believe it."

"Believe it or don't. It doesn't make it any less true."

Fin sounds hurt, but I don't have time to deal with that right now. I've finally got my gear straightened out. It's time to do this thing. I set the earcones into my ears and pull on my haptic gloves.

Whispers have carried news of the final all around Wayfinders, and I'm surrounded by a circle of kids now. Stick stands by my side. The kids' eyes are fixed on the display above my head. While I'm in the Game competing, they'll be out here following my every move.

I take out my last two coins, rubbing my fingers over their smooth surface. I've been saving up for a month to afford this session, skipping one meal every day. Without my deep diver position in Papa Grady's crew, there won't be any more coins after this. If I don't win now, I'll never get another chance.

My palms are sweating. My mouth is dust-dry. I slip the coins into the slot and the start button blinks red in the center of my display. This is it. If I ever want to find Ianna, I have to win now.

I meet Sticks' eyes and force myself to grin. Nothing to worry about. This will be no different from the hundreds of practice runs I've done. No different than the qualifying runs I aced.

Raindrops. Easy and cool as falling water.

I settle my goggles over my eyes and the virtual world flickers to life. The entrance portal pulses before me, the Guardians' logo, a gold shield rotating within a circle of red, bright in the center.

I take a deep breath and step into the Game.

5

The virtual scablands of the Game is perfect. Canyon walls rise up around me, red and white layers stacked to the sky. The spiky limbs of reaperplants sway in the hot breeze, little whirlwinds spinning away across the sand. I'm sure the wind would smell of hot, dry stone if I had the gear to smell it.

A huge black-and-white checkered banner stretches across the canyon from wall to wall. The starting line. The hum of the spectators fills my earcones. Their avatars gather along the rim of the canyon or hover over the course in Hummingbird fliers and personal Dart rigs.

My armor is red and custom, with fins on my shoulders and wrists. A warpknife shimmers across my back. The armor is my pride and joy, won piece by piece over dozens of games. I've been putting it together for over a year and I still haven't gotten the entire suit: my right arm remains a drab, factory-standard grey.

The other competitors wink into existence one by one, their gravbikes parked beside them. They are all tall and beautiful, perfect teeth flashing in the sun. They could be anyone in real life, but I know that they're not. They're Sunrisers, every bit as perfect in the real as they are here.

A tan boy with ash-blonde hair and pale eyes stands in the starting box beside me. My head only comes up to his shoulder. His armor is an exact replica of the Guardians' suits, all graceful curves and polished silver. He glances at me and his lip curls in a sneer.

I look away, suddenly ashamed of my incomplete armor. It looks like I'm the only rockhead who made it into this final. I pretend to adjust something on my gravbike.

"Jmini, show me the course."

"Course map active," Jmini replies primly. I'm not wearing my helmet yet, so the overview projects up from the chassis of the bike.

This game isn't laid out like a normal game. Normally you work with a team to achieve an objective, each member bringing in a different set of specialized skills. But this qualifier is just for Chasers. Which means no team, just gravbikes and speed.

I suppose you could call it a race. A race with deadly obstacles.

My eyes are on the map, but I don't really see it. I'm thinking about the Sunrisers I'm competing against. Kids brought up with every advantage. I bet the haptic rigs they're using make mine look like garbage.

Who am I kidding? Mine is garbage. Garbage held together with solder and electrical tape.

I look up at the spectators lining the rim of the canyon. Sitting beneath umbrellas, sipping drinks with ice in them.

I don't belong here. Those people aren't here to see me. They're here to see their sons and daughters become Guardians. Watch them carry on the family tradition.

I wonder if it's even possible for me to win. I may be the fastest Chaser in Canyon City, but that doesn't mean dust when I'm competing against Sunrisers. Maybe their gravbikes are factors faster than mine. Maybe I haven't got a chance.

Dust that.

I grip the copper circles pressed against my chest, feeling the sharp edge cut into my skin. Ianna's out there somewhere. I promised my dad I'd take care of her.

I don't care what kind of gear they have, or who their parents are. I outran a Rock Horror to get here. They're all going to eat my dust.

I slide my helmet on and straddle my gravbike. Squeeze the

handlebars between my gloved fingers. The bike rises, humming softly, hovering half a meter above the ground. The chassis is red, matching my armor. The bike feels good beneath me. Solid but light as a feather, ready to pivot and leap at my command.

Down the line, the other contestants do the same. A dozen riders, poised in mid-air. Weight shifted forward over their handlebars. Sun gleaming off their armor.

The rectangular starter's platform moves out and hovers above the banner. The crowd goes quiet. The world holds its breath.

The starter's platform blinks red. Once. Twice.

Then it lights green.

As one, we surge forward.

It doesn't take long for the field to start thinning. Two hundred meters in I see a flash out of the corner of my eye. On the far side of the canyon a gravbike goes spinning out of control, trailing smoke. It slams into sandstone and bursts into flames.

"Dust storms," I breathe. "What was that?"

"Side cannon," Jmini informs me. "The rider beside him blasted out his stabilizer."

I wince. With the kind of gear these guys have, they feel everything. That rider is in a world of pain right now.

"Good to know. Keep your eyes open, Jmini. These Sunrisers will have weapons we're not used to seeing."

"Aye aye, Capitan," Jmini says, putting on a ridiculous accent.

I grin and shake my head. Greica is dozens of light years away from the seas of old earth, yet I've got an AI who thinks he's a pirate.

By the time we hit the first turn, two more riders have flamed out. I watch for incoming fire, but the other Chasers are too focused on taking each other out to be concerned with me yet. They don't think I'm a threat.

My gravbike's been able to keep up with the pack so far. They may out-gun me, but it doesn't look like they're going to run away from me. One piece of good news at least.

The canyon breaks up ahead, splitting into several smaller canyons, which then split into the fractured areas that give the scablands their name. I frown as I study the map.

"Which way, Jmini?"

Three routes light up on my display, traced in blue, green, and white.

"These all seem close to equal in length. The blue route appears to be the most open route. Green or white are slightly shorter, but require tighter maneuvering and decreased velocity."

"Which way should I go?"

"Most of the other competitors seem to be heading toward the blue route. You can play it safe and stick with the pack, or take a chance on one of the others. I suppose the real question is, are you feeling lucky enough to gamble?"

No, the real question is, can I afford not to? If I play it safe, the Sunrisers' superior equipment will give them the advantage. If I want to get ahead, I have to take a chance.

"Green line, Jmini. Run up the flag for lady luck."

"Aye aye, Capitan."

A rider with blue-grey armor peels off after me as I slip into the narrow slot canyon. A camera drone follows overhead, sunlight glinting off its fist-sized shell, streaming everything out to the spectators.

The rider immediately opens fire, their front cannons blazing away. A shot catches me on the left leg, and my left hand burns as my patched haptic rig shifts the pain to the closest area of contact. I curse, gritting my teeth.

"Spines! Evasive pattern!"

Jmini shifts the gravbike into stuttering evasion, shifting velocity and direction. The other rider sticks tight thirty meters behind us, their cannon fire kicking up dust and rocks all around me.

I study the upcoming terrain on the map and smile as I see a thin sandstone spire a hundred meters ahead.

"Smoke bombs and control back to manual on my mark . . . Drop!"

A trio of small cylinders explode in a white cloud behind me, momentarily obscuring the other rider. I lean my gravbike hard to the right, fishtailing in a tight circle around the spire. Seconds later, I come back around to where I started, only now the blue rider is in front of me.

"Fire dragonflies!"

The tiny missiles leap across the gap. The other gravbike explodes in a rain of steel. I whoop as I pass through the debris cloud.

"Nice shooting, Jmini."

"Yarrr, Capitan."

A fierce grin stretches my face. I lean into the handlebars and the gravbike leaps beneath me as I throttle up, shooting down the empty canyon. I have a feeling it's going to be smooth sailing from here.

6

Two minutes later, I'm not so sure.

Sweat drips down beneath my visor, running into my eye, making me wince and blink. My riding armor is soaked and heavy, the dark burn across my left forearm stings like it's full of fire ants.

I glance at the time in the corner of my display, blue numbers running backward. All the time I have left to complete the run. As I watch, it rolls below four minutes. 3:59. 3:58.

Jmini's voice fills my earcone. "You'll rejoin the main route ahead. Five canyons converge soon after that. At the first branching you want the soft right, not the hard right. After that, it's a straight run to the flag."

"Raindrops," I mutter.

I tighten my grip on the gravbike's handlebars and goose the throttle, the bike accelerating like it's being shot out of a rail gun. The bike hums, building vibrations that travel through my gloves and up into my shoulders.

We rocket out of our slot, back into the main canyon. The silver rider in the Guardian gear is there. His bike shoots over the sandy floor, a silver bullet, matching me speed for speed.

I glance at my rear display. Empty.

"Other riders, Jimini?"

"Negative, Capitan. Looks like there's only two of you left."

Fierce hope surges through me, with fear following close behind. If the silver rider is the only one left from the main pack, he must have taken out all the other Chasers. This guy is dangerous.

Something flashes, and I tap my brakes and swerve, pure instinct taking over. His side cannon sprays the dust in front of me, missing my nose by centimeters.

"That's the same trick he used on that rider back at the starting line," I gasp. "Almost got me too."

"He's probably full of them," Jmini says. The artificial calm of his voice is a jarring contrast to the pounding of my heart. "I'd watch out for this one, if I were you."

"Oh, would you? Thanks, Jmini. I never would have figured that one out on my own."

"Always here to help."

The canyon is several hundred meters wide here, so I veer to the far side, keeping a careful distance from the other Chaser. Ahead, I see the place where the five canyons come together. I lean low over my handlebars, the gravbike surging like an uncoiling rock hound.

I have a feeling the biggest obstacle is still ahead.

The ambush hits right where I thought it would, five blocky attack dozers lurching out as we shoot into the area where the canyons converge. Even though I'm expecting the Outsiders, my stomach still sours with fear. I can't match their armor and weapons in a fight. If I let them box me in, they'll use their flamethrowers to burn me to char. Game over.

At least they'll keep the other Chaser occupied. I hope.

I throttle hard, trusting my instincts. I zip past the flanking Outsiders, leaving only a single dozer between me and the spur canyon I want. It's a huge, looming beast, bristling with sleek rockets and the ugly mouths of guns. An enormous scoop is welded onto the front of the dozer, the steel plate nearly filling the canyon from wall to wall. If the dozer gets in front of me with that scoop, I'm squashed. I grit my teeth and accelerate again, the gravbike kicking and whining in protest.

I veer to one side, angling around the dozer. Sun glints off the scoop as the Outsider turns with me, blinding me for a second. A gusting crosswind pelts me with dirt and pebbles as loose scree skitters beneath the gravfield. The dozer's guns bark. I wrestle the bike into an evasive pattern, the shots kicking up little puffs of dirt around me. My breath hisses through gritted teeth.

The timer on my display ticks down relentlessly. 2:45. 2:44.

I'm closing in on the canyon wall, but the dozer is closing the distance just as quickly.

"Thirty meters. Twenty. Ten," Jmini informs me, the AI's voice calm and dispassionate. "Collision imminent."

"Tell me something I don't know," I growl.

The scoop of the dozer scrapes the wall in a shower of rock, and I can see the mutant driver perched on top of the great beast, his yellow teeth bared in a hideous grin. It looks like I'm not going to make it.

Which is exactly the way I planned it.

I yank the handlebars hard and lean to the left. The gravbike goes into a skid, showering the scoop with a seven-meter-high plume of gravel. I lean into it hard, slewing the bike so low to the ground that my kneepad skips across the dirt, the skin-shredding rocks flashing by centimeters from my face. I feel the gravbike lurch, losing traction, and the skid goes from controlled to dangerous in an instant. I start to fall, the ground rushing up to shred me with teeth of red rock.

Then I hit the scoop, and the gravbike isn't on the ground anymore. I switch to magnetic mode, and the magfield latches onto the thick steel, holding the bike perpendicular to the ground. As I shoot across the front of the dozer, the great expanse of the scoop hides me from the driver's view. My lips peel back in a grin of my own. I've got him now.

Just before I reach the end of the scoop, I kill the magfield and slide the gravbike back down to the earth, pivoting sharply around the corner of the dozer. Before the driver realizes what's happening, I'm past the metal beast and accelerating away into open canyon. I leave the Outsiders behind, scattered like reaper spines on the wind.

I whoop in triumph. Now it really is game over. I'm the fastest rider in Canyon City, no one can catch me once I really get going. I feel like the gravbike and I have been melded together into one flesh, as if the cycle's struts are smooth extensions of my skeleton.

Then the silver rider pulls up beside me.

"Dust storms! What does it take to get rid of this guy?"

"You could try not brushing your teeth for a month, I hear that really pushes people away."

"Not the time for jokes, Jmini."

The silver rider's side cannons flash and I swerve again and again. I've gotten the hang of them now. Their barrel glows a split second before they fire, which makes them predictable.

He realizes this too, so he throttles up and swerves directly toward me, slamming his gravbike into mine. My bike slews wildly, kicking up huge plumes of dust as I struggle to maintain control.

He does it again, but I'm ready for it this time, and lean my bike into the impact. He's not going to knock me off that way.

The third time he hits me, he takes it a step further. Just before impact, he launches himself across the gap, latching onto the back of my armor like a deranged rock beetle.

I swerve wildly, fighting to keep control of the gravbike with the added weight. He locks his arm around my throat and pulls, trying to haul me off the bike. I swing my elbow back into his ribs, but his grip only gets tighter. He's bigger and stronger than I am, but I've got the better position. We struggle back and forth, each trying to knock the other off the bike. The gravbike veers unpredictably beneath us as our weight shifts, and a sandstone boulder almost takes my head off.

I'm getting tired. I don't know how much longer I can hold on.

It's my turn to do something unexpected.

"Jmini, full chest plate maglock on my mark. And . . . now!"

I yank down on my handlebars and lean forward as Jmini activates the maglock. The magnetic field jerks my chest plate down toward the chassis of my bike. As the steel surfaces lock together, I slam on the brakes. The maglock is the only thing that keeps me from flying over the handlebars. I slam forward inside my armor like I've hit a wall. The air huffs out of me.

My attacker is not so lucky. Inertia tears him from my back and he flips over the front of the gravbike, skidding and tumbling in the dust.

I lay there in a cloud of drifting dust. It hurts to breathe.

"Twist, are you all right? Can you hear me?"

It takes a few tries, but I eventually get some words out.

"Yeah, Jmini. I think so. I mean, everything hurts, but other than that, no problem."

"Well, I hate to interrupt your little interlude, but you might want to check your timer."

I turn my eyes to the blue numbers in the corner of my display. 0:58. 0:57.

"Spines," I groan. "Where's the flag?"

"It's three hundred meters ahead of you. The same place it was before you took up the sport of extreme brake testing."

I start to laugh. It hurts, and I groan, but that just makes me laugh harder.

Laughing and groaning, I pull my protesting body upright in the saddle. I throttle up, veering around the mangled armor of my fallen rival.

0:26. 0:25.

The flag juts from the rock ahead, halfway up the canyon wall. I throttle up and wrestle the gravbike onto a rising spar of rock, then yank up hard on the handlebars as the bike launches me into space.

I snatch the flag with five seconds to spare.

The spectators gasp, then their roar fills my earcones. Faintly I hear the kids in Wayfinders screaming. Hands clap my shoulders and back.

My stats scroll down on my display, glowing gold. Gold. Top rank.

The canyon shifts, blanking out. Then a new pop up flashes before me. The Guardians' logo, a gold shield rotating within a circle of red. My breath catches as text fills the screen:

"Congratulations. You have won an invitation to the Guardian training center. Pass through to enter."

7

I knuckle my scratchy eyes, scrub my hands over my face in frustration. Stick is passed out on the floor beside me, curled on a scrap of rug like a cat.

I've been up all night, trying to gather information on Guardian training. Scouring old servers, looking under every electronic rock I could overturn. Hours of searching, and all I've been able to find out is that the winners of the tournament go into Merrimac, the Guardian training facility. That's it. What happens after that is anyone's guess.

"I don't suppose I can talk you out of it."

Fin shuffles out from behind dusty piles of junk, clutching a steaming cup of coffee. His magnifying lenses are shoved up onto his forehead, his grey fringe sticking out in all directions. A strand of cobweb trails from his left ear.

"You think I should report to the scrap vats instead?" I snort. "Besides, becoming a Guardian is the only way I can find Ianna."

He frowns, the corners of his mouth gathering wrinkles like a slow-motion avalanche.

"I had a student once, years ago. Bright kid, like you. He got invited to the Guardian training center too. I never saw him again."

"Maybe he lives in Sunrise now."

"Maybe. But not even one visit in all these years? I think he'd want to show off his shiny armor, if nothing else. Word on the street is, that training center is dangerous. A lot of kids go in and they don't come back out."

"I have to go, Fin. For Ianna. For my dad."

My eyes don't waver, and he sighs, sips his coffee. He looks tired, and suddenly ancient.

"Be careful, all right? Those Sunrisers are a nest of sand stingers. Never trust them. They might hold the weapons, but we were born down here. Canyon City belongs to us. Remember that."

He puts his arms around my shoulders and presses my face to his smock, his chin whiskers tickling my ear. He smells like coffee and overheated circuits. Like the dad I no longer have.

Tears well up in my eyes, catching me off guard. I've been so focused on moving forward, I never realized I'd be saying goodbye. Fin has meant so much to me since my dad died. I wonder if I'll ever see him again.

I blink back the tears and pull away.

"Thank you, Fin. For everything. I'll come back, I promise."

Stick follows me out of Wayfinders, quietly coming up beside me when I stop across the street from Merrimac.

"Are you really going in there?" His voice is full of awe. And with good reason. Rockheads like us don't go into Merrimac. Not ever.

"Yeah. I guess I am."

"Will you come back?" His voice wavers, and his lower lip shakes like he's on the edge of tears. I squat down and look him in the eye. His dark skin is smudged with crimson dust.

"Yes, Stick, I'll come back."

"Promise?"

"Promise."

I can tell he doesn't quite believe me, but he wants to, so he nods and tries to smile. I smile back and ruffle my hand over his close-cropped hair.

"Take care of Fin for me, ok? He's old. He needs someone to watch out for him."

Stick nods seriously.

"Good. Thank you." I ruffle his hair one last time, then I stand and take a deep breath. Merrimac awaits.

It doesn't look like much from the outside. Crimson walls, thick windowpanes - your typical government building. I stare at it from the shade of a tall reaperplant across the plaza, running my eyes up the wall of rock above the door, following the windows up. I count all eight levels, and squint at the lip of the plateau. Sunrise is up there, sitting above us like some golden goose.

Inside the white-tiled lobby I stumble to a halt. The air is cool and smells like rain. An indoor waterfall trickles down the wall. After a lifetime of breathing hot dry dust, I can't decide which is more shocking, the coolness or the waterfall. I don't know how long I stand there, looking like a rockhead, before the receptionist breaks me out of my stupor.

"Your name?"

I tear my eyes from the waterfall and track the voice to a man with a face like a puckered raisin, seated behind a small slate desk.

"Twist, uh, I mean Theo. Theo Maro."

He looks up and to the side for a moment, clicking his tongue. Then his eyes focus back on me.

"Yes, I've got you on the list."

List? I drool as I realize he must have data implants that let him access the net anywhere. I'd give my last spit for implants like those.

"Through there," he says, gesturing to a heavy metal door. "Strip and put on the uniform you find in the cubby. Leave your belongings there. Then proceed through the door at the far end of the changing room."

I squeeze the straps of my backpack tight, thinking of my gloves and goggles inside.

"What about my gear?"

"Gear will be provided."

"But what will happen to my stuff?"

"It will be incinerated. No outside materials are allowed in the testing area. Candidates are allowed one personal item only."

"One? Incinerated?"

My heart tries to leap out of my chest. My gear is my most precious possession in the world.

Jmini clears his throat in my earcone.

"I'd like to register a formal complaint."

"You and me both," I mutter. I back toward the door. "You can't . . . I mean . . . Can't I just leave my gear at home?"

The words fasten around my neck like a lead chain as I remember I don't have a home. I've been reassigned to the scrap vats. The room is suddenly too hot, too small.

Wayfinders then. I'll leave my gear back at Wayfinders.

But the man is speaking.

"That's out of the question. Once you check in, your training has begun. There is no postponement and no second chances. You are free to leave. But you may not come back."

I've got my back against the wall beside the door, unable to move. One personal item. I can't let them incinerate Jmini. I can't let them take my pendant either. And I definitely can't abandon the tournament. I'm frozen between unacceptable options.

A scrawny girl with charcoal skin steps through the front door, letting a blast of heat in with her. She's tiny and looks like she's maybe ten years old. The kinky hair on her head is barely higher than the desktop.

She strides right up to the desk, and the man tells her what he told me. As the girl turns toward the metal door she catches sight of me huddled against the back wall. Her eyes measure and dismiss me. She passes through the door without breaking stride.

That's it. If she can do it, so can I. There's no halfway here. If I'm in, I've got to be in all the way. I square my shoulders and wrap my fingers around my pendant. I take a deep breath.

"I'm sorry, Jmini," I whisper.

Then I remember Stick.

I whirl around. Sure enough, he's still standing across the street, watching me through the window. I crack the door and motion him over with my hand.

Jmini whispers in my ear, "But who will navigate the ship, Capitan?"

"I'll have to find my own path now, my friend. Help Stick find his way."

I take out my earcone & stretch my hand out to Stick. "Here. Can you take care of Jmini and my gear for me?"

His eyes are as big as gears as I hand over my earcone and backpack. He nods solemnly.

"Thanks, Stick."

I ruffle his hair one last time, before turning to march through the door opposite. I wipe my eyes with the back of my hand as I pass through.

Neat rows of cubbies stretch away to both sides, filling the room beneath a low, unfinished ceiling. There are no signs, so I follow rustling sounds of movement to my left. I find two boys and a girl halfway down the row, placing their clothes in the cubbies. Sunrisers.

One of the boys is tall with ash-blonde hair. He looks familiar, but my gaze is drawn to the second boy. He is one of the biggest humans I've ever seen. He sports a shaved head and a braided rat-tail down the back of his neck. He has to duck to keep from cracking his skull on the ceiling.

The girl is facing away from me, but turns as I enter the row. She's got long legs and tanned, red-gold skin. Her hair falls to the top of her shoulders in dark curls. Her stomach is smooth and flat, her breasts high and small. I know these last bits because she's standing in her bra, a brown shirt half-lifted above her head.

"Take a flash, it'll last longer," she snaps.

I turn away, blushing.

"Sorry."

"Dust-sucking rockhead," the giant boy growls.

I glare at him beneath my brows, but I'm better off pretending I didn't hear his insult. His arms are as big around as my legs. One of the most important survival skills in Canyon City is knowing when to pick your battles.

I find the little girl from the check-in desk halfway down the next row of cubbies. She's pulling a loose brown shirt over her head that matches the pants she's wearing. She doesn't look at me directly, but I can tell she's watching me out of the corner of her eye, like a speckled cave lizard waiting to see which way I'll move.

I take a cubby a safe distance away from her, and pull down an identical set of brown clothes. The fabric is soft, but feels sturdy, and there are drawstrings at the wrists and ankles to adjust the length. One size fits all.

When I glance down the aisle again, the girl has disappeared, leaving me alone with the empty cubby mouths gaping at me. Which suits me fine. I didn't want her watching me change anyway.

I replace my clothes with the brown shirt and pants, and press my fingers against my chest, tracing the copper circles that hang there. I don't care what they say; the pendant stays with me. Nothing will make me give that up.

Tears well as I turn away from the cubby. I miss Jmini's voice in my ear already. Stick better take good care of him. I chomp hard on my lip, focusing on the physical pain as I fight down the emotion. I wipe my cheeks dry with the back of my hand. Now is not the time for this. Maybe later, when my training is over.

There's no going back. Maybe life is like the Game after all. Once you've passed a level, you can't return to it. You have to keep moving forward.

8

We gather in a large room deep inside the rock. It looks like a natural cave that's been extended and hollowed out, the ceiling is so high it disappears into shadow. It's deep enough that it's a little chilly, and I have to rub the goosebumps from my arms. There are about fifty of us standing around in our brown clothes. Most of the kids are clearly from Sunrise, including the ones I ran into in the changing room. They stand together in clusters, as perfectly sculpted as sandstone spires. The ash-blonde boy from the changing room sneers down at the rest of us.

It burns my ego, but I have to admit that if I was one of them, I'd probably sneer at us too. Compared to the Sunrisers, the handful of Canyon City kids are a sad-looking bunch. Most seem to be around my age, except the scrawny girl from before, who is definitely the youngest. We look undernourished and desperate. Even wearing the same clothes as the Sunrisers, we stand out like reaper plants in a rock garden.

"Not exactly what I was expecting," a boy says. He's a head taller than me, with thick fingers and freckles scattered across the bridge of his pug nose and over his cheeks. His doughy skin looks gray. One of his wrists is wrapped with tape, and brown heat-shield stains cover his hands and arms up to the elbow. He must be a welder. He rubs a hand over his bristly clay-colored hair.

"What were you expecting?" I ask.

"I don't know. Goggles and gloves? Not this."

"Did you get in through the Game?"

"Yeah. I'm Rory. Gunner." He extends the hand without the tape.

"Twist. Chaser," I say, pumping it once. His grip is strong. "Level twenty-two."

He whistles low, and eyes me up and down, impressed.

"You must be fast."

"Fastest rider in Canyon City. What about you?"

"Oh, I'm just a fifteen," he mumbles.

I scrunch my nose up, puzzled.

"A fifteen? And you got through the tournament?"

"Yeah," he says, folding his arms defensively. "What's wrong with that?"

"Well, nothing, I guess. It just seems strange is all." I flounder, wanting to change the subject. I nod toward his taped wrist. "Hurt yourself?"

He smiles wryly and rubs it with his good hand. "Yeah, I sprained it in the qualifier. Even with crappy haptics, the game hurts, you know?"

"Yeah, I know. I got this yesterday." I roll up my sleeve and show him the bubbly scab where the blaster burned across my forearm.

"That'll be a nice scar," someone says. I turn to find the little kinky-haired girl staring up at me.

"I'm Shadow," she says before I can ask. "Covert, twenty-fiver."

Now it's my turn to whistle. Twenty-five is the highest level there is.

"A spy, huh?" I say.

"And a good one," Rory adds.

"Best in Canyon City," the girl replies, echoing my words with a tight little smile.

"How old are you?" I ask.

"Old enough," she snaps, jutting her chin forward in challenge.

"I didn't mean anything by it." I raise my hands in surrender and turn to Rory. "Apparently some people are prickly about their age."

"Don't mind him," Rory says to Shadow. "He's just jealous. If you're really a twenty-fiver, you can be whatever age you want to be."

Shadow squints at him, suspicious, but before she can decide if he's serious or not, a deep voice interrupts us.

"Old enough for what, exactly?" The big guy from the changing room puts his hand on her head and leers down at her. "Yeah, I guess you're old enough to clean my boots."

Shadow whirls and punches him right between the legs. I gape at her. The big guy's face slowly crumples.

The ash-blonde Sunriser steps up and pushes Shadow to the ground. Instinctively, I push him back. Someone punches me in the side of the head, then Rory leaps forward and tackles them. In seconds there are limbs flying everywhere. We Rockheads fight hard, but the Sunrisers are bigger, stronger, and better fed. And there are more of them. A lot more.

Rory screams as the big guy grabs his injured arm and twists hard. I'm flailing away, trying to return punches, but there are a lot more that are hitting me. Then someone kicks the back of my knees and I go down, curling into a protective ball as the blows rain down on me.

Mercifully, a siren blares across the chamber, and everyone jumps back. A voice booms out of hidden speakers.

"Welcome to Merrimac, candidates. My name is Instructor Castle."

I gingerly pick myself up off the floor. I feel like I've been trampled by Horrors. A projection of a bald man appears in the air above us. He's got a deep tan and a square jaw; his lined face radiates vigor like desert rocks radiate heat. I'd bet good coin he's the type of maniac who goes for a ten kilometer run every day before the sun rises. When he speaks, he exposes big, square teeth, bleached white as bone.

"Congratulations, you've made it into the Guardian tournament."

I hear my surprise echoed around the room. Instructor Castle grins.

"What, you thought you'd already made it through the tournament? No. That was just the qualifier. The real tournament starts now. If you've made it this far, it means you're good. Very good. Some of you probably think you could walk out that door and become a

Guardian right now." He chuckles, but his blue eyes are hard. "Let me assure you that is not the case. No matter how good you think you are, the Guardians are better. Beside a full Guardian you are as competent as an infant."

He lets that sink in for a moment, and we all squirm beneath his intense gaze.

"Those of you who survive the training will become a part of the most important force in the scablands. Make no mistake, the Guardians are all that stands between this settlement and destruction. Every day we are under attack by Outsiders and Rock Horrors. Every day the Guardians repel these threats.

"Being invited to join this force is the highest honor imaginable. You should be proud to be standing here. You need more than skill to become a Guardian. You need desire and toughness, brains and resourcefulness. At the end of the tournament, twenty-five of you standing before me will earn a place in our graduating class. The other twenty-five will not. Many of you will not even make it that far."

There's a flutter of shock and dismay around me. One of the Sunrisers laughs. My mind whirls with panic, and I squeeze my hands into fists so tight that my nails dig into my palms.

I knew this was too good to be true. I knew Canyon City kids didn't simply become Guardians. I look at the assembled crowd around me. The Sunrisers look smug and unsurprised. The Canyon City kids look shaken.

Sweat slicks the back of my neck. Half of us.

If we're going to be sent home, why invite us in the first place? Why are we even here?

As if in answer to my thoughts, the man speaks again.

"I can tell from your faces that some of you think the game is rigged. I can see those of you who grew up in Sunrise relaxing. You think you've got it made. Let me assure you that you do not. We will take the best twenty-five candidates, no matter where they are from. And you can be cut from the program at any time. Do I make myself clear?"

The Sunrisers nod soberly. It makes me feel a bit better to see the smirks wiped from their flawless faces.

A projection fills the wall behind him. A list of names in blue runs down the left side: Desert Wolves, Sand Stingers, Dust Lizards, Midfalcons, Rock Hounds, and a handful of others. On the right are point totals in white. All the points read zero.

"This is the leaderboard. It's how we will track your progress. You will collect points as a team, based on your performance in classes and in game simulations. Fall too far down the board, and you will fall out of Merrimac entirely.

"You will also be tracked as individuals." The board changes, listing fifty names in blue. I find Theo Maro near the bottom. "These scores will be secondary to your team scores, but they will still carry weight. If your team is dropped from the board, a high individual score may save you from expulsion. Or it may not." He chuckles, and a smattering of nervous laughter echoes him.

"I know you're all eager to get started, so I won't keep you any longer. Your first challenge is simple."

Huge spotlights come to life, illuminating the darkness behind the projection as the man continues. They reveal five doors set into the far wall of the cavern.

"Upstairs you'll find your team and bunk assignments. Find out where you go, and get there. The first ten trainees to arrive get ten points each."

"That's it?" the Sunriser girl with the curls asks. "Seems pretty simple."

"Appearances can be deceiving."

"This is in the flesh?" someone in the crowd pipes up. Their voice shakes. "I think there's been a mistake. I was invited here through the Game."

"Indeed, you were. As were most of your companions. Prowess in the game proves that you possess certain skill sets that will be valuable should you become a Guardian. But they are far from the only skills that you will need. Before we waste our time training you, we have to be sure you possess certain … other qualities."

"Such as?" another voice asks. I'm startled to realize it's my own.

"If you were listening to my speech, you'd already know the

answer to that. Can anyone enlighten this young man? What do you need to become a Guardian?"

"Desire and toughness," Shadow calls out. Her voice does not wobble. "Brains and resourcefulness."

"Nice to see someone was paying attention," the man says. His blue eyes measure the little girl for a minute, before turning to the group of Sunrisers. "This tournament will not be the cakewalk you think it will."

"What are the rules?" the Sunriser girl asks.

"Win. Survive. Nothing more."

The big Sunriser with the rat tail grins at this, and exchanges wolfish smiles with the ash-blonde boy. A chill runs down my spine.

Other mouths open, but the man holds up a hand, silencing them. "Hang on to the rest of your questions. I'll answer them once you've gotten settled in. Good luck. May the sun be at your back."

The projection disappears, leaving us all standing around gawking at each other uncertainly.

"Well that was unexpected," Rory says. He runs his hand over his injured wirst, wincing. "What do we do now?"

In response, Shadow takes off running. A collective gasp goes through the crowd as we watch her scamper through one of the doors and disappear. Then, like a herd of startled springtols, we all leap for the doors as one.

9

I choose the center door, the same one Shadow took. As I step through, an elbow slams into the side of my head, sending me reeling into the wall. I cling to the rough stone as the huge Sunriser with the rat-tail storms past me. He boots me in the face on the way by, spinning my head around. As the world sways and blurs, everyone else storms past me too. I curse and do my best to stumble after them.

It's crowded in the passage. More than one kid goes down, victim of a quick elbow or tripping foot. Rory goes down right in front of me, crashing headfirst into a wall. Nobody stops to help him.

"Hey, are you all right?" I squat down beside him, help him sit up against the wall. Bright blood spreads over his face from a gash in his skull.

"Fine," he says. His eyes are wide and unfocused.

I pull the ties on the sleeve of his shirt, loosening the extra fabric. I fold it into a ball in his hand, then lift his hand over the wound.

"Hold this here. You're bleeding. Press hard, ok?"

He looks at me and blinks, his eyes slowly focusing on my face. Then he jerks back, as if suddenly realizing where we are.

"What are you doing?" he asks suspiciously.

"Helping you, dust brain."

"I don't need your help." He pushes me away and levers himself back up to his feet. He staggers away down the passage. "I can take care of myself."

"Yeah, all right. Of course you can." I shake my head and jog after him.

We follow the hum of voices to the end of the hall, and find a crowd standing before a big leaderboard set high on the wall. As we approach, at least a dozen kids dash off to find their bunks. Clearly we are not going to be in the first ten.

I duck under arms and squirm past elbows, making my way to the front. Halfway down the board, I find my name listed under Team Three: Dust Lizards. The other members of the team are Shadow, Rory, and a couple of names I don't recognize.

Rory and I grab a chunky yellow tablet from a slot in the wall, and follow a map down the hall. The interior of Merrimac is amazing. It's hollowed from the very heart of the Mesa, halfway between Canyon City and Sunrise. The red sandstone corridors are wide and airy, the floors and ceiling polished and smooth, with no hint of the unfinished stone you usually see in Canyon City. The floor is tiled with polished white granite, and there's not a hint of dust in the milk-blossom scented air. Service bots of all shapes and sizes move about, intent on their single-minded tasks.

We step between a pair of gleaming HAMRdroids, into an alcove off one of the main corridors. A heavy metal hatch is set into the floor. Through the hatch and down a metal ladder, we find ourselves in a roughly circular, windowless room. Five carbon shells are spaced around the room, their covers sleek and shiny.

"Full immersion shells," I whisper.

I pop the nearest one open reverently, fingering the blue padding within. It flows around my hand like living sand. Maybe leaving my old gear behind wasn't such a bad thing after all.

Below each shell is a locker, containing three sets of clothes, a chunky yellow tablet for personal use, and a shiny watch. I pick the watch up. The steel casing is cool beneath my fingers.

"We're supposed to wear those at all times." Shadow's sitting on the bed of her shell, the lid propped open behind her. Her feet dangle, swinging back and forth. She looks like she's been here a while.

"Ok." I slip the band around my wrist and turn to face the rest of the team.

A gangly Sunriser with protruding front teeth sprawls in an open shell. He's all elbows and knees, leaning over his tablet, face scrunched into an annoyed scowl. I stare at his legs. They are shining steel. I wonder if he's got real legs under there or if he's half-droid. I want to ask, but his expression says, "Do not disturb."

Standing next to the fifth shell is a huge islander girl - almost as big as the boy from the changing room. She's got shaggy black hair that covers her eyes and stands silent, her hands interlaced in front of her, dirty fingernails tapping out a rhythm on her knuckles. She must be from the greenhouses, there are a lot of islanders in that part of Canyon City. I've never met one though. They don't really mix with outsiders.

Rory stands in front of his shell, his stained arms crossed in front of his chest. He's scowling at the islander and the droid boy.

"Well. It looks like we're the Dust Lizards," I say, attempting to break the ice.

No one reacts to my statement. I raise an eyebrow at Shadow. She just shrugs.

"Maybe we should start by introducing ourselves. I'm Twist. Chaser, level 22."

Again, I'm answered by silence. Shadow rolls her eyes and goes next.

"Shadow. Covert, twenty-fiver."

Rory glares at the others. The gangly boy hunches closer to his tablet. The big girl gives no indication that she's even noticed our existence. Rory scowls and huffs, but finally gives up and opens his mouth.

"Rory. Gunner. Level 15." When the others still don't react, he slams his hand down on the metal of his shell. The bang makes us jump. "Don't all talk at once."

The boy shifts in his shell, his adam's apple moving up and down. His eyes never leave his tablet, but he croaks out, "Grab. Mapper. Obviously, I'm not supposed to be on this team."

"What's that supposed to mean?" Rory demands.

Grab's eyes flick up at Rory, then quickly down again.

"One of these things is not like the others. You figure it out," he says.

"You think you're better than us? Is that it?" Rory takes a step toward Grab, his fist clenched.

"Can we at least finish our introductions before we start beating the dust out of each other?" I say, stepping between them. "Is that too much to ask?"

Rory stares hard at me, then shrugs and turns his back.

"Whatever you say, Chief."

I exhale, then turn to stare at the girl, still tapping away at her knuckles.

"You must be Knott."

"Himene'e polau," she says.

I stare at her.

"What the dust does that mean?" Rory demands.

"Singo tat," Knott clarifies.

"Maybe she doesn't speak standard," Shadow ventures.

I curse.

"Dust storms. How are we supposed to coordinate our runs if she doesn't speak standard?"

"You need aural implants," Shadow says. "Don't worry. Inside the shells, we should be able to communicate just fine. The AIs will translate for us."

I throw up my hands in disgust.

"OK, fine. I guess talking isn't our thing. What a team. Go Dust Lizards." I grab the bottom rung of the ladder. "We've got a little time before our meeting. I'm going to go explore, if anyone wants to join me. Rory, you want to come get the medrig to close that wound on your scalp?"

Rory looks at his bloody sleeve in surprise, like he'd forgotten all about it.

"Yeah, I guess I should do that."

• • •

As we're coming out of the medrig room, we follow the sound of excited voices to a big lounge at the end of the hall. About a dozen students are there, gathered around a gigantic wall screen. One entire wall of the room is windows, floor to ceiling. Through them, I can see down East Canyon, far beyond the wall. It's a bright sunny day, without a cloud in the sky.

I stop three steps into the room, my mouth hanging open. I've never been this high up before. Looking out those massive windows makes my hands and feet tingle. My knees feel weak.

I tear my eyes away, focusing instead on the wall screen as I struggle to control my breathing.

The screen shows a transport caravan. Half a dozen long tankers. Smoke billows from two of them, and tiny figures appear to be firing at them.

I forget all about the height as I realize what's happening. The tiny figures are Outsiders. The caravan is under attack.

I watch the figures swarm the breached transports. They scurry like plakbeetles as they take the goods from the transport into a cave mouth. Back and forth they go, practically running. I wonder what their hurry is, then I see what's got the other trainees so excited, and I understand.

A team of Guardians rockets onto the scene. Their cannons cut down the Outsiders, scattering them like dust. In seconds, the raiders have disappeared back into their caves, and the caravan is safe.

A cheer goes up from the assembled crowd. I realize that most of them are standing near the windows now, pointing outside excitedly. Looking past them, I see a plume of smoke in the distance. I cautiously creep in that direction.

"Can you see them from here?" I ask no one in particular.

"Nothing more than the smoke, really. But if you squint your eyes, you can fool yourself into thinking you can."

I turn my head toward the voice and find the Sunriser girl from the changing room standing beside me. We're the same height, and her bright, griecagin-blue eyes are startling against the red-gold of her skin. Her brown hair curls forward along the line of her jaw.

"Still pretty close though," Rory says. He's standing on the other side of the girl, scowling at me like I've interrupted something.

"Do they normally hit caravans that close to the city?" I ask, my eyes drawn back to the girl.

She shrugs and her lips curve in a tiny hint of a smile. Her eyes meet mine. My blood surges.

"Sometimes. They've been getting more brazen lately. My grandad thinks we should send the Guardians out to exterminate them once and for all."

"That's exactly what we should do," Rory agrees. But the girl keeps her eyes on me.

"I'm Twist," I say, extending my hand.

"And why should we care?"

The ash-blonde guy muscles up behind her, looking at me like I've just stepped in his pudding. His eyes are an unsettling translucent grey. My head barely crests his shoulder.

My mouth drops open as I realize why he seems so familiar. He looks just like the guy in the silver armor I beat in the qualifier. But how could he lose and still be here?

He sees my reaction and cocks his head suspiciously.

"What is it?"

"I just . . . you look familiar is all. Did you compete in the chaser qualifiers?"

His face darkens.

"That was my brother, Julius. It was a travesty he even had to compete. Our uncle should have been able to get both of us a place in the training class. When I find out who eliminated him . . ."

My mouth goes dry. His brother? I breathe a prayer that he never finds out I'm the guy he's looking for.

I force myself to meet his gaze, trying to mask my fear with false confidence.

"Well, like I said, I'm Twist. I just thought you might want to know whose name you'll be seeing at the top of the leaderboard."

He stares at me like I'm a shellbaby that's started speaking. The girl looks amused though, so I turn my attention back to her.

"And you are?" I offer my hand again.

Her smile widens, flashing bright white teeth.

"I'm Kass. And this is Octav," she says, inclining her head toward the tall boy. She takes my offered hand. Her skin is soft and warm and an electric charge shivers down my spine at the touch.

Behind her, Rory's face is stormy.

A deep voice growls above me, "You can call me Genghis."

I whirl around to find the massive guy with the rat-tail frowning down at me. This close he's as big as a dozer, his muscles look like tumors multiplying out of control. His bicep is bigger around than my thigh. He doesn't look friendly.

I'm saved from having my head ripped off when our watches all flash at once. A message scrolls across the screen, "All trainees report for the introductory session."

"Well, this has been great," I say, backing away. "Let's do it again sometime."

My smile stays frozen all the way to the door.

10

—————

A spindly service droid directs us to a big conference room. There are rows of chairs facing a lectern at the front of the room, but everyone is slow to sit down. Instead, we're milling around the room checking each other out, like flecks of pepper in a pot of soup.

I count heads. Out of the fifty of us in the room, I only find nine that look like they're from Canyon City. Not good odds.

I search the room for Shadow, and find her seated near the back. Her dark eyes look like they're taking it all in: weighing, measuring, and categorizing everything and everyone. I start toward her, then hesitate. She's Covert, and I'm sure she can gather more information without me going back and calling attention to her.

Castle strides into the room with a silver cane and takes his place behind the lectern. He looks smaller in person.

"Take your seats," he barks, and I find myself moving without having consciously decided to move. He's got one of those voices that pulls your strings like a marionette. I grab a seat next to the aisle out of instinct. Poised to escape.

I laugh at myself. If only escape were that easy.

Castle watches as we settle into our seats, his expression blank. And I don't mean that he's keeping his face blank. I mean that his face shows as much emotion as a dead plakbeetle. He speaks in a conversational tone, but his crisp voice carries easily over the room.

"Welcome to Merrimac. The training you are about to embark upon will be the most difficult thing you will ever do. You will be pushed to your limits, and well beyond them. Only the best of you will make it. Some of you may not survive. This isn't a game anymore. This is about the survival of our colony.

"The Outsiders want what we have. If there were no Guardians, they would tear down the wall tomorrow. The Horrors would be right behind them. Together they would kill every man, woman, and child in Canyon City. I do not exaggerate when I say that we are all that stands between civilization and death." He pauses to let that sink in.

"There is good news, however. Those of you that complete the training will be part of the finest fighting force ever assembled on Greica. The Guardians are the stuff of legend. Of myth. Of our enemies' nightmares. And now, more than ever, they are desperately needed. You are desperately needed.

"My name is Instructor Castle. You will call me Instructor. I am the head of this program. There is no higher authority within these walls. If I tell you to get down on the floor and lick my boots clean, the only question I want to hear from you is, 'How shiny do you want them, Instructor?' Is that understood?"

There are nods and mumbles around the room.

"I can't hear you. Is that understood?"

There's a ragged chorus of, "Yes" and "Yes, Instructor."

Castle's eyes go cold.

"That was pathetic. You," he snaps, pointing at a boy in the front row with his cane. I'm horrified to see that it's Rory. "Do you think that was an acceptable response to a direct question?"

"Yes, Instructor," Rory says, his voice going a little squeaky at the end.

"Yes, you think it was acceptable?"

"Uh, no. No, Instructor."

"Well which is it, yes or no?"

"No. No, Instructor."

"Are you making fun of me, Trainee?"

"No, Instructor." There's a quaver in Rory's voice that knots my stomach.

"Get up here and give me fifty pushups."

Rory gapes at him.

"Instructor," he squeaks, "My wrist is injured, I don't think…"

"You are not here to think, Trainee! You are here to move when I say move!"

Rory does, scrambling out of his chair to sprawl facedown beside the lectern. He does a few shaky pushups, but it's obvious he's never going to get anywhere near fifty. I'm amazed he can do any with that wrist.

"What do you think you're doing, Trainee?" Castle barks, snapping his cane down across Rory's back. Rory yelps and collapses onto his stomach.

"Did I say you could lie down?" Castle demands, hitting him again.

"No, Instructor." Rory pushes himself up off the floor, but Castle cracks him with the cane, knocking him back down again.

"Get up," Castle commands, hitting him again, and again. "If I don't get fifty pushups, you are going to be one sorry sack of dust."

Rory tries to push himself up, but Castle's blows catch him on the elbows and wrists, knocking his arms out from under him. Eventually, Rory gives up and rolls into a fetal position, trying to cover his head with his arms. The silver cane beats upon his legs and back like a metronome.

"Fifty! We are not leaving this room until I get fifty!"

"I'll do them, Instructor!"

Castle's arm stops in mid-swing, his head whipping around toward the voice. I'm horrified to discover that I'm on my feet, and he's looking right at me. Note to self: In the future, consult with brain before taking idiotic actions.

"Did you say something, Trainee?"

Spines. Well, there's no backing out now.

"Yes, Instructor," I say. I square my shoulders and try to look like my courage isn't dribbling down my leg. "You said you want fifty pushups. I'll give them to you."

Castle smirks at me.

"Well, I didn't realize you two rockheads were sweet on each other. I'm sorry if I was too hard on your girlfriend here." My face burns with shame, but I don't rise to the bait. "All right, Trainee. I see what you're trying to do. You don't like your little anal probe being singled out. You think that as trainees, you're all in this together. Rise together or fail together, am I right? OK, I respect that. You can get up here and give me fifty."

I take a deep breath and start toward the front of the room. I can feel everyone's eyes boring into me. At the front of the room, I drop down and start doing the pushups.

"Let's all count together," Castle says, and fifty voices begin to count in chorus.

"One. Two. Three."

"If you can't do all fifty," Castle raises his voice to be heard above the counting, "by your own philosophy, that means it's not just you that fails. It's everyone in this room. Well then, if you don't give me fifty pushups, every trainee in this room goes without dinner tonight."

I don't reply, focusing on my muscles, pressing my body up and down.

"Fifteen. Sixteen. Seventeen."

At twenty I start to slow down. By thirty the muscles in my chest are burning.

At forty my arms are shaking, but I grit my teeth and push on. Just a few more. I can do this.

I feel something small and hard press down between my shoulder blades. It takes me a couple of pushups to realize it's the tip of Castle's cane. I struggle on, the pressure increasing with each pushup.

"Forty-four. Forty-five. Forty-six."

It takes every ounce of strength in me to push myself up off the floor again. It feels like Castle is leaning his whole weight on the cane.

"Forty-seven."

I lower my chest back down, the polished granite looming in front of my eyes. Sweat drips from my eyebrow. Three more. Just three more.

I strain to push myself up again, every muscle screaming, my arms shaking like a candle flame in the wind. I get halfway up and stall. I can go no further. I grit my teeth, growling with effort, putting every-thing I have into straightening my arms.

I can't.

I collapse to the floor with a groan that's echoed by every trainee in the room. My cheek rests in a puddle of my own sweat.

"Aww," Castle mocks. "So close. Well, it's a good thing nobody's hungry in here. Now get back to your seat and stop wasting every-one's time, Trainee."

I slink back to my seat, my hands curled into fists, feeling the hostile stares of the others. I'm shaking with exhaustion, embarrass-ment, and rage. Castle cheated, and there's not a dust-sucking thing I can do about it.

11

Castle looms over me, leering, his silver cane a cattle prod. I back away on all fours, but he just laughs and lunges forward, inhumanly quick, jabbing the point into my ribs. Electricity courses through me and my teeth clench, slicing through my tongue. The metallic taste of blood fills my mouth.

Ianna runs forward, eight years old again. She looks exactly as she did the last time I saw her, wearing yellow sneakers and her red polka-dot scarf. Her almond eyes are wide and scared. She tugs at his arm, but he just laughs, casually backhanding her small body into the door. I lay helpless as Castle turns and plunges the cattle prod straight through the center of her chest. Blood bursts from her mouth, and I scream and scream as the light in her eyes goes out.

An alarm blares through the barracks.

I sit up, gasping, my heart hammering against my ribs, the nightmare vivid as a fresh wound. My sheet is sweat-soaked and twisted. I struggle to calm my panic as the rest of the team emerge from their shells around me, yawning and cursing.

"Report to the track in five minutes," a tinny voice bellows through the wall speakers. "If any of you are late, there will be no breakfast for the group."

"Dust-licker," Rory mutters. There's a chorus of agreement as we scramble to pull on our workout clothes.

Rory hasn't even looked at me since the pushups debacle. As soon as we got to the barracks, he crawled into his shell and ignored everyone for the rest of the night. Talk about ingratitude. I mean, I know I failed, but you'd think a guy could get some credit for trying to help.

At least the others speak to me. Mostly they curse my name for costing them dinner. But still, it's talking.

We manage to drag ourselves out to the track with at least three seconds to spare. Which is a good thing, because if we had to skip breakfast on top of missing dinner last night, I'm pretty sure the group would be ready to turn cannibal. And I know exactly which dust lizard they'd spit first.

Instructor Salin sets us to running around the track. Salin is a sallow, whip-thin cord of a man with short grey hair that recedes in wings from the top of his forehead. He's so long and lean he makes greyhounds look fat.

The movement feels good and I lose myself in the steady rhythm of my feet, slowly shaking off the last remnants of the nightmare.

I outdistance most of the group, but as I'm coming around to lap a handful of Sunrisers, Octav's foot catches mine and I collect a face full of dirt. Ghengis jogs by, snickering as I pick the rocks from my palms. I stay away from the other runners after that.

Salin has us run for half an hour, then climb stairs for another half. By the time he sends us off to shower and get breakfast I'm wobbling on my feet, and so hungry I could eat flitter-bat guano.

In the cafeteria, I grab a tray of food and take a dazed seat at the first empty place I come to, my mind on one thing and one thing only. I devour my breakfast so fast I can't even remember what was in it. Something with eggs maybe?

Now that my stomach is satisfied, I finally notice my surroundings. I realize I'm the only one at the table. Apparently my pariah status extends to mealtimes as well. Correction, I'm not the only one at the table. Sitting way down at the end, as far as he can get from me without sitting on the floor, is Rory. He is studiously not looking at me.

"It wouldn't kill you to say thank you, you know," I say.

Rory flinches as my voice hits him. Then he looks confused.

"Thank you? For what?"

"For sticking up for you."

Rory looks as though someone's plugged an air compressor into his anus. I watch him inflate, his face turning red.

"Stick up for me? You stuck up for me?"

"Easy, Rory. People are watching."

"You think you stuck up for me?" He's yelling now, his face so flushed it's purple. I'm afraid he might burst his stitches. "You humiliated me in front of everyone. The next time you want to help me, why don't you just stick a knife into my back. It'll be more effective."

"Come on, Rory. I…"

"Leave me alone!" He snatches his tray from the table and stomps off.

I look around and find everyone staring at me. I give them the old one-finger salute and stomp off in the other direction.

After breakfast, our group has range weapons practice with Instructor Asa, an icy calm, dead-pale woman with close-cropped blonde hair and lips so thin I'm not sure they exist. She spends what feels like five hours explaining to us how our gun works, then she makes us take it apart and put it back together at least a hundred times.

The whole thing feels like an enormous waste of time. I mean, who fires guns by hand? In the game, all of the weapons are controlled by the AI because, as everyone knows, AIs can target you and shoot you dead before you've even registered that there's a threat. If you have to rely on firing a gun by hand, you are so screwed you might as well just fire it into your own skull.

Instructor Asa doesn't seem to realize any of this, however, so we put tiny pieces into tiny holes and detach wires and crimp them to other wires until I'm cross-eyed from eye strain. I spend a lot of time on my hands and knees on the floor, trying to find tiny screws that have disappeared under the table.

"Typical rockhead," Asa scoffs as I dive under the table once again.

"Don't worry, you probably won't be staying in Merrimac long enough for your failure here to impact you."

I grind my teeth, but say nothing. One lesson I learned from my run in with Castle: it's better to keep my mouth shut around the instructors.

My sole consolation is that nobody else seems to be any good at this either, and Asa spends her time inspecting our work and telling us in detached, clinical terms how much we suck dust.

The only exception is Grab, who has a brief, quiet conversation with the Instructor, then spends the rest of his time in the corner doing mysterious things on a mini datapad. Where in the five canyons did he get a mini datapad anyway? The datapad in my kit is oversized and yellow and apparently made for kindergarteners. Someone needs to have a conversation with the instructors about fair treatment.

Finally, Asa lets us into the firing range. Unfortunately, this turns out to be just as big a waste of time as the rest of it. We're not allowed to use our targeting computers. Or the smart-projectiles.

Instead, Asa tells us we have to, "Still your mind and body. Focus only on the target. Be consistent."

We have to look through a scope and line up the target with our naked eye, which is utterly ridiculous. Twitch your wrist even a couple of millimeters as you thumb the switch, and you end up missing the target completely. It seems I've taken Asa's advice about being consistent to heart because I miss almost every time.

Again, I'm consoled by the fact that nobody else seems to be hitting the target much either. The exceptions this time are Octav and Rory, who gleefully turn target after target into smoking piles of ash. I guess I see why Rory got an invitation to Merrimac now.

Next we report to a big room with padded mats covering the floors. The instructor here is a squat, dark-skinned, shaven-headed person named Instructor Skinn. Skinn has a round, asexual face, thick fingers and powerful shoulders atop a slim, feminine waist.

"I am here to instruct you in hand-to-hand combat," Skinn tells us in a warm mid-range voice.

I figure I might do ok at this one. I mean, my first choice is always to run from a fight, but when push comes to shove, I know how to take care of myself. It's one of the first things you learn as a kid growing up in Canyon City.

As it turns out, I'm wrong again.

Skinn doesn't teach us how to punch or kick. Or bite, which is always a Canyon City staple. Instead Skinn takes the biggest kid in the group, Ghengis, and brings him up to the front of the class.

"I want you to attack me," Skinn says.

Ghengis furrows his brows, his mouth twisting skeptically.

"Now," Skinn barks, and we all jump.

Ghengis shrugs and half-heartedly tries to grab Skinn. Skinn avoids Ghengis's meaty paw and slaps the big guy across the face so hard the sound echoes off the walls. Somebody in the group laughs, I think maybe Octav. Ghengis's jaw drops in surprise, then his face darkens with anger.

"Again," Skinn says.

This time Ghengis rushes the smaller instructor, trying to use his weight to bear Skinn to the ground. Skinn moves incredibly fast and does something that involves a sudden bend and twist. Ghengis goes flying through the air and lands on his back on the mat.

The room goes silent. I think half of us are trying to figure out what just happened, while the other half are waiting for Ghengis to get up and rip Skinn's arms off.

"Thank you for that demonstration, Ghengis," Instructor Skinn waves him back over with the rest of us. For a moment I think Ghengis is going to charge the instructor again, but then he shrugs and pretends indifference as he strolls over to us. I let out a breath I didn't know I was holding.

Skinn shows us a couple of strange holds that let you use your opponent's weight and momentum against them. Then we're paired off to practice. To my surprise, I get paired with Kass. Just standing next to her makes my face warm.

"Seems like a big waste of time, doesn't it?" I say, to cover my embarrassment.

"How so?"

"Well, I mean, we're not going to be battling any Outsiders hand-to-hand are we? Why do we need to learn this stuff?"

Kass doesn't look amused.

"You never know what's going to happen out there. Guardians have been captured and stripped of their gear before. You have to be ready for anything."

"Oh," I say, feeling foolish. "I didn't know that."

"I'm sure there's a lot you don't know." She smirks. Then she softens her words by adding, "But that's why we're here isn't it? To learn?"

"Yeah, I guess it is."

"Stop thinking you know everything ahead of time. If you pay attention, you might actually learn something important."

"Right."

"Now try to attack me."

I hesitantly try to grab her arm. Kass latches onto my wrist and pivots, pulling me forward. The world flips and I land on my back on the mat, my breath huffing out of me. I stare at the ceiling for a moment, admiring the swirling grain of the sandstone.

"Something tells me you've done this before," I say.

"I might have had some training." Kass smiles, her blue eyes sparkling. I have a hard time breathing, though I can't tell if it's from the flip or Kass's smile. "Ok, your turn."

She comes at me fast. I do what Instructor Skinn showed us, but when I try to flip Kass, I'm the one who ends up on the ground. Anger makes my face warm, and I brush away the hand Kass offers to help me up.

This time I don't hesitate when I attack her, and instead of trying to grab her arm, I go low, wrapping my arms around her legs and wrestling her to the ground.

"Well that was unorthodox," she says.

"It got the job done," I retort.

I'm lying on top of Kass, her face a handspan from mine, dark hair curling around her neck. I'm acutely aware of her belly pressed against mine, her breasts rising and falling with her breath. My blood surges, singing through my veins, making my fingertips tingle.

"All right, I'm not a mattress." She pushes me off and rolls to her feet.

We go back and forth. Regardless of who is doing the attacking, Kass ends up flipping me onto the ground more often than not. I slowly start to get the hang of it though, and eventually I manage to throw her.

"It's about time," she says. "I was beginning to think you were a little slow."

"We didn't all grow up in Sunrise," I snap. "Some of us had to work for a living. Don't worry. You Cloudheads may have a head start, but Rockhearts learn fast."

"Rockhearts?" Kass laughs. "That sounds like you're about to have a coronary."

"It means we're strong where it matters. Inside. Something you Cloudheads wouldn't know anything about."

"You don't know anything about me," Kass snaps. "I trained for years to get into this program, and no dust miner off the street is going to take my place."

We're standing nearly nose to nose. I can smell the sweat on her neck.

"We'll see," I say. "You better run fast, because I'm coming up hard on your tail."

"This dust-licker bothering you, Kass?" A large hand clamps onto the back of my neck and lifts. Suddenly I'm standing on my tiptoes, struggling not to choke. The bulk of Ghengis looms in my peripheral vision.

"Bothering me? Hardly. He's nothing but a fly on a dung heap." Kass flicks her fingers and walks away.

Ghengis turns me so that I'm staring up into his scowling face. His breath reeks of garlic.

"Careful, little sewer-fly. I will squash you flat."

He lets go and I collapse to the floor, wheezing.

Well. That could have gone better.

12

My watch goes off as I'm leaving the locker room, the blue alarm circle pulsing around the rim as it buzzes. The message says we've got our first run in ten minutes. My stomach twists. This is it. Game on.

My teeth are clenched as I slide down the ladder to our barracks room. Shadow and Knott are already present.

"I guess we don't get a practice run," I say.

Shadow shrugs as she opens the lid of her shell.

"No problem. The Game is the Game. We'll know what to do."

I don't know if she believes that, but it's reassuring to hear it anyway. I nod and turn to my own station.

Despite my nerves, I can't help but smile as I run my hand over the sleek shell, breathing in the scents of metal polish and spun carbon. I've always dreamed about gear like this. It's so far beyond my old patched-together gear it isn't even in the same universe. This gear is so clean I feel dirty standing next to it.

I open the lid and carefully lower myself into the shell. The shock pads flow around me like sand, firm yet soft, encasing my limbs completely. A clear mask comes down over my face and cones insert themselves into my ears. Then the shell seals around me and it's so dark I can't even see the mask anymore. Total darkness. Complete silence.

But it's a different darkness than the kind I'm used to. It's not the cool smell of dust and rock. It's too warm. Suffocating. Unexpected panic rises in my chest. My breath is hot and stale inside the mask. I try to move my arm and can't. I'm buried alive. I thrash, fighting against the sand.

Help. Somebody help me.

Then fans whir to life, blowing cool air over my face. I suck it down in big, grateful gulps.

The display lights up, and I find myself in a familiar menu room. Choices and options hang around me like bunches of fruit. I jerk my arm toward the nearest one and the sand slides smoothly around me. I can move again. I take another deep breath, my heart rate slowly backing away from cardiac arrest. I glance around, but don't see any other avatars in the room.

"Anyone else here?"

"Present." Shadow's voice comes through my earcones.

"Where are you?" I ask.

"Menu room."

"Huh. We must each get our own individual menu rooms. Raindrops."

I examine the choices hanging around me. There's all the usual options: different builds, weapons, armor, etc. But as I look, I realize that there's a degree of specificity to these that's far beyond what I'm used to. For instance, not only can you choose the type of brakes you want on your gravbike, you can also control exactly how fast they'll slow you down. If you want, you can dial them all the way up to where they'll stop you dead on the point of a cactus spine at 100kph. I have no idea how you'd stay on the bike if you stopped that fast. Or what it would do to your body if you did. I'm pretty sure it would hurt.

All the gear is chock full of micro-level options like this. How fast do you want your ammunition to travel? How many centimeters do you want it to penetrate? Are there any materials you do not want it to penetrate? How many rounds do you want in your magazine? How many pulse charges in your battery?

I wander around the choices, overwhelmed. I could spend hours in here, agonizing over things I've never even considered before.

Carbon or steel foot pegs? Night scope in blue or green?

Fortunately, Shadow calls me back from the brink.

"The run is in two minutes. Don't get lost in the options. Just find your standard packages. They're the choices we're used to. Pick one and gear up. We can explore the in-depth options later."

Sound advice.

Since we don't know anything about the run, I pick a gravbike that suits my style: fast and maneuverable, with lots of speed, light weapons, and not much armor to slow it down. For my personal armor I pick the X-J6, the greaves and elbow plates locking around my limbs like an old, familiar friend. The inside of the helmet smells like hot silicon and carbon.

I breathe it in and straddle the gravbike inside the virtual garage. Some of my tension slips away. For the first time since I got here, I feel comfortable. This, at least, is something I know how to do.

The garage dissolves and I'm sitting on the gravbike in a deep canyon. A striated wall blocks the low-slanting morning sun on my right, the shade throwing a chill over the sandy ground. The heating plates in my armor kick on, warm against my skin. There's some cactus and a few spindly reaper plants here and there, but mostly the canyon is clear and straight. Nothing but red rocks and white sand as far as I can see.

"Jmini, what've you got?"

The voice that replies is not British and fussy. It's female, and icy cold.

"There is no Jmini here. I am Hiroko."

"Load Jmini," I say, my voice rising. "I want Jmini."

"I'm sorry. That is not permissible."

Tension comes slamming back down on my shoulders. I forgot I had to leave Jmini with Stick. Jmini is my right-hand man. He knows what I need before I ask. Chasing without him will be like cave diving with one arm.

"The objective is up," a strange, resentful voice says through my earcones. It takes me a minute to remember it belongs to Grab.

The map flashes up in my display. It shows my team as a cluster of colored dots in a canyon, surrounded by a sea of dark, unmapped territory. Somewhere out in the dark area, a red dot blinks, showing the location of our objective.

"Well that's helpful," Shadow says.

"I'm on it," Grab croaks. "Drones are in the air."

I watch the mapped area expand as Grab's drones move away.

"Opposition?"

"Team one: Sand Stingers," Shadow supplies. "I'm pulling up their personnel files now. It seems like a straightforward snatch and grab. First to the prize wins."

"Then we'd better get moving," I say.

"Way ahead of you," Rory growls.

I see two bulky suits of armor moving down the canyon in front of me. Rory and Knott. Rory hugs the canyon wall, staying behind cover, dashing from boulder to boulder like a sniper. Knott strides right down the center of the canyon, looking like she's out for a Sunday stroll.

"Well, that's one way to draw fire," I mutter.

"You do your job. Let everyone else do theirs. That's what a team is for," Shadow tells me.

I bend over the handlebars and rev my gravbike, feeling the faint vibration thrum through me.

"Not like I have much choice, do I."

"Here's our opposition."

Shadow sends me a batch of personnel files. Flipping through them, I discover Kass and Octav are both Sand Stingers. Dust storms.

I chew my lip, watching the map expand in the corner of my visor as my team moves out into the canyons. This is the hardest part, the waiting. As the Chaser, it's my job to retrieve the objective. But I can't do that until we know where it is, and my team has taken care of whatever nasty surprises are out there waiting for me. So I sit. And wait.

My mind goes back to Ianna. I remember my sister as a baby, her tiny fist clutching my finger. Eyes so wide you could fall right into them and never hit bottom.

When our parents died in the Outsider attack, Ianna was all I had left. We bounced around for a while, six months here, three months there, never finding a foster home that fit. The instability drove us together like strands of ivy twisting.

For a while we ended up with an old seamstress named Granny Zazo. She harbored a lot of foster kids. New ones would come and go every few weeks. We were some of the lucky ones. We were there almost six months.

I think she only kept us around for the extra credits she got from the colony. She certainly never seemed to like us much.

Still, even though she was a drunk and an abusive shrew, she had her moments. When she was in the right mood, she could tell jokes and stories like nobody's business. Some nights we'd all sit around the living room floor and listen to her stories for hours. I remember Ianna falling over on the dirty carpet, bright tears in her eyes, helpless with laughter. It wasn't a perfect life, but it was a life.

Until the day they sent me away to Papa Grady's camp. I never did find out where they sent Ianna.

My hand trembles as I finger the firing stud on my handlebar. I'm going to be a Guardian. When I get my badge, I'll find her. Even if I have to tear down every sweatshop in Canyon City to do it.

"Twist, wake up! You've got incoming!" Shadow's voice drags me back to the present.

A glance at my display shows that my crew has been busy while I've been gathering dust. Rory and Knott are nearly a kilometer ahead of me and have split off into separate canyon spurs. Shadow has disappeared from the feed entirely. I assume she's gone into a stealth mode.

Grab's drones have been busy little bees, mapping out nearly three kilometers of the canyon system ahead. They're over halfway to our objective. It looks like your typical scablands maze of broken spires, sheer walls, dry ravines, and rockslides waiting to happen. A real mess, in other words.

But what catches my eye is the pair of hostiles coming in fast across the mesa, blinking red in my display like a pair of evil sirens.

"Drones?" I ask. My mouth goes dry and I crane my neck back to peer up at the sky, trying to get a visual on them.

"They're airborne, so that'd be my guess, yeah," Shadow says. "But who knows what kind of gear they've got in here. Get moving and be ready for anything."

I take her advice and throttle up, training my helmet cam on the tops of the cliff walls around me.

"Hiroko, eyes up."

"Acknowledged." Hiroko says without a trace of sarcasm.

I sigh. I miss Jmini already.

There's no time to dwell on that though, as the first drone comes buzzing over the lip of the canyon. I see it glinting in the sunlight. Then it drops, disappearing into the shade of the cliff face. It's smaller than I expected; if it hadn't been for the sun I doubt I would have seen it at all. Hiroko's got it locked though, so even though I can't see it, my display gives me a pretty good idea of where it is.

I accelerate again, hoping to leave the thing in the dust. The canyon floor blurs beneath me, the gravbike purring over the smooth sand. Wind pushes at me, forcing me to crouch low over the handlebars as I lean first one way and then the other, whipping the gravbike around boulders and sandstone spires. I'm impressed with the shell all over again. The g-force pushes at me and I feel every vibration. It's like I'm really out there, skimming the canyon floor.

My lips peel back in a wild grin.

A glance at my overhead display wipes the grin away as quickly as it came. The drone is still there.

"Does that thing have any weapons, Hiroko?"

"Uncertain. If it does, it will have to get close to use them. A drone of that class does not have the capacity for a long-range weapon."

"Good to know."

As if on cue, the drone dives, plummeting down the side of the canyon toward me. My earcones fill with … the sound of a chicken clucking? A voice follows a moment later,

"Run little chicken run."

The voice sounds familiar.

"Octav? Is that you?"

"Right the first time. Congratulations. At least your first run won't be a total waste."

My head fills with the image of Octav on the firing range, burning target after target. A chill goes down my spine as I realize I've got one of those targets on my back now.

"Dust storms! Hiroko, take that thing out!" I lean hard, twisting the gravbike beneath me, snaking and fishtailing as I take evasive action. I don't hear the sizzle of my cannon discharging. On my display, it looks like the drone is right on top of me. "Hiroko, what are you waiting for?"

"I cannot discharge the weapons properly while you are weaving in such an unpredictable pattern. The probability of a hit is greatly decreased. You must turn control of the gravbike over to me so I may calculate shot trajectories with accuracy."

"Are you insane? I'm the driver, you're the gunner. That's the way this works. Just take out the drone!"

"Negative. You must set the gravbike to autopilot."

"This is ridiculous!" I fume. Jmini never asked to take control of my bike. He might have made snarky comments, but he did what he was told.

A green beam lances past my head, exploding a rock to my left. Red shards ping off my armor.

"Now he's shooting at me! Take the dust-licker out, Hiroko!"

"I'm sorry, I cannot…"

"Manual override. Transfer weapons control to me."

"I do not advise…"

Another beam streaks down, puffing the ground beside my foot.

"Do it, Hiroko! Now!"

"Weapons control transferred."

A blue targeting cross flicks up on my display.

"Auto-track drone," I command. It's not a perfect solution, but the targeting system will at least keep the cross close to the drone. I just have to pick the right moment to shoot.

Driving with one eye on the sky is incredibly difficult. As I'm skidding through a patch of loose sand, a half-buried rock kicks the bike off-balance. Fighting to regain control, I sideswipe a yellow sand spire.

Pain burns my lower leg as the rock scrapes the skin raw. Suddenly I'm not such a big fan of the high-quality shell haptics anymore. I would have hardly felt that with my old, patched together gear.

I flick my eyes back to the targeting display. I see a green flash and swerve the gravbike as hard as I can. The beam sears through my thigh.

"Dust-licker!"

I give the gravbike every bit of throttle I can, twisting and leaning wildly, desperate to escape. My breath rasps in my throat. Sweat rolls down my forehead.

In the corner of my display, the drone is still above me, slightly behind and to the right.

I'm in an open part of the canyon now, and I see it flashing in the sun. For an instant, the cross hairs line up perfectly.

"Fire!"

The drone explodes in a puff of smoke.

I howl in triumph and slow, straightening up on the gravbike. I roll the tension from my neck as relief floods through me. Take that, Octav. Then Hiroko has to go and spoil it.

"Second drone incoming."

13

———

My display shows the drone angling down on the far side of the canyon. Worse yet, it's in front of me, so I'll never get past it without a fight.

"No rest for the wicked," I sigh, leaning down over the handlebars as I throttle up.

"Hiroko, analyze terrain for cover."

There's a full five hundred meters between me and the drone, most of it dotted with boulders and sand spires. If I can find the right path, I've got a chance. It's all about picking the location of your battles. Any foe is beatable if you fight them under the right conditions.

"Cover found," Hiroko says, lighting up three areas on the display.

I study the map with one eye as I rocket forward. The rockfall on the north side of the canyon looks too unstable, I don't trust that it won't go sliding away beneath me the moment I try to ride over it. There's a cluster of cave mouths to the south, but I dismiss that as well. Caves would be all right if I was on foot, trying to hide, but I wouldn't want to take my gravbike in there.

That leaves option number three, a thicket of crumbling sand spires two hundred meters up the canyon. I chew my lip as I examine the map. It's risky. Some of the gaps between the spires don't descend all the way to the floor of the canyon, and if I'm not careful, I'm likely to round a spire at full speed and hurtle face-first into a wall of solid stone.

Still, it's the best chance I've got.

"Hiroko, find me a way through those spires."

Sweat trickles down the bridge of my nose as Hiroko calculates. The spires draw closer, as does the drone. The chicken clucking fills my earcones again, making me grind my teeth. Octav is really starting to get under my skin.

"Come on, Hiroko."

One hundred and thirty meters. One hundred. Seventy-five. The gravbike is screaming beneath me, going flat out. The drone is a glittering streak on an intercept course, plummeting like a meteor out of blue sky. It's a toss-up which of us will arrive first. Fifty meters. Thirty-five. Twenty.

Dust storms. I'm not going to make it.

"Analysis complete."

On the map, a snaking blue path appears, winding away through the sand spires. The entrance is … not the one I'm headed toward.

I brake hard, yanking the gravbike to the left. It slews and skids, bouncing and protesting beneath me. My forward momentum tears at me, trying to pull me off the bike. I hook my left foot beneath the foot peg and clamp onto the saddle with my thighs, my joints threatening to pop out of their sockets under the strain. In my peripheral vision, a bright streak goes shooting past me: the drone, caught off guard by my unplanned course correction. That'll buy me a few seconds.

I get the bike under control and onto the path Hiroko's mapped out. The sun disappears as I slip between the spires, flickering out again in blinding pulses as I flash across the gaps between the spears of rock. It makes it almost impossible to see as my visor clears, then polarizes, then clears again, faster than my eyes can keep up.

"Digitize display."

The real world blinks out as Hiroko turns my visual field into a digital rendering, the jumbles of fallen rocks and spire walls reduced to 3-D line drawings around me. It's not a perfect solution, but at least now I can see. I just have to hope Hiroko doesn't miss something and send me slamming into an invisible boulder.

The maze of spires is everything I hoped it would be. The slot between them is narrow and deep, and too twisting for the drone to dive on me from above. If it wants me, it will have to come down to my level to do it. The drone has disappeared from my screen for the moment, so I take a second to check on the rest of the crew's progress as I wind my way through the virtual canyon.

Grab's drones have got the whole run mapped now, the entire canyon system laid bare from above. Shadow is still nowhere to be found, but Rory and Knott's icons are flickering, indicating heavy engagement. A click over to the common channel gets me an earcone full of curses from Rory. His feed shows that he's pinned down in a crevice, but managing to hold his attackers off. For her part Knott is… Spines. Knott is trading blows with a Waste Horror. The thing is easily four meters high, with unhinged, snakelike jaws and arms like thick cables. One of those arms cracks forward like a whip, wrapping around the torso of Knott's armor. The big girl grunts and plants her feet, straining backward as the creature tries to reel her in. Her feet start to slip on the sand.

Then I've got my own problems, as a cannon blast just misses me, bringing a spire down in a cloud of billowing dust.

"Stupid drone." I see it behind me now, skimming about three meters off the ground. It's bobbing up and down, not letting me get a target lock on it. That's ok, I've got a better idea.

I slow a bit, letting it get closer. The back of my neck itches; I can feel Octavs's targeting computer lighting me up. The path I'm following is twisty enough that he can't get a shot off, but still, it makes my skin crawl.

Finally, I see what I've been waiting for: a narrow slot between two spires, barely wide enough for the gravbike to pass through. I slow again, letting the drone creep up another few meters. The timing has to be just right.

I flash through the gap, counting the seconds until the drone hits the gap. Just before it does, I light up the sides of the spires with my cannons. They explode in a shower of shards, turning the gap into a shredder. The drone doesn't come out the other side.

I whoop and pump my fist, baring my teeth into the wind.

"Take that, dust licker!"

Now, let's see about getting the flag.

Suddenly the world goes gray, and everything freezes around me. Game Over scrolls across the sky.

What the dust?

My display goes dark, and I'm back in my shell. It cracks open, disgorging me, blinking, into the light.

Around me, the others are sitting up in their shells too. They look just as confused as I do.

"What was that?" I ask. "What happened?"

"Someone else got to the objective first," Shadow says. Her mouth is twisted and sour.

"What do you mean, somebody else got there first?"

"While we were busy defending ourselves, their Chaser went straight for the objective. Not a bad strategy, actually." She shakes her head in grudging admiration.

"Octav was using the stupid drones to distract me." I groan.

"Great job, Chaser. You didn't get within a kilometer of the flag," Rory sneers. I scowl and ignore him.

"Why didn't anyone tell us what they were doing? I would have approached the whole thing differently if I'd known."

"I suppose that's my fault. And Grab's." Shadow scowls, glaring at the Mapper. "Why didn't you tell me the other team was moving on the objective?"

The lanky boy swallows and ducks his head, his adam's apple bobbing.

"I thought you'd be monitoring my feed. That's how we usually coordinate at home."

"It would have been nice if you told me that. Then I'd have done it."

"Well, I guess we know what we need to do next time out." I turn and swing my feet down to the floor.

"Yeah, and in the meantime we just got dusted," Rory gripes. "This is the sorriest excuse for a team I've ever seen."

I start to retort, but all of our watches buzz before I can form the words. The message scrolling across the surface says, "All trainees report to room twenty immediately."

"Oh good," Rory says. "Now we can share our failure with everyone."

I don't even know what to say to that. It's hard to argue with the truth.

14

———

Room twenty buzzes with excitement. The other trainees bounce around the room in clumps, laughing and joking, high on the adrenaline of their first runs. My team sits with our arms folded, frowning.

Castle strides into the room and everyone slides their butts into seats. One group doesn't notice him enter, and they're still talking when he steps up to the podium.

"What's your team?" he barks. The trainees turn, startled to find everyone looking at them.

"We're the Midfalcons, Instructor," a sharp-faced boy stammers.

"I'm deducting one point from your score for every second of my time you waste, Midfalcons." Castle checks his wristwatch. "You're at ten points and counting."

The sharp-faced boy pales and scrambles for the nearest seat, the rest of his team piling in around him.

"That's better," Castle grunts. He grips the podium with both hands, running his eyes over the crowd like a sniper assessing his targets.

"Congratulations on your first runs. As you learned today, you must be ready for a run at all times. Just as they do in real life, runs will come at you without warning. You could be called to a run before breakfast. In the middle of the night. Just as you're finishing a five-kilometer cross-country run. You must be ever vigilant. That is what it means to be a Guardian.

"As of today, you will be on guard every minute of every day. Your team will be closer to you than your mothers. Closer than your fathers, brothers, or sisters. You will eat as a team, sleep as a team, train as a team, and defecate as a team. You will succeed as a team or fail as a team."

My team doesn't look happy at this news, and in all honesty neither am I. Rory hates everyone, Grab's incompetent, Knott doesn't speak standard, and Shadow is the youngest trainee in the room. And we just got our butts handed to us in the first training run. Things are looking grim, to say the least.

"Let's check the leaderboard."

A projection lights up the wall behind Castle. Each team is listed in blue, their points total in white. The Sand Stingers are at the top with fifty points. I wince as I see that we are at the bottom with only fifteen.

"This is how you stand after the first run. Congratulations to the Sand Stingers for obtaining the objective."

I follow his eyes and see Kass and Octav smiling. Kass sees me looking and winks. I clench my teeth and turn my eyes back to Castle, heat rising in my cheeks.

"And before we forget, I'm deducting thirteen points from the Midfalcons for wasting my time."

The Midfalcons' total drops to nine, and they switch places with us on the board. Well, at least we're not last anymore.

"Lest you think this is all just a game, let me remind you that this training is very, very serious. The Outsiders have been stepping up their attacks. Last night they raided us again, took out three of our transports. Killed innocent people. Our intel indicates that they are raising an army. We need more Guardians, and we need them now. We're going to train you as quickly as we can. You will be pushed to your limits and beyond. We are counting on you. Do not let us down."

For just a moment, Castle's guard slips and I see his fear. He means what he's saying. The Outsiders really are coming.

I shiver. I haven't thought about what being a Guardian really means. I only wanted to find my sister. I didn't think the colony might actually needing protecting. My mouth goes dry as I picture myself facing an army of Outsiders. Canyons full of Horrors with pincers and cable-thick arms. I wonder if I've made a horrible mistake coming here.

"This leaderboard is how we will monitor your progress," Castle continues. "Top scorers earn rewards. Low scorers earn the opposite. Sand Stingers, your performance has earned you double dessert at dinner tonight."

A whoop goes up from Kass and her crew.

"Midfalcons, your position on the lowest rung has cost you dinner tonight. Perhaps you will be hungry for victory tomorrow."

The Midfalcons groan, but I sigh with relief. If it wasn't for Castle docking them points, that would have been us.

15

———————

"Today you take your first real step to becoming a Guardian. Today you receive your first warpknives."

Instructor Asa stands beside a rack of warpknives, hanging blade down. My breath catches in my throat as I run my eyes over the black handles, the slim crescent-shaped blades soaking up the light like unpolished granite. Warpknives. Real warpknives. I've dreamt of this moment my whole life.

"The warpknife defines what it means to be a Guardian. It symbolizes your duty. It symbolizes all that is right and true in the world. Once you receive a blade, it is yours. Keep it with you at all times. Eat with it. Sleep with it. Cherish it as you would your father, your mother, your brothers and sisters. This blade is now a part of your family. Care for it, and it will care for you. Treat it well and I guarantee that someday it will save your life."

We line up and shuffle forward. My stomach starts to flutter. I can't believe I'm about to hold a warpknife. An actual warpknife, just like in the stories.

Then I'm at the front, and Instructor Asa is placing the blade in my hand. She sneers down at me.

"Try not to cut your own arm off."

I clench my jaw and turn away from her. She can say whatever she wants. All I care about right now is the warpknife in my hand.

The knife feels lighter than I expected, the grip soft against my palm. The blade itself is as long as my forearm, fingertip to elbow. There are several power studs on the hilt. I tentatively run my thumb over the edge of the blade. Deactivated, it isn't even sharp.

I feel like a five-year-old kid with a stick as I take a few experimental cuts and thrusts with it. How many times did I imagine that stick to be a warpknife? Now here I am, holding an actual warpknife. I catch myself grinning, and see the same expression on the faces of the other trainees as well. In this moment, we are all five years old again.

"All right, children. Enough playing," Instructor Asa snaps.

We stop flailing about, but the grins remain.

"At full power a warpknife will cut through anything. This is what they are famous for, and the reason they were developed. It doesn't matter what kind of armor your opponent is wearing. Whether it's thick steel, energy shields, or the bone plating the Horrors have, if you can get close enough to use your warpknife, you can pierce it. They also have a number of lesser-known capabilities, including practice mode, which we will be using extensively in training. In practice mode, the warpknife's cutting field depth is limited to one millimeter. Meaning you can draw blood on your opponent, enough to let them know they're hit, but not enough to do any real damage. However, the core of every fighting technique is not the weapon, but the body. And most importantly, the footwork."

Asa spends the next hour showing us proper fighting stances. Where to place our feet, how to move them to advance, how to retreat. You have to keep your knees bent and stay low, shuffling forward and back one foot in front of the other, and after an hour of moving in a semi-crouch my thighs are burning.

Then we finally get to draw our blades.

Asa pulls Kass up to the front of the class, and uses her to demonstrate a six-guard system, which means that our defense is built around six basic parry points: High center, left, and right, and low center, left and right.

"Economy of movement is key. In a fight, fractions of a second can mean the difference between a successful parry and getting your arm sliced off. Your parry position should be exactly wide enough to deflect your opponent's attack, but no wider. You want to reach each position with as little movement as possible. Keeping your movements small will allow you to switch between attack and defense quickly and efficiently."

Asa demonstrates by having Kass attack her, and it's immediately obvious what she means. In the first demonstration, she parries tight, deflecting Kass's thrust with the tiniest movement of her wrist, so that the warpknife misses her shoulder by millimeters. In an instant she counterattacks, extending her arm in a lightning thrust, pressing the tip of her warpknife against Kass's chest before the girl has a chance to recover. The second time around, she parries wide, with a sweeping movement of her forearm. It takes her a noticeably longer amount of time to bring her arm back in line for her counterattack, which allows Kass time to recover as well, and she successfully deflects Asa's counterattack.

"Keep your blades deactivated for now," Asa says. "We don't need any blood on your first day."

Asa pairs me with Knott and sets us to alternating thrusts and parries. Knott moves with deliberate efficiency, her form tight. For her size, she's very quick. She's not just a big bruiser, there's skill in there as well.

After ten minutes of doing the same movements over and over, my excitement starts to dry up. Repetition is boring, even with a warpknife. Still, I remember the unarmed throws Instructor Skinn taught us, the careful balance and precision required to make it work. I imagine warpknife fighting is no different, so I do my best to stay focused and in form despite the monotony.

"You look like you've been fighting with warpknives for years," I say to Knott. "Is there something you islanders are keeping from the rest of us?"

She starts and shakes her head shyly.

"Oh, so you can communicate when you want to."

"Less talk, more practice, rockheads." Instructor Asa cuffs me on the side of the head, knocking me to the ground.

Knott glares at Asa's back as she walks away.

"Ke sai, ithio," she mutters darkly.

I shake my head as I get back to my feet.

"You know, it's really hard having a conversation with you." She shrugs and taps her ear, then points at mine. "Right, I need audio implants. I don't think that's going to happen anytime soon. Now that I think of it, Shadow said you'd be able to communicate just fine inside your shell, but I don't remember hearing a word from you during our run. I wonder if I could rig up some earcones that would receive signals from you as if they were implants?"

She shrugs again, then comes in fast with a thrust that beats my parry, poking me hard in the shoulder with the tip of her warpknife.

"All right, I get the point!" I wince and rub my shoulder. "Less talk, more focus."

The ghost of a smile floats across her lips.

After an hour I can barely lift my arm, and my legs feel like blocks of wood. I don't remember stick-fighting being nearly this tiring. I'm relieved when Asa finally sends us to the changing room.

I strip off my sweaty padding and hang my warpknife in a locker. The other boys are laughing and shouting, in high spirits from our first day of blade work. Unlike most rooms in Merrimac, the changing room has been carved out of the sandstone and left mostly unimproved after that. The ceiling, walls, and floor swirl with rough red and white waves, layers of stone, each one the compacted sediment of hundreds of years. Lifetimes laid bare.

I cross the center of the room to get some water, stepping carefully on the slick wet stone. I've just reached the faucet when a voice rings out.

"He's so small! Like a toy soldier!"

Hoots and laughter echo from the walls.

I feel my cheeks grow hot, but I don't look up. Instead, I turn on the water and bury my face in the flow. Maybe if I ignore them, they'll go away.

"Did your mom forget to feed you? Is that why your growth got stunted?"

"They probably couldn't afford food. That's why she had to turn tricks at night."

"That true, rockhead? Was that your mom I saw standing on a corner last night?"

My blood surges in my ears and I whirl around, trying to figure out who said it.

"My mom's dead, dust-licker," I snarl, my fists balled tight. I glare around the room. All I see are laughing faces. As my words hit them, some of them have the decency to look ashamed.

"Was it your breath that killed her?" Ghengis says, slowly and distinctly. Fear cools my rage as he steps out from his cubby, facing me. Dust, he's gigantic. My dread must show on my face because he smiles and cracks his knuckles. "You got something to say?"

This is not good. I've got no weapons, and I'm surrounded by Sunrisers who don't like me, facing a freak of nature who's ready to pound me to pulp. My chances of winning this fight are about as good as a sand flea farting against the wind.

If I run, I'm dead though. They'll torment me every chance they get. That's the way bullies work. Show them you're afraid and it's blood in the water.

I force myself to unclench my fists. Stand there before them as if their eyes mean nothing. Like they are beneath my notice.

There's a look kids get in Canyon City when they've been kicked around too often. We call it dead eye. When you see it, you know there's nothing more you can do to that person, because they are beyond caring about anything. Even killing them would only be a release.

I meet Ghengis's gaze and give him my best dead eye look. This is no different than facing down gang thumpers in Canyon City. Or wild dogs. You can't let them see your fear.

I hope my hands aren't shaking.

"Only the game matters." I run my eyes over all of them. "Words mean nothing."

I make myself walk out of the changing room with my head held high, like I haven't got a care in the world. Fighting every instinct that's screaming at me to run.

Somebody clucks like a chicken, and the others snicker and laugh. But no rough hands grab me, no fists slam into my ribs.

Fortunately, our barrack is empty when I get back. The chills catch up with me all at once, taking my legs right out from under me. I collapse onto my shell, arms wrapped around my stomach, shaking uncontrollably. I stare at the wall for a long, long time.

16

———————

I hear someone enter our barrack. I track their footsteps as they cross the room, then I hear tools jingling. I cautiously roll over and raise my head.

Grab is fiddling with his legs. He's lying on his stomach, and he's got an access panel open on the back of his left thigh. A tiny toolkit is laid out in the shell beside him. I watch him for a few minutes as he tries to adjust something inside the hatch. The position of it makes the operation awkward, and he has to twist and stretch. I can tell he's having a hard time seeing what he's doing in there.

My curiosity finally gets the better of me. I slip from my shell and step silently across the barracks. Inside the access panel, the leg is full of tiny gears and shining pistons.

"So your legs are fully mechanical," I breathe, impressed. "Did you make them yourself?"

He flinches and hunches his shoulders up.

I watch him try to grab a wire that's come loose with a tiny set of pliers. He touches it to the wrong lead, and his leg sparks and twitches.

"Spiny darkness!" He looks up at me in frustration. "Would you leave me alone? You're making me futz it all up."

"It looks to me like it's the position of the panel that's making you futz it. I don't think you can get that wire under the inverter without breaking your back."

His eyes open in surprise.

"You recognize an inverter?"

"Sure. I know how to do more than dig around in the dust. I built all my haptic gear from scraps. I can get that for you, if you want."

He squints up at me, suspicion in his eyes.

"Why?"

"Why would I help you?" I shrug. "We're crew now. It's just what you do. Besides, your legs are the wettest thing I've ever seen. I've been dying to get a look inside them."

I grin, and he relaxes a little at the wonder on my face.

"All right. If you could get that wire under the inverter for me, I'd appreciate it."

He hands me the tiny pliers and I lean down over the hatch. I marvel at the incredible complexity of the bio-electrical system. Grab's twisted around on his elbows watching me, as concerned as a mother hen.

"You want me to solder this?"

"No, just slot it back in and click the clamp."

"Ah ok, I see it."

I slide the wire under the inverter and click it into place. It's easy if you can see what you're doing.

"All fixed." I hand the pliers back.

He reaches back and closes the hatch, rolling onto his side. He cautiously flexes his leg.

"That's got it. Thank you."

"What happened to your real legs?" He flinches, and I quickly add, "If you don't want to talk about it, that's fine."

"No, it's ok. I lost them in an accident when I was a kid. Crushed by a transport truck."

Despite him saying that it's ok, talking about it clearly makes him uncomfortable. I change the subject.

"I've been thinking about Knott. How we need aural implants to translate what she says. What if we built translators into our earcones? Would that work?"

His scratches his ear, his mouth twisting to one side as he thinks.

"I can think of a couple of ways that might work. Let me research a few things and get back to you." He pulls out his tablet and starts jotting down notes.

"I could help."

"That won't be necessary." He waves me away absently.

I can tell he hardly even knows I'm there anymore. Fin used to get like that. Completely engrossed in an idea. I shake my head and leave him to it.

I'm surprised to see that the rest of the team wandered in while I was helping Grab. I guess he's not the only one that gets engrossed.

"Castle must have meant what he said about being ready for a run at any time." Shadow pulls open her shell. "It looks like we're sleeping in these things."

"Imagine waking up with the lid of the shell closed over you?" Rory shudders. "Creepy."

I stand in the center, looking around at the open shells.

"No, this is a good thing. We've got shells anytime we want them. Which means we can train anytime we want. We may have been thrown together by chance. We may not even like each other. But we're a team now. Crew. You all heard Castle, we live as a team or die as a team.

"Today sucked. We weren't ready, and we got whipped. Personally, I don't intend to let that happen again. We've got everything we need right here. The instructors may train us, but it's up to us to become a real crew. We can work harder than anyone. Train harder than anyone. We can be number one on the leaderboard, and wipe the smirks off those stupid Sunriser's faces. What do you say?"

They look at me in silence. Grab's still looking at his tablet; I don't think he heard a word I said. Rory gives a sarcastic clap and goes back to rooting around in his locker. Knott stands silent, which is no surprise. I think her face looks thoughtful, but I could be projecting.

Shadow looks at me with a bemused expression. Then she laughs and moves forward.

"That was the worst speech I've ever heard," she says, shaking her head and grinning. Then she turns to face the others. "But no matter how terrible his delivery was, I think Twist is right. Nobody wanted us here in the first place. Even you Grab. If they stuck you on a team with a bunch of Rockheads, something tells me you weren't exactly popular with the folks upstairs. Imagine how much fun it will be to make them all suck our dust."

The room is silent, and my spirit sinks. My little attempt at team-building is a failure. I should have known better than to open my mouth. I've never been a leader. I don't know why I thought that would change now.

I look at Rory. He doesn't look back, but his shoulders hunch up around his ears, and I can tell he feels the weight of my eyes.

"Eat dust, Twist." He raises a one finger salute in my direction. "You can keep your team-spirit guano."

Grab bobs his head up and down over his tablet in quick, birdlike movements, completely oblivious.

Knott turns away.

I look at Shadow, who shrugs and gives me a sarcastic victory sign. I sigh. I guess that's as close to victory as we're going to get today.

17

The dusty old lounge at the end of the hall has one wall made entirely of windows. The canyon spreads out before me, yawning away into the distance. Far below, Canyon City seems small and inconsequential, little more than a cluster of winding streets and jumbled boulders. My fingers and toes tingle with the height. I belong underground, down in the caves where the light doesn't reach. Where there are walls all around, keeping you safe. Up here, you're exposed. Up here, there's nowhere to hide.

"It's quite a view, isn't it?" Shadow comes up and gazes out the window beside me.

"Yeah, it's something," I agree. I stay well back from the glass. "It's a little overwhelming, actually. I've never been this high before."

"You haven't? What did you do down there?" She cocks her head at me, indicating Canyon City with her chin.

"I was a miner. Well, deep diver, actually. I'd go down in the black places where no one had ever been before, ferret out hidden greicagin deposits."

"Ah, that makes sense. You're used to going down, not up."

"What about you?"

"I've always been a climber. Trees, rocks, you name it. If I could get on top of it, I would. I love being up above everything, the wind in my hair, able to see for kilometers. I think I've spent half my life with people chasing me off one thing or another."

"It sounds like we've got the full range of heaven and earth covered between us," I laugh. I flick my eyes toward the ceiling. "Did you ever climb all the way up?"

"To Sunrise, you mean? No, too risky. Their security is tight. I did climb to the top of Southspire though."

I whistle, impressed. Southspire is the second tallest spire in Canyon City. It tapers to a long, narrow point that crests only thirty meters below Sunrise.

"What did you see up there? Could you see over the rim of the canyon?"

"No, the canyon rim is still a good hundred meters above that. The view was impressive though." Her eyes shine with the memory. "Canyon City looked tiny from up there. Even the walls, like I could pick them up between my fingers. There was a midfalcon circling below me, if you can believe it. I saw beyond the walls and far down the canyon, all the way past three prongs."

"What did you do for work? Let me guess, you were a chimney sweep."

Shadow smirks, looking up at me out of the corner of her eye.

"Nothing that ... official."

I glance around to make sure we're alone. I lower my voice.

"Were you in a gang?"

"Not the kind you're thinking of."

She walks up and leans her forehead against the glass, gazing down at the city below. It makes my skin crawl, and I have to fight the urge to snatch her back from the brink.

"So what kind then?"

"We were more of an independent crew than a gang. Bunch of street kids lifting things to survive."

"What kind of things?"

"Everything, really," she shrugs. "Whatever we could get our hands on. Whatever we thought we could sell. Which turns out to be pretty much everything."

I glance around again, the conversation making me nervous. But the hallway is still empty.

"You never got pinched? By the gangs? Or the Guardians?"

"I did once. When I was five. I stole a block of cheese from a vendor in the market. The vendor didn't see me, but some gang thumpers did. They took it easy on me because I was little. Gave me a warning. Only broke two of my fingers." She holds up her left hand and I can see where her ring and middle fingers are slightly crooked.

"It looks painful."

"Hurt like spines," she concedes. "Made lifting things a lot harder for a couple of months, that's for sure."

"But you kept doing it anyway?"

"It's not like I had a choice."

"Why not? There's got to be plenty of things you could do. Scavenging metal, or mining, or … lots of things."

"Do you know how many kids there are in Canyon City?" she asks, turning to look at me.

"No."

"Well there are a lot more kids than there are jobs that won't kill you, that's for sure."

"Good point," I say, thinking of the scrap vats. "Is that why you're here?"

"Damn right. Stealing loses its charm after you've done it half your life. Besides, I'm older now. Big enough for the gangs to take seriously. If I got caught lifting stuff on their turf now, they'd leave me dead in an alley quicker than a flash flood."

"No wonder you're Covert." I grin. "You've been training for it all your life."

"Best training there is," she says, grinning back. "Compared to Canyon City, hiding out in the game is jelly easy."

I steel myself and step forward until I'm standing next to her, the glass almost touching my nose. Below my feet, the wall of the canyon drops away in a sheer cliff face. Cold fear tingles through my fingers and toes. One more step is all it would take to fall.

"So does this mean you can get things?" I ask softly, my voice little more than a whisper.

"Depends on the thing," she says just as quietly.

My heart hammers in my throat, a ringing rising in my ears. I try to swallow down the panic, but it's no good. Sweat beads across my forehead.

I step back and sink onto the arm of a chair, panting. Shadow smiles and steps back beside me.

"You'll get used to it."

"If you say so."

She waits for me to get my breathing back under control before cocking an eyebrow at me.

"So?"

"I need my Jmini. I left him with a kid named Stick. Hiroko is no good. She almost got me burned by those drones last game."

"Challenging." She gazes thoughtfully out the window.

"Does that mean no?"

"No, it means I'm not sure. We haven't been in here long enough for me to get the lay of the land. I'll have to scope it out first, see what I can do."

"That's fair. When will you know?"

"I'll let you know."

"Sooner would be better than later."

"Isn't it always?"

"What would you want in return?"

"Don't know. Depends on how hard the job turns out to be."

"Whatever it is, I'll pay it."

"Yeah?" She looks up at me, her eyes laughing. "Did you get rich when I wasn't looking?"

I feel my face flush.

"I just mean … It's important to me. I'll find some way to make it right, whatever the price is."

"Big words," she says, her face suddenly serious. "You better mean it. This could be a real risk."

"I do," I respond, just as serious. "We're crew now. I've got your back."

She stares at me for a minute, then nods.

"Yeah, all right."

I slash my warpknife across my palm, watch the blood well up in a thin red line. Shadow does the same and we clasp hands, pressing our bloody palms tight.

"Crew." Shadow's small, dark eyes are fierce.

"Crew." I hold her gaze solemnly.

"I'll let you know about your order."

I listen to the heels of her boots click away down the hall. Beyond the glass, the scablands spread out in an endless jumble. There's a lot of open air out there. A lot of room to fall.

18

———————

"Today, your training moves to the next level," Instructor Asa tells us. "Today we go outside the perimeter."

I chew my lip inside my helmet. We've been working with the armor for a week now. It bumps up your strength and reflexes, makes you bulletproof, even allows you to fly in short bursts. Inside Merrimac, I feel indestructible with it on. But beyond the wall? Out in the scablands with the Outsiders and Horrors?

Asa sees our expressions and sneers.

"Do not worry, little rock babies. The area we will be visiting has been cleared. It is completely safe. And on the very small chance that it isn't," she smiles her thin-lipped smile. "I will be with you."

I'm not sure if this reassures me or terrifies me. A little of both, I think. If there's one thing I've learned in our training sessions, it's that Asa is one scary lady. Violence flows through her veins the way most people have blood. If something can be killed, you can bet she's going to kill it.

The spookiest part is how unemotional she is about it. She'll throw you across the room or shoot you down with the same flat expression she wears at dinner. I'm glad she's on our side, but still, she is one scary lady.

We follow Asa down a ramp & up into an open-backed transport. The sun sparkles across the silver plates of our armor. Six shining figures sitting beneath the bluest sky I've seen in days. The striped walls of the canyon bracket the road. As the transport starts to roll toward the gate, my throat tightens and my breath speeds up. I look around at my team for reassurance. Five armored figures plus Instructor Asa, up against the scablands and a world full of Horrors. It doesn't seem like enough.

Then it clicks, and I get it. Them making us sleep in our own little barracks. Keeping our success dependent on each other. The all-for-one-and-one-for-all muck they've been spreading on so thick since the day we arrived in Merrimac. This is what it's for. This moment right here. Outside the wall, if we don't have each other's back, no one will. We're in it together, all the way.

Shadow catches my eye and nods, her face shaded within the snug embrace of her helmet. I can tell she gets it too, which makes me feel a little better. Even if nothing else good comes out of my time in Merrimac, I know I've made one true friend. No matter what the rest of the team does, Shadow's got my back. The vice around my throat loosens, just a little.

The towering metal gates swing open, earth vibrating with the grinding of massive gears. I see sunlight glinting off Guardians standing on the towers that flank the gates. They seem small and insignificant. Too far away to make a difference if the Outsiders come rampaging down upon us.

My breath hisses between my teeth. Our whole lives, we've been told there's nothing but death outside the perimeter. Unspeakable Horrors. Things that will rip your head off and spit down your throat.

And now we're going out to face them.

I grip the bench hard with my gauntleted fingers as the transport rolls through the gate. It's all I can do to not vault from the transport and run screaming back into the compound. I've never wanted to cower beneath a blanket so much in my life.

I can tell the others feel it too. They shift in their seats, heads jerking around, trying to look everywhere at once. Faces pale and sweating, jaws clenched tight. Even Knott looks green around the gills.

Not Instructor Asa, of course. She sits carved like a statue, eyes staring straight ahead. To be fair, I'm sure this isn't her first time outside. She's probably been beyond the wall dozens of times, maybe hundreds. I wonder how many trips it takes before the panic subsides. Five? Ten? Twenty?

Watching the gate swing shut behind us, I bite my lip so hard I taste blood. There goes our escape route. Now we are truly alone.

The transport rumbles forward, jostling me in my seat, the six massive tires kicking up a plume of white dust behind us. The canyon floor is wide and smooth, white sand packed hard as rock by the weight of countless vehicles. Just like in the game, the canyon walls are striated red and white, and pitted with the dark mouths of a hundred caves. Carrion eaters circle high above, riding thermal currents. Spiky reaper plants cluster in pools of shadow, scenting the air with peppery blooms. I've seen this part of the canyon in a million sims. It's as familiar as the old welcome mat before the front door of Wayfinders.

Then we round a bend in the canyon, and everything changes. I watch the gate disappear behind us, and hold my breath as the rest of the wall is swallowed up by the landscape. Canyon City is gone. Now we're in the scablands proper.

"Seal up," Asa orders.

I shut my faceplate with relief, the pressure changing in my ears as the helmet seals. There's a soft whir as the climate control system activates, blowing cool air over my face. The canyon looks different through the visor, more the way I'm used to seeing it on my headset. I know it's silly, but now that I'm fully sealed up in my armor, the situation feels a lot less real. I draw in a deep breath of suit-cooled air, forcing my anxiety down.

I'm surprised by how much the canyon changes as we move. In less than an hour, the red and white striped sandstone gives way to mottled gray rock, pocked with perfectly round caves that look like air bubbles. After another kilometer, the transport stops in a small box canyon. The floor of the canyon is in shadow, and the air circulating through my suit grows cooler.

"Step down," Asa barks, and we do, clambering awkwardly off the back of the transport, clumsy in our armor.

I should clarify that we're the ones who are clumsy, not the armor. Guardians can do somersaults at a full sprint in these suits. But it's going to take us a while to get to that level of skill.

"I feel about as comfortable as a cat in a tin can," Shadow gripes, echoing my thoughts.

"I guess that's why we're here, right?" I say.

Shadow just makes a face behind her visor.

Asa makes us do sprints back and forth across the floor of the canyon to warm up. Then we run laps around the outer edge, where we have to pick our way across jumbles of scree and loose rock. I lose my footing and go down three times. I'm pleased to discover that the armor cushions my fall so well it feels like I'm coming down on the gymnastics mats back in Merrimac, instead of a bunch of jagged rocks.

I don't feel bad for falling. Everyone else does too and, except for Knott, they all fall a lot more often than I do. Poor Grab spends as much time on the ground as he does on his feet. I wonder if it's because of his metal legs, or if as a Mapper he's just not used to using his body very much.

After we run, Asa has us scale the canyon wall.

"Focus on the wall in front of you," Shadow advises. "Don't look down."

"Yeah, we wouldn't want you to fall and go splat," Rory jeers.

I bite back a hot reply and give Shadow a grateful nod. The tension has been building with Rory, like a volcano bubbling up beneath the surface. Sooner or later there's going to be an explosion, and he and I will have this out once and for all.

Now is not the time though.

I keep my eyes on the wall in front of me. Don't look down. Don't even think about down. Stay focused on the wall. Handhold, foothold, handhold, foothold.

It's easier than I expected. The grey walls are swiss-cheesed with little nooks and crannies, and the augmented strength of the armor makes holding on a snap. We scuttle up to the top of the canyon, quick as real dust lizards.

At the top I turn, blinking in the sudden sunlight. The high plateau of the scabland stretches out around me, smooth and flat as far as the eye can see. Dark canyon-veins rift the earth all around. For a moment, I can't breathe. My entire life has been down inside one of those rifts. I'm literally on top of the world. It seems so big and empty, the sky stretching out forever, the horizon impossibly far away. I find myself squatting down, one hand on a boulder, trembling as if I'm afraid the wind is going to lift me away.

It makes me feel better to see I'm not the only one. I catch a glimpse of Rory's face, his mouth a wide-open O inside his helmet, his eyes showing white all around. Knott is doing a little better, but I can tell by the rigid way she's standing that she's not exactly comfortable. Only Shadow and Grab seem unfazed, but she's a climber and he was raised in Sunrise, so they don't count.

That thought makes me pause. No wonder the Sunrisers think of us the way they do. They live up here in the open air. A world full of light and space. We spend our entire lives in a big crack in the earth, living inside the rock. Canyon City has always seemed so big to me, so full of life. But looking around at the dark canyon-veins surrounding us, the empty space stretching on forever above, I understand for the first time how small our world really is. We're just a bunch of sand-mites scrabbling around in the dirt.

This thought makes me clench my fists with anger. I mean, I've known my whole life that Canyon City is a penal colony. That we're all prisoners. But it wasn't until now that I understood what that truly meant. The world we've been denied our whole lives.

Asa calls up from the canyon floor,

"Now use your grav boots to float back down."

I turn to peer down into the canyon and stumble backward. Whoa. We're a lot higher than I thought. The fear that gripped me in the lounge comes back, even stronger. My hands and feet are tingling so bad they're practically numb. I fall to my knees, then forward onto my hands as well. On all fours, I stare at a scattering of smooth pebbles on the ground, my breath rasping in and out of my throat.

Rory laughs, but it sounds forced, as if he wants to laugh at me, but doesn't actually find the situation all that funny. I hardly even notice. I've got bigger problems than Rory right now.

Shadow kneels down beside me.

"It's just like coming up. Don't look down. Focus on what's in front of you."

"Except in this case, what's in front of me is a thousand meter drop." I try to laugh, but it comes out as a sob.

"Instructor Asa? We could use some help up here," Shadow says.

"Not my problem, rock baby," Asa says cooly. "He's your teammate. You take care of him."

"Thanks for nothing," Shadow mutters under her breath. "Fine, we'll figure it out. Anybody have any suggestions?"

"Toss him over the edge," Rory says. "If he catches himself, fine. If he doesn't, maybe they'll assign us a better Chaser next time."

"Funny, Rory. Not helpful," Shadow snaps. "Anyone else?"

The only answer is the wind whistling across the plateau.

19

———————

"Maybe Knott can carry him," Grab says hesitantly.

I'm still staring at the pebbles, but I can feel Shadow considering this.

"Yeah, that might work," she says finally. "Knott? What do you think?"

There's silence on the comm, and I laugh softly as I realize I was waiting to hear a response from Knott. As if that would ever happen.

There's a crunching of footsteps over the gravel, and a pair of big boots comes up in my peripheral vision. I stare at them for a few seconds, wondering what they are doing there. Then something grabs the back of my belt and hauls me into the air.

"Waaaggghhhhh," I shriek, which I'll admit isn't helpful at all.

I find myself draped face-down over Knott's shoulder, staring at the backs of her legs. I try to struggle, but her grip is like a double-welded strut. Nothing short of an earthquake is going to break it.

"Hey, can we talk about this?" I squeak. "I don't think this is such a good … Aaaaaaggggggggghhhhhhhhhhhhhhh."

This last bit comes as Knott leaps off the edge of the cliff. We plummet toward the distant ground.

I lose all control of my body. As the canyon wall rushes past me, I thrash and scream and weep like a two-year-old at nap time. My stomach remains up on top of the cliff somewhere. I wrap my arms around Knott's torso and shut my eyes, squeezing with every muscle I have, her shoulder plate digging into my ribs. The fall lasts forever. I age ten years in ten seconds.

Then we stop moving.

I hang there, upside down and panting, eyes shut, still squeezing Knott like a demented constrictor.

"It's ok, Twist," Shadow says. "You can open your eyes now."

My lids are so tight it feels like I should use a crowbar, but I eventually get my eyes open just in time to have the world flip again as Knott sets me back on my feet. My legs fold, and I sit down hard.

"Thanks, Knott," I mutter. I'm glad the polarization in my mask makes my face hard to see, because I'm sure my cheeks are redder than the canyon walls.

The rest of the team are carefully not looking at me. Except for Rory, who's doubled over with laughter. The prick.

"OK, you've gone high, now you go low." Asa points to a large opening in the cliff wall. "I want you to clear that cave in under ten minutes. Get going."

Relief floods through me. This is something I can handle. Maybe I can make up for losing it up on the mesa. I take a deep breath and stand, shrugging my armor back into place.

"Two one two," I bark out the formation. "I'll take point."

My faceplate clears and the helmet lights kick on as I step through the opening. The cave is about ten meters in diameter, with a sandy floor and smooth ceiling and walls. Fifteen meters in, it takes a sharp turn to the right, and we leave the daylight behind.

A weight leaves my shoulders along with the light. This is my world now. In the dark, under the earth, surrounded on all sides by rock.

The passage splits, and I stay at the juncture while Shadow scouts down one branch. When Knott arrives, she takes over the junction and I scout the other passage. Grab and Rory stay about thirty meters back, covering our retreat. When we've cleared a hundred meters or so of passage, Shadow and I return to the juncture and compare notes, then decide which way we want to proceed. Repeating this maneuver at every split we come to, we work our way deeper into the caves.

It's a big system, but dead simple in caver terms. Everything is man-sized. No tight cracks, no belly crawls, no face-first wriggles through a jumble of fallen rocks. The most difficult thing we have to do is crouch under a low ceiling a few times. Yawn.

I'm out scouting a long branch, and starting to wonder how far we need to go before we can declare the cave clear, when I see a flash of movement ahead of me. I freeze, wondering if I'm seeing things. That happens when you're alone in a cave. Your brain gets lonely and starts imagining faces in the walls, friends in the flickering shadows.

I hold for a minute, carefully studying the passage ahead, waiting to see if the movement repeats. It doesn't, so I push my apprehension aside and continue forward. Half a dozen steps later, I wish I'd listened to my instincts.

The loudest noise I've ever heard lifts me up and slams me against the passage wall. Thick grey dust fills the corridor, swirling in the beam of my headlights. The only thing keeping me breathing is the filters on my helmet. I hear a loud crack overhead and plunge forward on instinct, my armored legs driving me down the passage with super-human speed. I get about five steps before the entire ceiling collapses, huge chunks of stone roaring down onto the place I was just standing. I dive and roll, skidding to a halt beside the passage wall, rocks rattling off my armor. Something heavy slams down on my left leg, and sudden pain makes me scream.

Things eventually stop falling and I lay there, panting and gritting my teeth against the agony in my leg. I shiver, fear turning the sweat on my back cold. Dust so thick you could stir it with a spoon fills the tunnel, obscuring everything.

I kill my helmet lights while I wait for the dust to settle. Whoever set this trap might be nearby, watching, and I don't want to give away my position. I flick on my night vision and infrared, but get nothing useful.

My leg is trapped beneath a large rock. I try to lift it off, but every time I shift, my leg shrieks with pain. Still, I grit my teeth and try, but

I've got no leverage from my position and it won't budge. I'm stuck until my crew finds me.

I watch the dust swirl and try to figure out what is happening. Outsiders. It has to be. The uniformity of the passages comes back to me, how easy they were to explore. As if they were regularly used. As if somebody maintains them.

Of all the dust-licking luck. First time out and we stumble upon an Outsider cave system.

Are they watching me right now? Do they know I didn't die beneath their little avalanche? And what about the others? Did the rest of the team get crushed?

No, I was a pretty good distance out in front. The others must have been far enough back to escape the rockfall. I hope.

The dust is starting to settle a bit, so I turn my headlamp onto its lowest setting, and dial my night vision up to the max.

"Light is not advised in this situation," Hiroko chimes in.

"If I want your advice, I'll ask for it, Hiroko."

I can see the dark outline of the fallen rock pinning my leg, and just beyond that a huge jumble of stone. The passage I just came down is completely buried. If I'm going to get out of here, I'll have to find another way.

I glance ahead of me. Still no movement or heat signatures.

I check my armor. Miraculously, all of the systems come up green. I lost my cannon somewhere beneath the rubble, so I draw my warp-knife. The blade glows a faint blue, the grip snug and familiar in my hand. I really hope I don't have to use it. I just had a mountain dropped on me, and I think my leg might be broken. The last thing I want to do is fight.

"Just let me get back to Merrimac in one piece," I whisper. "That's all I ask."

Speaking aloud reminds me that I haven't tried my comms yet.

"Shadow, are you there? Grab? Instructor Asa? Anyone?"

"There is no comm signal," Hiroko says.

Which is pretty much what I expected. Comms don't work very well through several tons of rock.

I use the warp-blade to carve small sections off the rock pinning my leg.

"This action is not advised. Standard procedure is to maintain position and await rescue."

"I'm not going to just lay here and do nothing, Hiroko."

"Standard procedure is to maintain position and await rescue."

"Yeah, I heard you the first time. You're annoying me, Hiroko. Deactivate."

"This action is not advised. Standard procedure is…"

"Deactivate! That's an order!"

Hiroko's status light goes dark on my display. I sigh. I really miss Jmini.

It takes a while, but eventually I manage to chip enough of the rock away to slide my leg out. It hurts like jagged metal sawing at my flesh from the inside, and when I stand up I can't put any weight on it. It's definitely broken.

Leaning heavily against the wall, I limp deeper into the cave. A glint near the floor catches my eye. I squat down to get a better look and discover a thumb-sized lens set at ankle-height. I look across and see a mirroring one in the wall opposite. Trip beams. I wonder if that's what set off the explosion back there.

I manually set my suit to scan for similar configurations and alert me from now on. Then I hop over the beam, jolting agony through my broken leg in the process.

Finding the beam makes me feel a little better. I probably just tripped an automated defense system. Automated systems are much less frightening than slavering hordes of Outsiders waiting to cut my head off.

I round a corner and the tunnel lights up with the glare of multiple beam-lights. I'm staring at half a dozen weapons, all pointed at me.

A voice calls out, "Drop the warpknife."

Well. So much for automated systems.

20

They take me to a small cell and strip me of my armor piece by piece. Someone throws a blanket at me and they leave me there, in my underwear, sitting on a stone bench carved from the wall. There's no door keeping me in the cell, but there are two armed guards standing just outside. It's pretty clear I'm not going anywhere.

My captors seem human, for the most part. They've kept their lights, and guns, pointed in my face, so it's been hard to get a good look at any of them. But their bodies are definitely humanoid. Outsiders, not Horrors.

I suppose this should make me feel better - if it were Horrors, I'd be dead already - but it doesn't. Everything that lives outside the walls of Canyon City hates us. They may not have killed me yet, but it's only a matter of time.

Curious faces appear from time to time at the entrance to my cell, and now that I'm not being blinded, I see my first impression was wrong. They're not entirely human after all. Their faces are odd colors, with patterns running along the edges of their cheeks. Strange growths speckle their heads.

I shudder. They're biomods. Not Horrors, but no longer human, that's for sure.

I wonder why they're keeping me alive. Are they going to question me? Torture me?

The joke is on them, because I'm just a trainee. Not even a real Guardian. I don't know anything.

Of course, even if I did know something, that's probably what I'd say. So there's no way they'll believe me at first.

I start to sweat. I don't want to be tortured. If they're going to kill me anyway, why don't they just do it now? Maybe I'll try to provoke one of the guards. Make them mad enough to shoot me dead.

Except that I don't want to die either.

Spines. This sucks.

A woman comes into my cell, carrying a small medkit. Her skin is earth-toned, and a fleshy, dark green crest rises in a ridge down the center of her skull. Her eyes are clear and green.

"I'm Sparrow," she says. "I'm going to set your leg for you, if that's all right."

I nod cautiously. If I've got to be a prisoner, I guess I'd rather be one without a broken leg.

She kneels in front of me and peels back the blanket. My exposed shin is swollen and bruised, with strange lumps pressing out against the flesh. It's so deformed I don't even recognize it. It's like someone else's grotesque shin has been grafted onto my knee.

Sparrow cleans the blood away with cool antiseptic wipes. I have to fight to keep from flinching away, but her touch is gentle and light. Once she's got it cleaned up, she carefully feels around the lumps, assessing the damage. Finally, she nods to herself and sticks an anesthesia disc onto my skin. I sigh with relief as the pain recedes into the distance. Then she hands me a folded-up scrap of towel.

"Bite down on this. The next part is going to hurt." She grips my leg firmly, one hand on my ankle, the other just below my knee. She looks me in the eye and counts down. "Three. Two. One." She yanks on my ankle hard and I scream, the pain bringing tears to my eyes. I grind the towel between my teeth. Then she gently probes my leg with her fingertips and nods. "That's got it aligned. The worst is over now."

She sprays foam over my lower leg, and I watch it harden into a cast. Then she smiles at me.

"You'll be good as new in a month or two. Don't try to walk on it until I can find you some crutches, ok?"

I nod warily. I don't know why this Outsider is being so nice to me, but it makes me suspicious.

Sparrow leaves me staring at the grey walls of my cell, the chill of the stone bench seeping up into my thighs. I wrap the blanket around my shoulders and huddle down inside it, my thoughts going round and round, fear blowing up like a sandstorm. I almost cry three times. I'm proud of the fact that I manage to choke back the tears each time.

After what feels like hours, a dark-skinned man enters my cell. He's tall and thin, with a long jaw and patterns speckling his bald head that look like lichen. The almond shape of his dark eyes reminds me of Ianna, and sadness and anger swirl in my heart, almost releasing the tears I've been fighting so hard to contain. I bite my lip savagely, and focus on the anger. These are the people who killed my parents. Now is not the time for sadness.

The man is rubbing his hands together nervously, his fingertips so heavily callused I can see the bulges. There's dirt under his nails.

He catches me looking at his hands and realizes what he's doing. He hides them behind his back, and stands up straight, shoulders back.

"What's your name?" He speaks quietly, but his voice sounds loud in the tiny cell.

I consider lying, but really what's the point? It's just a name, it doesn't mean anything.

"Twist."

"Twist." He purses his lips as if he's tasting the word. "And what were you doing in our tunnels, Twist?"

"It was just a training exercise. I didn't know there was anyone in here."

He frowns and I see the disbelief in his eyes. Sweat slides down the back of my neck. I can see it coming. It's only a matter of time before they start sticking blades under my fingernails. Panic tightens my chest.

"I swear. I'm just a trainee. Our instructor told us to make sure these caves were clear, so that's what we were doing. Please, I don't know anything."

"Where are you from, Twist?"

"What?"

"Where are you from? I can see you're not a Sunriser. Where did you grow up?"

"Canyon City."

"Obviously. Where in Canyon City?"

I don't see why it makes any difference to him, but I take a deep breath and start to tell him about my childhood in Canyon City. The words come slowly at first, but as I speak they acquire a life of their own. Like they've been building up inside me, just waiting to come out.

I find myself telling him everything. About my parents dying in an Outsider attack. How Ianna and I bounced around for years, holding tight to each other. How I was sent to Papa Grady's camp and never saw her again.

"It's your fault. You killed our parents." My eyes are full of tears as I look him right in the eye. "You killed our family with your dirty bomb. Why would you do that? They never hurt anyone."

I'm surprised to see that the man's cheeks are wet too.

He's trembling and looks like he's holding himself upright through force of will alone. He tries to speak, but has to stop and collect himself. He licks his lips. Tries again.

"Twist, what … What's your real name?"

"Theo. Theo Maro."

The man moans and sways a little, like he's going to pass out. I don't know what's wrong with him, but this is definitely not the way I thought this interrogation was going to go.

"Theo." Tears glisten in his eyes. "What would you say if I told you your father is not dead?"

I stare at him like he's grown a second head. What game is this guy playing?

"I'd say you're crazy."

He nods, like he expected that. Takes a shaky breath and blows it out. He waves me over on the bench and I scoot to one side, making room for him to lower himself down beside me.

Things have officially gotten weird.

"The Outsiders aren't what you think." He's got a look of intense concentration on his face, like every word that comes out of his mouth could be the difference between life and death. "The Guardians paint us as terrorists. Planting bombs in Canyon City. Killing innocent people."

"That's because you are. You killed my dad!"

He chokes and nods. I can see his jaw muscles working as he grinds his teeth together, holding back some strong emotion.

"That's what they want you to think. It's the key to their power. Keep everyone frightened. Focused on an external enemy. That way they never question. Never see what the Guardians are doing."

"Of course you'd say that."

He nods again, his face calm and serious now.

"Yes, I would. You're right to question my words. You should. Think for yourself. Question everything. It's the first step toward freedom."

He shifts on the bench, turns his body so that he's facing me.

"You were born on the first day of spring, just before sunrise. I still remember your mother's eyes when she held you for the first time. The way they shone. Your tiny fist clutching at her hair. It was the happiest moment of my life."

I blink in confusion, trying to make sense of his words.

"What are you saying? How do you know that?"

His dark eyes catch and hold mine.

"I know because I was there, Theo. I know because I'm your father."

21

———

"You're lying." I'm pressed up against the wall of the cell, as far from the Outsider on the bench as I can get. "You're just trying to get me to trust you. My dad is dead. He died in a bombing."

"Who told you he was dead? The Guardians?"

"The bombing happened. I saw the burned-out building."

"You're right, it did happen. But it wasn't Outsiders who planted the bomb." He's speaking calmly, as if every word coming out of his mouth isn't dust-crazy.

"Then who did?"

"Who benefits from keeping everyone scared of the Outsiders? Scared people think they need saving. They're happy to let the Guardians control them in order to save them."

"That's insane. Why would the Guardians kill their own people?" I'm leaning away from him now, shaking my head over and over. "My dad died. Whatever game you're playing here isn't funny."

"No," he says soberly. "It's not."

Something in his voice plucks at me, and I look at him. Really look at him.

It's been a long time, but I still remember what my dad looked like. I've got this memory of him sitting by the window, laughing at something I'd done. He's got dirt smeared across his cheek, and there are bags under his eyes. But he's smiling, and his eyes sparkle in the sunlight coming through the window.

The guy sitting beside me is thinner, and looks ten years older. His hair is gone, replaced by those weird lichen splotches. Deep, sad lines crease his forehead and bracket his mouth. His eyes are still sparkling, but now it's because they're brimming with tears. They look like they've cried a lot over the years.

But his face is still shaped the same. His mouth still pulls up to one side when he talks. And his eyes are still shaped like dark almonds. The same eyes he gave to Ianna.

"Dad?" I sway in my seat.

He nods and chokes out, "Yes. It's me, Theo."

He pulls his pendant out from beneath his shirt, the twin to mine. Three copper circles, intertwined.

Then his arms are around me and we're both blubbering.

"Why? Why did you go?" I push him away, glaring. "You left us!"

"I'm sorry. I had no choice. I had to get out of Canyon City. The Guardians were hunting me. It was the only way I could protect you."

"Protect us?" I'm shaking now, hot anger roaring up inside of me. I shove him hard, and he sprawls on the dirt. "You left us alone! How was that protecting us?"

He holds his hands out helplessly.

"I didn't have time to plan. The bomb almost got me. I panicked; I had to make a split-second decision. The scablands is no place for kids. You were too young. Your sister was even younger. I thought you were safer in Canyon City. So I left you." His face crumples, falling into old, sad lines. "It was the hardest decision I've ever made. Not a day goes by I don't regret it."

I look down at him, kneeling in the dirt. A broken old man. Part of me wants to forgive him. He was in a bad situation. He made a bad choice. It happens. People make mistakes.

Then I remember Ianna.

"Ianna's missing because of you. They took her away. I haven't been able to find her for three years," I hiss. He flinches, my words stabbing deep. I hate myself for adding to his pain, but I can't stop the anger pouring out. "All those years of sleeping in shelters. Scrounging through garbage. Working for Papa Grady. It's all your fault. None of that would have happened if you hadn't left us."

He nods and looks even sadder. I can't stand it.

"It's all your fault!"

I fling myself at him, swinging my fist wildly. I hit him in the chest, the shoulder, the head. He doesn't even defend himself, just puts his face in his hands and takes it. Years of frustration pour out of me. I punch him over and over, screaming, tears and snot pouring down my face.

I pound on him until I can't lift my arms anymore, and then I collapse against him and he puts his arms around me. I bury my face in his shoulder and deep, painful sobs tear out of me, ripping away at my insides, one after another.

"It's ok," my dad murmurs. "I'm here now."

I sob until I can't breathe, and that makes me hiccup, which makes me laugh. I feel my dad smile too, and that makes me cry some more. But it's an exhausted, gentle cry now. Slow tears seeping into my dad's shirt.

My dad's shirt.

It finally hits me that this Outsider really is my dad. My dad is alive. My dad's shoulder is warm beneath my cheek. My dad's hand is gently patting my back.

It's such a strange thing, to have your dad back after he's been dead for so many years. It feels like a dream. A bizarre, nonsensical, wonderful dream.

We sit there like that for a while. Dreaming together.

Eventually I collect myself and sit up, wiping my eyes with my sleeve. Dad reluctantly lets me go.

"I got snot all over your shirt."

He chuckles.

"Best snot I've ever had."

I laugh too, then I sit there, suddenly uncomfortable. What do you say to your dad who's been dead for years?

"What's that stuff on your head?" I finally ask.

"We call them scabs." He grimaces. "It's some kind of local lichen.

Inside the city they innoculate against it, but out here it grows on everything."

"Did it make your hair fall out?"

"No, my hair did that all by itself. The scabs don't really hurt anything, as far as we can tell. They just look strange."

"Can I touch them?"

His eyebrows raise, but he shrugs and nods.

"Sure. If you want to."

I slowly reach out and touch the top of his head. His skin is warm and smooth, and I can feel the hard bone of his skull pressing against my palm. The scabs are little patches of green and brown and orange, some as big as two fingers across. They raise up a little from his skin, bumpy and rough.

"I see why you call them scabs."

"Yeah. They feel like scabs, don't they?"

"Are you sure they're not bad for you?"

"As sure as we can be of anything out here. We've all got them. That's what comes of living on an alien planet, I suppose. I'd say blame your grandparents, but it wasn't their decision to get shipped off to a penal colony, was it?"

"The Guardians. Does everything come back to them?"

"Well, no. The Guardians are just the local enforcement agency. Everything really goes back to their bosses at IEC."

I hadn't thought about it before, but it makes sense now that he's said it out loud. The only thing Canyon City produces is greicagins, and all of the gins we pull out of the mines get loaded onto Interplanetary Extraction Coalition cargo trains. Of course the IEC control the Guardians. I can't believe I never thought about it before.

"Did they found Canyon City? Is the IEC the whole reason there are people on this planet?"

"Yes. It takes a lot of money to found a colony. They don't get started without a very serious economic incentive. The greicagins supplied that incentive. They're one of most concentrated sources of energy we've ever found. Of course, they had to offset the cost somewhere, and they did that with cheap labor."

"Prisoners."

"Slaves, essentially." His mouth twists, his eyes becoming hard and angry. "Generations of them. Labor doesn't get any cheaper than that."

My mind is racing to catch up, but I think I'm getting the picture.

"Is that why you became an Outsider? To fight the IEC?"

He smiles, and warmth rises in my chest at the pride I see in his eyes.

"I always knew you were a smart kid. You got it on the first try."

"But was it worth it? Worth leaving me and Ianna behind? Worth living out here in the scablands?"

He shakes his head and looks down at his hands, clasped in front of his knees, then tilts his head back and runs a hand back and forth over his scalp, staring up at the ceiling as if he's trying to read the answers in the crevices in the rock.

"Worth it? I honestly don't know. All I know is that I never felt like I had a choice in the matter. Once you understand what the right thing to do is, you can't do anything else. You do what you have to do. And the cost is what it is."

I nod, but I don't really understand. I keep thinking of Ianna, on her own for three years, at the mercy of gangs and bosses and who knows what else. I can't see how anything would ever be worth that.

22

Dad brings me a pair of crutches and takes me to a cafeteria to get some food. I'm shocked to see that the cave system is actually an underground base. The corridors are clean and wide. Strings of lights along the ceiling keep everything lit. I wonder how big it is.

I also wonder if Asa knew it was here when she sent us in. She couldn't have, right? She wouldn't send a bunch of raw trainees in to clear out an Outsider base. The Guardians must not know it's here.

Which is crazy, if you think about it. An Outsider base this big, hidden this close to the walls of Canyon City? Unreal.

"Did your people capture the rest of my crew?" I stumble to a halt, my breath catching at the sudden thought.

"Who?"

"The rest of my crew. They were right behind me when the tunnel collapsed."

My dad shakes his head.

"No. They must have been on the other side of the cave-in."

I sag over my crutches, relieved. At least my crew is safe.

Dozens of people bustle past as we walk. There's no uniformity to them, they seem to wear whatever they like. And what they like seems to be ragged, dirty clothes with holes in the knees and elbows. They wear goggles and scarves around their necks, and headlamps on their foreheads. Almost all of it is home-patched, mismatched gear, which makes me smile and think of Wayfinders. Most of the people don't look twice at me as they hurry past, intent on mysterious errands of their own.

"They seem busy."

"They are. Busy evacuating." My dad grimaces.

"Evacuating?"

"This base has been compromised. It's only a matter of time until the Guardians find it now. We can't risk it. We'll pack up and go somewhere new."

"I guess that's my fault."

"Don't blame yourself. You were following orders. I'd trade a hundred bases to have you back with me."

He ruffles my hair and I feel my grin get wider, pushing out at my cheeks. I realize I've been grinning like a fool for a while now, walking around beside my dad. I probably look stupid, but I don't care. I got my dad back from the dead. I think I'm allowed to look stupid for a while.

My dad takes me into the cafeteria and gets us bowls of lentil soup. The soup's nothing special, but I still can't stop grinning.

"This is the craziest day of my life," I say.

He smiles back at me and nods, like he knows exactly what I'm talking about.

"Tell me about yourself. What do you like to eat? What kinds of things do you like to do? Tell me everything, I've got a lot of catching up to do."

So I do. I tell him I like almond cakes and goat's milk and bread fresh from the baker's oven. I tell him about my colored rock collection, and the pure blue marble I found that sparkles like a cat's eye when you hold it up to the light. I tell him about the Game, and Wayfinders, and Fin. His face gets thoughtful as I talk, but he doesn't interrupt me, just lets me ramble on about all the stuff he's missed over the past three years.

I get thirsty after a while, and my dad goes off to get me some water. I sit there at the table, chewing on lentils, staring at all of the

Outsiders around me. I see now that the markings around their faces are really spots where they've got scabs growing.

There seems to be a ton of different varieties. I see blues and blacks and yellows and reds, as well as more of the greens, browns, and oranges my dad's got. A lot of people have covered the scabs with tattoos, geometric designs spreading around their faces like a lion's mane, but I can still see the bumpy texture underneath the ink.

Most of the Outsiders look thin and weathered, like my dad. I guess it must be tough to live out here, hiding all the time. I wonder where they get their food. Do they steal it? Grow it themselves? I know the water on this planet is potable if you filter it. I guess that's one thing they don't have to worry about.

I study a woman at the next table over. She's got her face bent over a tablet, so engrossed in reading something that her soup's getting cold. Her red hair is cut short the way miners keep it, and I can see patterns of scabs running along her scalp underneath. I wonder how she got here. What she had to give up. Does she have a family back in Canyon City? Do they think she's dead?

The thought makes me sad. I wish I could tell them, tell all the kids. Dust, I wish I could tell everyone. Run down the street crying out, "Hey, they're not dead! They're alive and they're fighting for you! They miss you!"

I hear raised voices across the cafeteria, and when I look over, I'm surprised to see my dad arguing with a short, thick woman with obsidian skin. She's got the longest hair I've seen here: a thick clump of dreadlocks tied back with a cord. My dad looks angry; I can see the color in his cheeks from across the room. The woman just stands there with her arms folded across her chest. She looks implacable, like a stone pillar in a sandstorm. Like my dad can talk and shout all day and it's not going to matter to her one bit.

The woman catches me looking at them and says something to my dad. He glances over at me, then looks away. He throws up his hands, shoulders slumping. Together, they start walking toward me.

When they get to my table, the woman looks at my dad expectantly.

"Theo, this is Tempest," he says, not meeting my eyes.

The woman does though, and her dark eyes hold mine. Her eyes aren't challenging like Castle's, or cold like Asa's. They are deep and gentle and understanding. Looking at her is like sinking into a warm cup of tea.

"Nice to meet you," I say hesitantly. I'm confused, torn between how upset my dad seems and how gentle Tempest seems. Something doesn't match up, but I have no idea what.

"May I sit down?" Tempest asks.

"Sure."

She sits directly across from me, while my dad perches on the edge of a chair to my left. Tempest isn't fat, but there's a thick solidity to her that most of the Outsiders don't have. It makes her seem strong and grounded.

"I'm not one to beat around the bush, and we don't have time for that anyway." Tempest's voice is thick and warm. "So I'll get right to the point. Your friends have almost cleared the collapsed tunnel. If you want to go back, you'll need to be there when they break through."

"I'm staying," I say instantly. Then I look at my dad's worried face, and I wonder if I've made a mistake. "That is, if you want me to, Dad?"

He looks up, startled.

"Of course I do!"

I smile and relief shivers through me, surprising in its intensity. I didn't realize how scared I was that he'd say no. That he'd leave me behind again.

My smile falters as I realize he still looks worried.

"So what's the problem?"

"The problem," Tempest says, "is that it's not that simple. We've been fighting a covert war with the Guardians for decades. I'll be honest with you. It's not going well. And losing this base will be a big setback for us."

"And?"

"And I believe you may hold the key to changing all that."

"It's not right, Tempest," my dad interrupts. "He's just a boy."

"It's not your decision to make," Tempest says, with just a hint of steel in her voice. "It's his."

My dad frowns and runs his hand over his scalp, but doesn't say anything more.

"What's my decision?" I ask. "I already told you, I want to stay here."

Tempest's eyes grab mine and hold them.

"What if I told you that you could help everyone here, help all the people in Canyon City, by going back to Merrimac instead?"

I look from her to my dad and back again.

"What do you mean?"

Tempest folds her hands together on the table, leans forward.

"First of all, if your friends do not find you trapped beneath that cave-in, they will know you are somewhere else in the tunnels, and they will come looking for you. There is no way we can get everyone out of the complex before they arrive. Lives will be lost, possibly on both sides."

I chew my lip. I don't want anyone to die.

"Second, and even more importantly, the biggest advantage the Guardians have in our war is that they are inside the walls, while we are stuck out here. They have access to better equipment, better weapons, better everything. If we had someone inside the Guardians working with us, we could neutralize that advantage."

I look at her blankly, not sure what she's getting at. Then it hits me and my jaw almost falls off of my face.

"You want me to spy on the Guardians?" I look at my dad to see if she's joking, but I can tell from his frown that she's not. "That's dust-crazy."

"You don't have to do anything more than what you've been doing," Tempest assures me. "Go back to Merrimac. Continue your training. Become a Guardian. That may be all you have to do for years, who knows? When the time comes for you to help us, we will let you know. At that time, you may be in a position to do what no other member of the resistance can do. You may be able to tip the balance of the struggle all by yourself. This is no small thing I'm asking. This could be the difference between freedom for every person in Canyon City, and more generations of slavery."

"You don't have to do it, Theo," my dad says. "Nobody can force you to fight. If you want to stay here, all you have to do is say so. We don't have to be separated ever again."

"It's true," Tempest says. "No one will force you to do anything. The decision is yours. But do not make it lightly. Your decision, right here and right now, could change the course of history."

I look at the long lines on my dad's face and I can't breathe for a moment. All I want is to live like a normal person. A person with a family. Is that too much to ask?

I can't ignore Tempest's words though. If my team comes looking for me, people will die. Shadow might die. My dad could die.

And staying here won't help me find Ianna.

Tears are running down my face, but I make myself look my dad in the eye.

"You said it yourself, dad. There's a right thing to do. And once you know what that is, you can't do anything else. I guess this is the right thing to do. I'm sorry. I have to go."

My dad sobs, and throws his arms around me, squeezing so tight I can hardly breathe. I bury my face in his shoulder, breathing him in, trying to lock this moment away, remember every detail.

After a minute, Tempest softly clears her throat.

"Thank you, Theo. You're a very brave young man. It's time to go now."

They take me back to the tunnel and Sparrow sprays solvent on my cast. I watch it bubble away into the dirt, gritting my teeth as my bones shift. Then they put me back in my armor and lever a big rock down over me, so it looks like I've been pinned there the whole time. My dad kneels down beside me.

"I'm proud of you, son. I wish you weren't doing this, but I'm proud that you are. Be careful in there. Don't do anything to draw attention to yourself."

"Thanks, Dad. I will. You be careful too."

With that, they're gone, and I'm laying alone in the dark, waiting for my team to find me. Waiting for my new life to begin.

23

"Are you ok? You seem a little off."

"What? Yeah, fine. I'm fine." I grip the hilt of my warpknife and crouch down, giving Kass the nod that means I'm ready.

It's been hard to focus in the weeks since I got back to Merrimack. I keep thinking of the Outsiders, wondering where they've moved to. If they're ok. If my dad is ok. Worrying about what they're going to ask me to do, and what the Guardians will do to me if I get caught.

Kass comes at me and I parry her first strike with my armored forearm, then leap back, dodging the backhand that follows it up. I stumble as I land. The medrig healed my leg, but I haven't regained all the strength in it yet.

Kass gives me a little smile.

"You're learning, Rockhead. If you ever get your brain out of the way, you might even be a decent fighter."

"Why do you say that?"

"That you might be a decent fighter? It's my naturally optimistic nature."

"No, that my brain gets in the way," I say, scowling.

"It's obvious. I see you trying to calculate every move before it happens. 'If she attacks *this* way, I'll counter with *that*. If she does *that*,

I'll do *this*.' That's all fine when you're mapping out strategy for a game, but in a warpknife fight, milliseconds can make all the difference. If somebody is already moving while you're trying to decide what to do, you're dust. Trust yourself. Know your strengths and let your body do its thing."

"So how do I turn off my brain?"

"Ask Octav. His brain is off all the time."

She grins, and I do my best to grin back.

It feels forced though. Which is crazy considering how beautiful Kass is. I mean, if I can't even bring myself to smile at a pretty girl, there's something seriously wrong with me.

Everything feels forced these days. Kass is right, I am thinking too much. It's like I'm standing back and watching myself through a window. I can't help it, I can't stop thinking about all the stuff my dad told me.

I've always known there was a gulf between Sunrisers and Rock-heads. The "haves" and the "have nots". But now I know the gulf is much bigger than I ever suspected. It's generations of slavery feeding IEC profits.

I look around at Merrimack, at the fancy equipment, and all I see is blood money. My parents, my grandparents, Fin. They worked their whole lives to build this. The Guardians and IEC managers live like this, while we do all the work and scrabble for food and die down in the dust and grit. Now that my eyes have been opened, I can't stop seeing what's going on around me. This enormous machine, running on human sweat and blood. It makes my stomach sick thinking about it.

"You're too easy on him, Kass. Let me show you how it's done." Octav puts a hand on her shoulder. Kass shrugs and steps aside, giving me an apologetic look.

Octav's warpknife glows green in practice mode. The setting stops the knives from penetrating anything more than a few millimeters, but it doesn't dull their sharpness, or the pain of getting cut. Even shallow gashes sometimes need stitches to close them up.

Octav's stance is different than Kass's, and unlike anything they've taught us at Merrimack. He holds his strike hand high, arm curled, and keeps the point of his blade aimed right at my chest. Almost like a sand stinger's tail. How fitting. His parry arm is a little lower than most people's, his feet more in a line. I sink into guard position warily, not sure what to expect.

"Did you know I have a twin brother?" he says casually.

"Oh really?" I try to keep my voice light, but tension thrums through me.

"Really. Some rockhead took his place here." His eyes narrow, watching my reaction.

Then he attacks in a blur, moving faster than I've seen anyone except Instructor Asa move. He feints toward my face, drawing my blade up, then lunges in and buries the tip of his warpknife in the meat of my thigh.

"Dust-eating Horrors!" I curse, hopping back. I rub at my thigh, watching as a spot of blood blooms on the fabric.

Cold anger burns in Octav's eyes.

"It's not a game, rockhead. My brother would have known that."

I scowl and raise my guard. The spine-sucker has my attention.

We go three more rounds, and three more spots of blood appear on my clothing. He's toying with me. No matter what I do, Octav slips past my defenses effortlessly.

I'm buzzing like a nest of kicked wasps by the time Asa calls a halt to the sparring session. Octav is glacial in his anger, and not even breathing hard. I want to kick his teeth in, except I obviously can't.

Naturally, our watches go off at that moment, calling all teams to battle stations.

"Dust-licking maggots." I limp down the hall, growling.

The games have been coming at us almost every day, at unpredictable times. They're training us to be ready to go at a moment's notice. Zero to Battle Stations in ninety seconds flat.

I understand why they're doing it. From a training standpoint, it makes perfect sense. But there's nothing worse than having to climb inside a shell when you're already angry, sweaty, and covered in blood.

Grab calls out as I'm climbing down the ladder into our room.

"Hey Twist, I've got those earcones you wanted."

"Earcones?"

"For translating Knott."

"Oh, right. Let's see them!"

He slips a pair of black earcones into my hand. They look the same as every other pair of earcones I've seen. I poke them into my ears and raise a questioning eyebrow at Grab.

"Just speak normally," he directs.

"Hello? Knott can you understand me?"

A synth voice answers me, rising and falling in musical amusement.

"I've always been able to understand you. The question is, can you understand me?"

"I can," I say, a grin spreading across my face.

"I've got some for everyone. I juiced up the receivers too, so our comm range should be better," Grab says.

"That's really wet, Grab. Well done." I clap him on the shoulder.

He smiles shyly, his eyes on his toes. As he hands out the earcones, he asks, "Anyone know what the game is today?"

"It's pin the tail on your mother," Rory quips.

"I already pinned the tail on your mother last night," Grab shoots back, to the surprise of everyone.

"Full point to the Mapper," Shadow declares.

Rory scowls and pulls the lid of his shell closed. I follow suit, pulling on my breathing mask and letting the blue sand flow over my body like frictionless ball-bearings.

We've seen three kinds of games so far. There's all-in, like we had on our first run, where all the teams compete over a single objective. Then there's face-off, where two teams battle head to head. The third type is an enemy-objective game where we have to go in and clear a bunch of Outsiders from an area and retrieve something.

This is my least favorite, for obvious reasons. I don't feel right killing Outsiders anymore, even sim ones. I keep seeing the faces of my dad and Tempest and Sparrow and all the other people I met in the underground base.

But if I'm going to keep my cover, I've got to act the way the old me would have acted. And the old me gunned down virtual Outsiders by the dozens.

This game turns out to be a new one, a hybrid of types two and three.

"It's a retrieval. Outsiders. Plus face-off. We're up against the Scorpions," Shadow says.

"Those dust-lickers?" I groan. "I've still got blood all over me from sparring against them."

"You'd better be faster this time," Rory growls. "I am not cleaning boots this week."

"But you're so good at it," I shoot back. "A natural born boot-licker."

I'm giving him the spines, but I know Rory's right. Rumor is they'll be cutting some teams from the program any day now. We're currently sitting below the middle of the scoreboard. We can't afford to lose this game.

"Scabland. Exterior. I've got the flyover," Grab announces.

Well, at least we've got the map to start with. That'll make things easier.

"Looks like three, no four possible roads to the objective," Shadow says.

"Four roads confirmed," Grab agrees.

"I don't like the look of the north route," I say. "Too many cave mouths in that narrow stretch half a kilometer in. Perfect place for an ambush."

"Agreed," Shadow says. "No north road."

"Spoilsports," Rory complains. "It's not all about retrieving the objective, you know. I want to kill some Outsiders."

"Don't worry your little head. You'll get plenty of chances for that," Shadow says.

"Promises, promises."

"Here's the plan." A map from Shadow flashes up in my display, with each team member's strike path traced in a different color. "Any objections?"

"What about this?" Knott's new musical synth-voice chimes in, accompanied by a close-up schematic of a bendy place on the map with key tactical points highlighted.

"Hmmmm, I see what you're saying there," Rory muses. "Good call."

Personally, I don't see what she's saying, but that's ok. Knott and Rory have developed a good rapport, and that's a big key to us clicking as a team. Your heavy-hitters have got to be on the same page.

My number one job is retrieving the package, so I focus on the areas Shadow has highlighted for me.

"Underground again?" I complain. "When do I get my time in the sun?"

"When you start pulling your weight," Rory says.

"I think you do enough pulling for all of us, Rory. Try to keep your hands on the trigger for once."

This draws snickers from Grab.

"All right team," he says. "Drones are away. It's go time."

I launch my gravbike, and reluctantly activate Hiroko. She'll probably get in my way as much as she helps, but Shadow still hasn't gotten me Jmini, and I'd be crazy to do a run with no AI at all.

The first part of the run is quiet. Skimming through empty canyons, taking potshots at the occasional Mini Horror. Yawn. Then I see the tunnel system approaching on my map.

"OK, Hiroko. Look alive."

All she says is, "I am ready."

I sigh. Hiroko's got no humor at all. Jmini would have never passed up a straight line like that.

I park the gravbike outside the tunnel entrance Shadow has marked for me and prepare to go in on foot.

"Watch the bike, Hiroko."

"Defenses engaged."

Grab's drones have infiltrated the tunnels, and they've mapped out several hundred meters on my display.

"That's quite the cave system," I observe.

"That's what your mom said," Rory chortles.

"Foul," Shadow says. "Grab already made a 'your mom' joke. I'm deducting a point for lack of originality."

"You suck spines, Shadow," Rory sulks.

"Every chance I get," she retorts, and I can hear the smile in her voice.

I smile too. Say what you want about Rory, but he always gets the banter going. Which is good. Banter keeps the team loose.

Knott and Rory come in from opposite sides, covering the main entrances. They encounter Outsiders almost immediately. Virtual Outsiders, I remind myself. It's just a sim.

I creep in through a smaller side passage, while Shadow is doing the same in another part of the complex. I see one of Grab's drones winking in the tunnel ahead of me. I grin and give it a one-finger salute.

There's no sign of the other team yet, which is probably not good. Kass is a smart tactician, and the Sand Stingers have been first or second on the leaderboard the entire time we've been here. I'm sure they're going to pop up at an inconvenient time.

I run into my first resistance about two hundred meters in, when I surprise a pair of Outsiders crossing an intersection. Their eyes barely have time to widen before Hiroko has them locked. Two shots and they're gone. I fight the urge to check their faces, see if I recognize them.

It's just a sim. Just a sim.

My earcones erupt with the sounds of battle.

"Holy mother of dust," Rory whoops. "You cut right through that one, Knott!"

A glance at my map shows me they've hit heavy resistance in the bendy place Knott pointed out earlier. That suits me fine. Let them distract the guards, while I slip in through the back door.

According to the map, the room containing the package is around the next bend. Hiroko flashes a warning: three heat signatures.

I creep close and peer around the corner. I see a huge storage cave, at least a hundred meters across. Crates of supplies are piled in neat stacks. My display highlights the package I'm after in green.

I freeze. From the other side of the cave, Kass and Octav cross toward the objective with a gunner covering their flank.

"Dust storms." I swear quietly.

I check my team. Rory and Knott are still in the thick of it. Shadow is invisible, as usual.

"Shadow," I whisper, "are you around?"

Soft static is my only answer. I squat with my back to the wall, chewing my lip. There's no way I can take them one-on-three. I'd be lucky if I could take any of them one-on-one. Then I hear a soft click.

"Yes." She's whispering so softly I can barely hear her. "I've got eyes on the package."

All right. Shadow's got my back.

Two-on-three then. Well, why not? Nothing ventured, nothing gained, right? I take a deep breath and prepare to make my move.

24

The gunner is the most dangerous of the three at a distance, so I need to take him out first. My cannon won't get through his armor, but maybe I can keep him off balance long enough for me to get close and finish him off with my warpknife. Of course, Octav and Kass will be trying to kill me too, so the first thing I need to do is create a distraction.

"Hiroko, stun grenades on my mark."

Hiroko gives me the green light, and I cue the countdown. It flashes in the corner of my display. Three, two, one.

I pivot, poking my left arm around the corner, while keeping the rest of me safely behind cover. The grenade launcher whuffs softly, and three spheres hurtle across the cavern.

The AIs in the Sunriser's armor react with blinding speed, sending them diving for cover while simultaneously targeting the incoming grenades. The first grenade explodes in mid-air, then the second.

But even inhuman speed has its limits, and the third gets through. It detonates amidst the trio with cavern-rattling force.

White dust blooms, obscuring everything. I'm already sprinting toward the last place I saw the gunner, my blue-tinged warpknife ready.

He sees me a split second before I see him, and his spatgun flashes, tagging me in the shoulder. I start to fall, but I'm already too close. My momentum carries me into him, my warpblade sinking into his chest before he can get a second shot off.

I crouch there for a second, elated, my heart thundering in my ears as I try to get my bearings. Where did Kass and Octav end up? Hiroko's having trouble locating their heat signatures through the debris, so I shuffle cautiously in what I think is the direction Octav fell.

For long seconds there is nothing but dust and silence and sweat burning into my left eye. Hiroko tells me nothing, of course. I swear she's the most useless AI ever.

A blur comes at me from the right. I turn to meet it, but I'm too slow. An armored boot catches me in the ribs, sending me sprawling on the floor of the cave. I go with the momentum and turn it into a roll, ending up back on my feet, warpknife extended to meet this new foe.

His stance gives him away. Red warpknife curled high. Then Octav's cold eyes come into view as he clears his faceplate.

"I know it was you," he says. "I'm going to take you apart for what you did to my brother."

Dust storms. I'm in serious trouble.

He advances and I retreat, peppering him with tiny snapdragon missiles from my shoulder mount as I go. They won't hurt him, but they might slow him down, which is all I can hope for at this point. If he gets within arm's reach of me, I'm dead.

"Give it up, Rockhead." His voice booms through his helmet speaker. "This game is over."

"Do you write your own dialogue, or do you pay someone to do it? I'm dazzled by your wit," I shoot back. False bravado is about the only thing I've got going for me right now, so I'm going to ride it for all it's worth. Admittedly, it probably isn't worth much.

I must have struck a nerve, because Octav lunges forward, his blade flickering toward me once, twice, three times. I retreat as quickly as I can, parrying like a stimmed-up desert dasher. I deflect his first two slashes, but the third catches me across the thigh, in exactly the same spot he poked me earlier.

"Dust-licker!" I curse, hopping on my one good leg. Unlike in the sparring room, his warpknife isn't in safety mode here, and the shell's haptics make it feel like that cut went deep. I can even feel warm blood seeping beneath my armor.

Octav takes a moment to gloat.

"Those who do not learn from their mistakes are doomed to repeat them."

"And those who spout cheap quotes always sound like an idiot," I growl. "But I guess in your case that's truth in advertising."

"Defiant to the last." He strolls jauntily toward me like some cheap sim villain. "That's what I admire about you, Twist. You're like one of those stupid little dogs that never knows when to shut up. Yapping away right up to the moment the wolf swallows you in one bite."

"Yeah, well…" I search for something clever to say as I hop backward. It's hard to be witty when you're using most of your brain power to keep from falling on your butt.

"Cat got your…?" His words become a gurgle as a white warpknife sprouts from the center of his chest.

"Enough with the cliches already." Shadow pulls her blade free from Octav's falling body. "That guy is really hard to listen to."

My relief lasts exactly five seconds, then a blue blur streaks the air and Shadow's helmet goes rolling away into the dust. With her head still inside it.

"I knew you'd come out if I waited long enough." Kass twirls her blade with a flourish.

Dust storms.

"That was rude, Kass. Don't they teach you manners in those fancy Sunrise schools?"

"Sure they do. If you notice, I killed her with one clean stroke. That is the height of etiquette."

"Little Miss Manners. Your mother must be proud."

"Oh, she is. Or at least she will be when my team graduates at the top of the leaderboard."

"You'll have to go through me first."

"I'm disappointed, Twist. You sound like Octav now. I expected more originality from you."

"I'm all out of clever at the moment," I grunt. My right leg is about to collapse from too much hopping and haptic agony stabs my left leg with every movement. I've got no time for clever. It's all I can do to keep from falling over.

"Well if you've nothing more to offer, I guess I'll take the money and run." Kass sheathes her warpknife and strolls off into the dust.

It takes me a moment to realize she's not going to finish me off. My face burns with shame. Never leave an enemy at your back is one of the first rules of engagement. Strolling away like that lets everyone know I'm not even enough of a threat to bother killing. It's the ultimate insult.

I hop after Kass, determined to prove her wrong, but my leg gives out and I fall facedown in the dust. I launch a few snapdragon missiles at her as a last token of resistance. Kass gives me the finger as they bounce off her armor. I can only watch as she takes the package and zooms away.

25

Kass and her crew preen in the cafeteria, holding court like royalty. Even Rory's over there, fawning over Kass. Octav shoots dark stares in my direction. I shudder. He's determined to get revenge on me for eliminating his brother.

Meanwhile, the leaderboard haunts me. We're buried in eighth place. Eight out of ten, almost two hundred points behind the Sand Stingers in the top position. We still haven't won a single game.

The only thing keeping us off the bottom of the leaderboard is Rory and Knott. Their individual scores are near the top of their categories, which pulls our team total up a bit. They can't do it all themselves though.

"We can't keep losing," I grumble, pushing cubed potatoes around on my plate.

"Not if we want to stay in Merrimack," Shadow agrees. "Word is, they're cutting the bottom half of the class in a week. If we don't get into the top five by then, we'll be gone."

"How do you know that?" Grab asks. Shadow just looks at him. "Yeah, sorry."

"We need a plan," I say.

"You could stop sucking," Knott chimes in. "That might help."

I scowl and push my potatoes some more. I can't even snap back because she's right, I do suck. My name is buried at the bottom of the Chaser's rankings. If I don't figure out how to stop getting slagged out there, I'll be gone in a week and none of this will matter. It'll be back to Canyon City for this rockhead.

I wonder how to get in contact with the Outsiders. If I flame out, there's no way I'm going down to Canyon City. I need to figure out how to get outside the wall. Back to my dad. Maybe we can find Ianna together.

I remember my dad's face as he knelt beside me in the tunnel. How proud he was that I'd chosen to go back to Merrimack. Sticking my head in the Horror's pincers to help fight the IEC. To free Fin, and Ianna, and all the people of Canyon City.

Will he still be proud of me if I flame out? Will I be able to help the Outsiders if I'm back in Canyon City?

I know the answers without asking. The Outsiders have plenty of people in Canyon City. They need someone in the Guardians.

I can't flame out. I have to be better. And to get better, I'm going to need some help.

"Shadow, have you got that thing I asked you for?" I lean close so the others don't hear. "Hiroko almost got me killed again last game. If we want to move up the leaderboard, I need Jmini."

"I think I've figured out how to get it," she says, keeping her voice low as well. "It's a two person job though."

"What do you mean? Stick's just a little kid. He'll give it to you if you tell him it's for me."

"My source tells me the kid doesn't have it anymore. And the person who does is going to want something in return."

My stomach drops.

"Is Stick ok?"

She shrugs.

"As far as I know. I was asking about the AI, not the kid."

Spines. If we get caught smuggling an AI in, we'll both get kicked out of Merrimack. Shadow probably doesn't even think about it, she's Covert. Breaking rules is what she does.

But I'm no good to the Outsiders if I get expelled. On the other hand, if I don't get Jmini back I'm going to flame out anyway.

I sigh. Damned if you do…

"OK. When?"

"Tonight, if you want." Shadow says this casually, as if we're talking about trading rocks. The girl's got ice in her veins.

Meanwhile, I'm instantly so tense my rectum could produce greicagins. I nod, afraid my voice will squeak if I try to speak.

The day passes in a terrible, panicked haze. I miss everything in target shooting, and almost kill Rory in the stall beside me when I forget to thumb the safety on my gun. Not that shooting Rory would be the worst thing in the world, but it would draw attention to me, and I'm trying to avoid that as much as possible.

Even running doesn't relieve my stress. Usually when I run, I lose myself in the rhythm of my body, my mind drifting into a state of calm. Today I run and run and my mind just keeps running right along with me, freaking out the entire time.

To cap it all off, we get matched against the Desert Wolves in blade practice. For those keeping score at home, that's the team captained by Ghengis, the biggest, craziest dust-licker in Merrimack. And of course Asa pairs us off together.

This is the first time I've been paired with Ghenghis, so I don't know what to expect. But I do know he put someone in the medrig last week, so being paired with him does nothing to calm my anxiety.

Standing across from me, he seems even bigger than I remember. In anyone else's hand, his warpknife would be called a sword, but for Ghenghis it's scaled just right. Which gives him a ridiculous reach advantage.

His warpknife glows green as he thumbs it into safe mode. He doesn't even bother to take a defensive stance, just beckons me forward with one massive hand.

"Come."

I try to decide how to get past his reach. Maybe if I wait for him to attack first I can parry and riposte? What if I feint left and go right? Or go low where he can't reach me?

While I'm still thinking, Ghenghis gets tired of waiting. He closes the distance between us with one massive stride. I'm still raising my warpknife when he clubs me with a fist like a sledgehammer.

The next thing I know, I've got my cheek pressed to the practice mat and I'm listening to the ringing in my ears, wondering what the dust just happened.

Ghenghis's deep laughter brings me back to the present.

"It's supposed to be warpknife practice, not bash-Twist-in-the-head practice," I complain, climbing slowly back to my feet.

"Blades," Ghenghis scoffs. "Blades are for worthy enemies. Dogs get beaten."

"Be careful, this dog bites," I snap, embarrassment and anger making my face blaze.

"And yaps," he says, unconcerned. "I have heard you are a yappy dog. Yap yap yap. Never know when to keep your mouth shut."

"Your sister didn't mind my mouth last night." It comes out before I can stop myself.

Ghenghis's jaw muscles bulge, and he squeezes the hilt of his warpknife so hard his fingers go white. My stomach drops past my feet. I've made a terrible, terrible mistake.

He bellows and steps toward me, reaching out with his free hand to throttle me. Panic shoots through my system and I move instinctively, dodging to the side while bringing my warpknife up. It slashes him across the wrist.

In the real world, his hand would be lying on the floor and there would be a lot of blood shooting out the end of his stump. Unfortunately for me, my warpblade is in safe mode, and it just leaves a long scratch down his forearm. Ghenghis doesn't even notice.

He whirls and grabs for me again, and again I move without thinking, scoring another long cut across his palm.

Blood drips down between his fingers, speckling the practice mat. I start to think I might survive this.

That's when Ghenghis remembers he has a warpknife too. He swings a wild overhead cut at my head, like he's trying to cleave me in two. If I didn't dive out of the way, that's exactly what would have happened, safe mode or not. He doesn't pause, just whirls and swings again and again, bellowing like a wounded bull. I dodge, parry, and riposte. Then dodge again. My conscious mind is screaming in terror, but fortunately for me, that same terror is keeping my conscious mind away from my body's control panel. I'm a creature of pure instinct, my fight-or-flight dial turned all the way up. Dodge, scramble, leap, roll, dodge, parry, repeat.

I don't know how long this goes on, but after what feels like hours, I notice that Ghenghis is gasping for air, his movements slowing with every swing. He's bleeding from a dozen cuts, bright blood slicking his arms. I'm panting too, but far from winded. My runner's stamina is serving me well.

As my panic drops and my conscious mind slowly resurfaces, I notice something else. There's a crowd circled around us. Everyone in the room has stopped sparring and is watching us instead. I see Rory, stained forearms crossed over his chest, and Knott with a small smile on her lips. Beside her stands Kass, her eyes shining.

Unfortunately, this makes me self-conscious. Which makes me start thinking too much.

Ghengis lunges toward me and instead of just reacting, I freeze for a fraction of a second, torn between dodging and parrying. In the end I do neither, and his fist smashes straight into my face. I stumble back and he follows, connecting again. This time I go down, the room spinning around me. I feel a boot thud against my ribs, but it's far away. My head is lost in a dark fog.

I'm dimly aware of Instructor Asa getting between us. She takes the blade from my numb fingers.

I feel like I'm watching myself from afar again. Watching someone else. Did I almost beat Ghenghis in a sparring match?

The faces in the crowd around me say I did. There's shock and grudging respect there.

Kass comes over while I'm stripping off my padding.

"That was quite a show," she says, smiling with her perfect teeth, dark curls bouncing.

"Yeah," I respond cleverly.

"You intrigue me, Twist. You're nothing like I expected rockheads to be. Maybe we should get to know each other better." She puts her hand on my arm, and an electric charge shivers through my body. "Do you want to hang out tomorrow night?"

I nod like a robot and croak, "Sure."

"Great." She smiles again, giving my arm a little squeeze. "I'll meet you in the rec room after dinner."

A goofy grin splits my face. As I watch her walk away, admiring the perfect sway of her hips, Rory shoves past me, scowling like a thunderhead.

I hardly notice.

She called me Twist. Not rockhead, Twist. I don't know whose dream I've fallen into, but I hope I don't wake up anytime soon.

26

———

My euphoria fades as the day goes on. By the time I meet Shadow in the lounge after dinner, I've achieved a perfect balance of floating-on-clouds-happiness and pissing-my-pants-terror. She stands at the window, watching the last rays of sunset streak the clouds, Canyon City a deepening bruise below. My mouth is dust-dry as I step up beside her. I do not look down. She waits until the last rays disappear, leaving a faint, sinking glow beyond the horizon. The first stars speckle the sky.

Finally, she speaks, "We have to go down there."

"I was afraid you were going to say that."

"It's up to you. If you want your AI, we have to go fetch it."

I chew my lip. I want to say never mind. I want to say I don't need Jmini. I want to say, don't worry about it, I've got this.

But the leaderboard tells me that's a lie. We can't afford to lose any more points, and Hiroko's as useful as a lead weight around my leg. If I don't want to be cut at the end of the week, I need Jmini. And I need him now.

"What do I have to do?"

Shadow leads me to an overlooked door set back in a nook in the hallway. It opens onto a narrow access corridor running behind the walls. Pipes and wires snake along the ceiling, descending periodically to rectangular panels with rusty metal doors.

"So this is how you get around." I brush cobwebs out of my face. Dust bunnies hitch along on the tops of my shoes.

"I love it," Shadow confides. "There's nothing more exciting than being in a secret place nobody else knows about. It makes me feel safe."

I walk into another cobweb and reel away, spitting.

"Imspiders make you feel safe?"

She thinks about this for a minute.

"That's not what I meant, but yes, I guess they do. Imspiders are secretive and solitary, lurking in the shadows and corners. Spreading their webs here one day and there the next. They aren't tied down to any one place in particular. I mean, they were engineered from earth spiders and took to Greica without missing a beat. I admire that."

"I've always wondered why they did that. Why bring earth spiders to Greica?"

"To eat the tiny Horrors."

I look at her to see if she's joking.

"I'm serious. Canyon City used to be full of little insect-sized Horrors. They chewed the hell out of the early colonists. The IEC tried lots of things to get rid of them, but none of them worked. Finally, somebody figured that if spiders did the job on earth, why not here?"

"Huh." I look at the spiders lurking in the corners with new respect. "So you see yourself as an imspider?"

"Yes, and I'm going to tie you up and suck all your blood out if you don't keep your voice down," she hisses. "It may seem like we're far from everything, but don't forget there are rooms on the other side of these walls. Sound carries."

"Sorry."

I follow in silence until we come to a circular metal hatch in the floor. The cover is thick and heavy, and it takes both of us to hinge it open, revealing an iron ladder that descends into darkness. Shadow switches on her headlamp, and I do the same.

In addition to the headlamps, we're both carrying a pouch of tools and our warpknives, just in case. As far as I'm concerned, if we have to draw our warpknives, it will mean things have gone way off the rails, and not in a good way. I really hope it doesn't come to that.

Shadow leads me down into a dark tube, our boots echoing on the metal rungs. I feel like I'm in a missile silo, and any moment something is going to come along and shoot me out the top of the tube. We step off the ladder into another maintenance corridor, and heave open another metal hatch to resume our descent into darkness. We repeat this operation for several floors. Shadow finally pauses beside what she says is the final hatch.

"It's going to get stinky down here," she warns.

"I sleep in a room with five teenagers. I've smelled the worst there is."

"Mmmhmmm." She doesn't look convinced.

We haul back on the hatch, and I stagger back a step. The stench that's wafting out may in fact be worse than the smell of Rory's feet, though it's probably too close to call.

"You take me to all the best places."

"Oh, you haven't seen anything yet," she promises.

This time the ladder takes us down into a natural cave, which swallows up the beam of my headlamp like an imspider cocooning a fly. The stench gets worse as we descend, and by the time we step onto a narrow shelf of rock my eyes are watering from the fumes. Before us is a dark, still lake of sewage, receding into the distant corners of the cavern. Piles of drift-turds line the shore.

"Charming." I cough.

Shadow covers her mouth with her sleeve and scurries away. I follow.

Thankfully, she guides me away from the lake of filth, down a long dry tunnel. After a few minutes, I feel the stirring of a fresh breeze in the darkness. After another hundred meters, I cautiously remove my arm from my face and test the air. Still stinky, but rapidly approaching breathable. Hallelujah.

The tunnel contracts around us until I'm stooped over and shuffling. We come to a rusty grate closing off the end of the tunnel. The bars are thick and black with age, a thick padlock clutching the hasp. Shadow squats beside it and beckons me over.

"Last chance to back out," she whispers. "Once we leave this tunnel, we'll have officially left Merrimack. I can't promise we'll be able to get back in,"

"What do you mean, we can't get back in? What's the point of all this if we end up stuck in Canyon City?"

"I didn't say we can't get back in," she corrects. "I said I can't promise it. I'm pretty sure we'll be able to get back. I wouldn't be leaving if I wasn't. But there's always a chance we'll get caught, and who knows what they'll do to us then. We could get the cages for all I know. I just want you to be sure you're willing to take the risk."

I stare at her, my brain spinning in circles. There are no good answers here. No safe bets. If I get caught, I'll be expelled. I could be locked in a cage on the wall. But if I don't get Jmini, I'll flame out and be sent back to Canyon City.

I take a deep breath and nod once. Sometimes you just have to roll the dice.

"All right." Shadow reaches through the bars and opens the padlock with a soft click. "Kill your headlamp. Help me with the grate."

The bars are thick and heavy and hinged at the bottom. Shadow ties a piece of rope to the grate, and it takes all of our combined strength to lower it down quietly. Still the hinges squeal, setting my teeth on edge.

Shadow shakes her head.

"I should have brought some oil. Let's go."

We emerge into a clear night. Neither moon is in the sky, and milky drifts of stars spill across the soft void. A cool breeze blows up from the south, carrying the peppery scent of reaper blossoms.

We're in a shallow ravine at the base of the mesa. Bits of old, dried turds cling to the lanbrush. This whole route must be an overflow storm drain for the sewer system above. Good thing it's not monsoon season.

Shadow motions for me to stay low, and we pick our way down the dry bed, keeping our heads below the edge of the wash. The ravine winds down to the base of the wall, where it plunges out through a small, semi-circular opening.

Shadow pauses with one hand on the huge blocks that make up the wall. Above us, one of the rusty cages they hang criminals in creaks in the desert breeze. Bones and rags are all that's left of the poor dust-licker. If we get caught, will I be the one to replace him?

I shudder. No good choices. No safe bets.

Shadow pokes her head above the edge of the ravine, peering down the length of the wall, cocking her head as if listening. Sitting on my heels in the dry wash, I try to listen too, but all I hear is the soft rasp of my breath. She motions me closer and points along the length of the wall.

"See that building over there?"

"Yes."

"When I say go, run for it as fast as you can. Don't stop until you're under cover of the roof."

I nod, not trusting my voice. The building is at least forty meters away. Forty meters of open ground. It's pretty dark out, but if any of the guards on the wall glance this way, there's still a good chance they'll see us.

I grit my teeth. No turning back now.

"Go!"

I scramble up out of the ravine, loose rocks skittering away beneath my boots. Dashing across the ground, I expect a shout and the sudden glare of floodlights every moment. I'm aware of each breath, every impact of foot on earth shuddering up through my bones. The building approaches with agonizing slowness.

Then I'm there, slamming into the wall at full speed, nearly braining myself on the bricks. I cling to it, gasping, as Shadow slips in beside me.

"All right," she says. "The hardest part is over. Now we just have to get in and out of Canyon City in one piece."

"Raindrops," I pant. "Jelly easy."

We slink around the building and slip off into the alleys.

It's weird being back down here. I've only been in Merrimack a short time, but already Canyon City seems different. The crumbling walls are dirtier than I remember, the garbage-choked alleys more foul. The squalid children huddled in the doorways seem thinner, their clothes more ragged. I thought I'd feel relief walking these streets again, but I don't. I'm repulsed. I can't believe people live like this. I can't believe I lived like this.

The next thing I feel is anger.

This is the IEC's fault. Things don't have to be this way. Canyon City could be clean and safe, the people properly fed. Instead they're left to fight over scraps like animals.

I wonder why I never connected the dots before. I guess when you're down in the filth, you can't see the full picture. It's only when you look back from somewhere else that you're able to understand it for what it is.

27

———————

S hadow takes us to the west side of town, walking openly now that we've made it into Canyon City proper. Our clothes earn us a few looks, until she trades a couple of street kids for a pair of filthy blankets, which we wrap around our shoulders.

"We just need to borrow them for a while," she assures them. Metal flashes as she hands them something. "Keep this as a deposit."

"Silverware?" I ask as we step around the corner. "You smuggled out silverware?"

She shrugs.

"Good metal's worth something down here."

I follow her down a progression of narrow alleys, until we come to a cellar entrance.

A pair of thumpers stand in an orange circle of light at the top of the stairs. They narrow their eyes when they see Shadow. She pretends to be unconcerned, though her smile looks brittle to me.

"Hedeg," she says, walking up to the one on the left. He's got broad shoulders and tattoos on the backs of his hands. A scar runs across the bridge of his nose. "Tell Jepet I've got some business to discuss."

"Jepet doesn't do business with thieves," Hedeg growls.

"Don't worry, those days are behind me. I'm legit now." She

unwraps her blanket. "Look at my fancy Sunriser clothes. You think a street thief's walking around in these?"

Hedeg frowns, and I can practically see the gears of his tiny mind trying to turn. Finally, he grunts.

"Wait here."

We stand in the alley, shuffling beneath the glare of the second thumper. I lean in close to Shadow.

"They don't seem to like you very much here," I whisper.

"Just let me do all the talking," she says, the smile never leaving her face. "Remember when I told you I got my fingers broken? It was Hedeg that did the breaking."

"Oh, that makes me feel so much better."

Hedeg returns and escorts us down into a low corridor. Cheap bulbs throw dim, yellow light on the walls. The basement is bigger than I expected, with passages winding off into darkness on either side of us.

"It's a rat's warren down here," I hiss.

"Even more than you think," Shadow agrees. "These tunnels cover most of the west side of the city."

I shake my head, amazed. Growing up in Canyon City, I thought I knew everything. It turns out there's a whole city below I never even heard of. Makes me wonder what other secrets could be out there, waiting to be discovered.

We end up in a large, rough basement. Heavy tapestries drape the walls, and thick, expensive-looking carpets cover the dirt floor. A fat man sits at a table, thick cushions piled beneath his spreading bottom. He's got a bald skull and a single massive eyebrow stretching across his forehead. The scents of saffron and cardamom rise from a bowl of stew on the table before him.

"Shadow." His voice is soft and sibilant. "Tell me why I shouldn't kill you now."

I flinch, but Shadow puts a hand on my arm.

"Where's the profit in that, Jepet? Dead people don't fill your pockets with chits."

"They don't steal from me either."

"As I explained to Hedeg, I'm done with all that."

"Forgive me if I'm skeptical." He sits back and laces his fingers across his stomach. "South winds never blow north."

"They do if they get into Merrimack."

Jepet quirks an eyebrow in surprise.

"Is that so?"

Shadow nods.

"Well. That is interesting." He considers us for a minute, the light from the flickering bulbs dancing across the shiny surface of his skull. His eyes are small and dark, but calculations spark in them like fire seeds. At last he says, "All right. Want can I do for you?"

"One of your people picked up my friend Twist's Jmini AI. He needs him back. And modified so he can run on Guardian hardware without getting zapped by antivirals."

"Interesting," Jepet's thick lips twist thoughtfully, "but not impossible. A program like that won't come cheap."

"I'm sure we can work something out."

Jepet smiles like a snake that's just spied its dinner. He gestures to the other chairs at the table.

"Step into my office. Now that we've established what I can do for you, tell me, what can you do for me?"

Shadow sinks into one of the offered chairs and shrugs, trying to look unconcerned. She sits a little too straight though, her shoulders held a little too high. She's nervous, which makes me nervous too.

She looks Jepet in the eye.

"What do you want?"

Jepet's oily smile spreads.

"I want a great many things. A warpknife, for instance. Such things are hard to come by down here."

Shadow and I both glance at the blades on our hips. The greicagins imbedded in the hilts glow faintly in the dim cellar.

"That might..." I begin.

Shadow cuts me off.

"No. If we come back without our blades, they'll know we left the compound. Name another price."

"Two hundred chits."

I gasp. Two hundred chits is more money than I've seen in my life.

Shadow laughs.

"Get real. Your little AI isn't worth more than twenty and you know it."

"If it's so cheap, you can get it from someone else. You know the way out." Jepet makes a show of returning to his meal.

My heart sinks. Shadow looks unfazed.

"I'm too tired to tromp all over town. We've got class in the morning, and I need to get some sleep. We're here, so we might as well deal with you."

"Oh, you do me great honor." Jepet slurps his soup loudly. "Make me a serious offer or get out of my office."

Shadow tugs at one of her kinky braids, thinking. Her eyes narrow and the corners of her mouth curl down toward her chin. She sighs.

"What do you want me to steal?"

"Steal? Why would I want you to steal something? I have all the things I need already."

"What then?"

Jepet looks up at her, his eyes suddenly sharp.

"I want your friendship."

Shadow and I exchange confused looks.

"My friendship?"

"Yes, your friendship. One can never have too many friends in the Guardians."

Understanding blooms in my head. Shadow gets it as well.

"You want an informant," I say.

Jepet looks hurt.

"Nothing so vulgar. Simply a friendly relationship. You scratch my back and I scratch yours."

"One favor," Shadow says. "I won't be your pet forever."

"Five favors, and you warn me if the Guardians are going to move on any of my operations."

"Two favors and two warnings. One from him and one from me. That's as far as I'll go. Take it or leave it."

Jepet considers, his eyes moving from her face to mine as he runs the tips of his fingers along his massive eyebrow. Then the oily smile spreads once more.

"It's always nice to make new friends. Hedeg will bring your merchandise." He summons the thumper with a snap of his fingers.

"What about Stick?" I ask.

"Stick?" Jepet looks confused.

"The kid you got Jmini from. You better not have hurt him."

Jepet laughs.

"Big threats from such a little Guardian cub." My hand goes to my warpknife, but Jepet just waves it away. "Oh, put that thing down. I'm sure your friend is fine. It's my understanding that the AI was purchased. We didn't take it from anyone. Isn't that right, Hedeg?"

The thumper nods.

I'm not sure I believe him, but I have no way of telling if he's lying either. I guess I have to take his word for it. For now.

We leave him there with his bowl of cooling curry. The spices cling to our clothes, the scent still with us long after we've left the cellar behind.

28

———————

In the morning, I'm haggard and worn from the night's adventure. Getting back into Merrimack wasn't any more difficult than getting out, but it was just as terrifying. By the time Shadow and I snuck into the barracks, I was ready to collapse. Still, I managed to slip the dataspike containing Jmini into my shell. Now all I can do is cross my fingers and hope it works.

So on top of being sleep-deprived, I'm wound tight with worry. If the program doesn't do what Jepet promised and the antivirals scan it, I'm burnt. I'll be kicked out of Merrimack quicker than a shellbaby pulling back into its burrow. And that's if I'm lucky. More likely I'll end up in a cage on the wall, like that poor carrion we saw last night.

Ghenghis walks past my table at breakfast, giving me the evil eye. His arm is bandaged up. Looks like our little sparring match hasn't left him with warm and fuzzy feelings.

I'm twitchy and paranoid, so when a hand comes down on my shoulder, I nearly leap out of my skin. My tea sloshes all over the table.

"Wow, you're jumpy today," Kass says.

I venture a queasy smile as I try to mop up the mess with a napkin.

"I didn't sleep very well last night."

"You're not sick, are you?" She takes a step back.

"No, no," I say quickly. "Just tired. It's the stress of, well, everything."

She nods.

"I get it. Being here puts a lot of weight on your shoulders. My family would be crushed if I didn't become a Guardian. My father's been preparing me for this since I was five."

"Since you were five?"

"It's a long story. I'll tell you about it tonight. If you still want to hang out?"

"Definitely! I mean, uh, sure, if you want to."

Her smile is dazzling, and for a second I forget all about the illegal Jmini in my shell.

"Meet me in the rec room at seven o'clock?"

"Yeah, great. That sounds good."

"Ok, I'll see you then."

I watch her walk away, wondering how in the world I managed to get a date with someone like Kass. Even if I'm sent back to Canyon City at the end of the week, at least I'll always know that I had a date with a Sunriser girl. How many rockheads can say that?

"Are you going to eat the rest of that? Or are you just going to sit there looking like someone dosed you with free love?" Shadow plops down beside me.

"Be glad I'm not dosed," I shoot back. "Otherwise I'd be trying to stick my tongue down the throat of everyone within reach. Starting with you."

"I'd advise against that." She smiles a dangerous smile. I feel a prick against my thigh and look down to see her warpknife uncomfortably close to cutting off my future generations. I sit extremely still.

"Aw, look. Shadow's playing with your junk already." Rory slides onto the bench across from us. "I knew it was only a matter of time. Hey, Knott! You owe me five chits!"

The big girl gives me a disappointed look.

"Hey, no. That is not what's happening here," I stammer.

"Save it," Rory interrupts. "I know what I saw. Was Shadow's hand in your lap or not?"

"Well, yes. But…"

"Case closed. Pay up." He holds his open palm out to Knott.

Shadow's warpknife flashes, leaving a bright red slash across his hand.

Rory yelps and jerks back. He shakes his head as he regards the wound. "If I can't masturbate because of this, you know who I'm coming to for help, right?"

"Please do." Shadow brandishes her warpknife. She gives him the same dangerous grin she gave me. "I'll be happy to help you trim the fat."

Rory scowls and wraps a napkin around his hand.

"You've got problems, you know that? We're crew. We're supposed to help each other out, not threaten each other with knives."

"I don't make threats. Only promises."

"Well you can keep your promises to yourself, thank you very much." He sighs theatrically. "This is awkward. Now I'm going to have to use my left hand for a couple of days."

"Way too much information, Rory," I say. "We're trying to eat here."

"You're the ones who started playing twiddle-the-twerp at the table. I was just going along with the mood." He dodges the piece of potato Shadow flings at his head, laughing.

I glance at the leaderboard as I mop up my eggs. It's always there, staring down at me like ... my fork falls from my suddenly shaking hand.

"Where are the Plakbeetles and the Midfalcons?"

Everyone turns to stare up at the wall.

"It's begun," Shadow says. "They're cutting the teams down."

We are in eighth place. There are now only eight teams on the board. Below us yawns an abyss, with Canyon City waiting at the bottom.

The rest of the day passes in a queasy blur and then somehow it's a quarter to seven and I'm standing before the mirror nervously pushing my hair this way and that. It won't lay down, and whenever I push it to the side I want it to go, a cowlick pops up right in front. I'm grinding my teeth, about to throw my brush through the mirror, when a large shadow comes up behind me. I tense and whirl around, but it's only Knott, looming in the doorway like a tree missing its forest.

"Meekro prov?"

"I'm sorry, Knott, I don't have my earcones in."

"I not talk good," she says haltingly, her words thickly accented.

I stare at her in the mirror.

"You speak standard?"

"A little." Her accent makes it come out as "leetle."

I shake my head.

"I can't believe you lied to us all that time."

"No lie. Only not all truth."

"Now you sound like Shadow." I laugh.

She steps up behind me and mimes brushing my hair.

"You want to fix my hair?" I crinkle my forehead at the big tank. It hardly seems like something she would enjoy. "Sure, if you want to. It certainly can't get any worse."

My brush looks tiny in her enormous hand. As she puts it to my scalp, a sharp memory of my sister doing the same flashes through my head. Ianna sitting on a stool, while I've got my legs crossed on the floor. Scolding me to sit still.

It must have shown on my face, because Knott stops and looks a question at me.

"I'm ok. Just remembering my little sister doing this when we were kids."

Knott smiles and makes some gestures that I can't follow.

"If you're asking about my sister, she's missing. I haven't seen her in years. She's the reason I'm here, actually. I thought if I became a Guardian, maybe I'd be able to find her."

Her face falls.

"I am sorry. Family is important."

"Yeah, me too, Knott. Me too."

There doesn't seem to be anything more to say after that, so she goes back to brushing my hair. After a couple of minutes she steps back and gestures to the mirror.

I gape at my image, astonished.

"That's amazing, Knott. The cowlick even looks like it's supposed to be there!"

She smiles, and before I know what's happening, her big arms enfold me in a hug. I stiffen, unsure what to do. It's been a long time since I got a hug from anyone. She's so large I feel like I'm being swallowed by a bear, but in a good way, if that makes any sense. She doesn't let go, and eventually I give in and tentatively hug her back. The whole thing feels awkward, but good. Really good.

She finally pushes me out to arm's length and pats me on the cheek.

"Thanks, Knott. I needed that."

She smiles and steps back.

"Man, Twisty." Rory leans against the doorframe, arms crossed over his chest. "You're getting all the female attention these days." He's trying to make it sound like a joke, but I hear the anger beneath his words.

Before I can retort, Knott steps toward him, balling her fists. Rory quickly retreats.

Knott shrugs and rolls her eyes at me. Then she gestures to the door and gives me a thumbs up.

"Thanks, Knott. Here goes nothing."

29

―――――――

The rec room is right in the center of the level, the hub that all of our free time revolves around. It's full of games, tables, and couches for relaxing. The Instructors never come near the rec room, which is both good and bad. It's good because it gives us an unsupervised space. And it's bad because … it's an unsupervised space to work out all of our teenage social hierarchies.

I avoid it most of the time, since as both a rockhead and a member of a team that's down on the leaderboard, I tend to be the butt of a lot of jokes. But today I enter the Horror's cave willingly.

I stop just inside the door and scan the room. Shells line one wall, and small groups congregate around them, vying for high-score bragging rights. In the center of the room are old-style standing games, like pool tables and foosball. Off to my right is the lounge area, with couches and tables.

I don't see Kass anywhere. Dread creeps down my spine. Maybe she's not coming. Maybe she just asked me to meet her as a joke.

Dust storms. Of course she's not coming. Why would a Sunriser girl want to hang out with a rockhead like me? How could I be so gullible?

I start to back out of the door. Maybe I can get away before anybody notices me.

I hear a voice behind me.

"There you are. I was worried you weren't going to show."

And there she is. Kass. Her eyes shine like miniature moons in the dark.

"Um," I stammer.

She laughs like I've said something funny and nods toward the refreshment stand.

"Shall we?"

I nod this time, not trusting my mouth.

"They've got these amazing Italian Sodas here," Kass says as we cross the room. "Do you like mandarin?" I nod again. I'm doing a great impression of a ventriloquist's dummy.

I can feel everyone staring at me, but I keep my eyes locked on the refreshment stand. Kass is the only one that matters.

We get sodas with whipped cream on them and sit on a beaten brown couch. I'm a little surprised to see something this worn out in Merrimack. I guess the furniture in the rec room isn't high on the list of things that need to look nice.

I sip my soda and cautiously look around, feeling profoundly out of place. Every other kid here is a Sunriser, with bronzed skin and perfect teeth. They look like they belong in Merrimack. I'm an interloper. An outsider.

The soda is the best thing I've ever tasted. The bubbles make it less sweet, but the whipped cream balances it out perfectly. I find my tongue and manage to say as much to Kass.

"I know!" she gushes. "I don't like things that are too sweet either. This is the perfect amount." She looks at me expectantly, like she's waiting for me to say something else. I take another sip of my soda, stalling as I flounder for a subject. Finally, I blurt,

"You said you've been training since you were five?"

She grimaces.

"Yeah, it's kind of a family tradition. My grandfather was a Guardian, and my father too. I don't have any brothers, so my father decided it was up to me to carry on the line."

"Sounds like a lot of pressure."

She shrugs. "In a way. I never really thought about it when I was younger."

"But now that you're here?"

She leans in close and speaks softly, "Now that I'm here I'm terrified I won't be good enough. My dad would be crushed."

"What about you? What do you want?"

She looks at me funny.

"You know, no one has ever asked me that? Everyone just assumes I want to be a Guardian."

"Do you?"

"I guess? I mean, it would be kind of a waste if I didn't become a Guardian. All those years of training for nothing."

"Let's try an experiment. If you hadn't had those years of training and were free to be anything you wanted. Anything at all. Starting right now. What would it be?"

She squirms and wrinkles her nose like she's accidentally snorted too much pepper and is trying to decide if she's going to sneeze or not. It's adorable. It makes me want to ask her more difficult questions, just so I can see that face again.

"I don't know. I've never thought about it before. You don't spend much time thinking about what you'd like to do when you already know you don't have a choice in the matter."

"I don't believe you. You know, I can see it in your eyes. Spill it."

"Promise you won't laugh?"

"Cross my heart."

She watches me dubiously to see if I'm going to crack a smile. When I don't she says,

"All right. But you can't tell anyone."

"My lips are zipped."

She giggles.

"That's a funny image."

"You're stalling."

She sticks her tongue out at me.

"Ok, fine! If I could be anything I wanted, starting right now, I would be," she looks around to make sure nobody else is listening, "a musician."

"A musician," I repeat, trying out the idea in my mind. "What would you play?"

"Piano," she says immediately. "My mother has all of these old piano recordings she plays around the house. They're so beautiful. It's the soundtrack to all of my best memories." Her face changes as she tells me this, her eyes wide and childlike. I feel like I'm seeing into a secret place she never shows anyone.

"What about you?"

"Me?" I squeak, surprised.

"If you could be anything, starting right now, what would you be?"

"A canyon racer." I blurt the first thing that comes to my mind.

"A canyon racer? Really?" She seems disappointed.

"Well," I stammer, "I like to go fast. And I'm good at it. It seems like it would be, uh, exciting. And challenging. And, um, stuff like that." I want to die. I want to shove my big stupid head up my big stupid butt until I suffocate and die.

"Yeah, I guess I could see that," she says.

We both sip our sodas. Awkward silence descends.

"Want to play pool?" she says finally.

"Sure."

It's a weird old game involving knocking colored balls into holes with a stick. There's a lot of geometry involved. Kass gets up close and presses against me when she's showing me how to shoot, which is really nice. I think it distracts me more than it helps with my shooting though.

Afterward we go for a walk, and end up in the lounge at the end of the hall, looking out the wall of dark windows.

"Do you ever think about the Outsiders?" I blurt.

"The Outsiders? The terrorists who keep blowing things up? What about them?"

"Well, did you ever wonder if they're really as bad as everyone says they are?"

Kass gives me a weird look, and I don't blame her. I'm mentally kicking myself for bringing up the subject.

"Why would I wonder that? They blow stuff up and kill people. Seems pretty clear they're bad people."

"Sure, but why do they do that stuff? I mean, they're people too, right? Why do you think they hate us so much?" I've got no choice but to press forward. I brought up the subject and now I'm stuck with it.

"They hate us because we're in here and they're out there," she says, shrugging. "What more do you need to know?"

"But how did they get out there? Where did they come from? What if the whole thing is one big misunderstanding?"

"Bombs are pretty easy to understand, Twist."

"Yeah, but...," I trail off. There's no argument I can make here without giving myself away. Better to just drop it. "Never mind. Let's talk about something else."

She eyes me warily.

"You're a strange one."

"Yeah, sorry. Sometimes I just say stuff. Don't pay attention to what comes out of my mouth."

"No, it's not a bad thing. I like that you're different." She reaches out and takes my hand, pulls me toward her. Her fingers are slim and callused. "The boys I grew up with are all the same. I know everything about them. They're boring. You're a puzzle. I like puzzles."

Her face is close to mine now, her eyes questioning. I'm frozen like a shellbaby out in the open, unable to advance or retreat.

"Thanks for hanging out tonight, Twist. It's been interesting."

She presses her lips to mine, expanding my insides like baking bread. Then she's gone, leaving me alone with the stars sparkling outside the windows. I can still feel her lips long after her footsteps have faded away.

I drift down the dark hall toward my barracks. Not thinking about anything in particular, just floating along in a warm haze, the feel of Kass's lips still fresh on my mouth.

The only warning I get is a flicker of movement in my peripheral vision. I start to turn toward it and then they're on me, a fist from the darkness snapping my head to the side. More fists follow, to my stomach, ribs, neck. When I go down the words and the boots join in.

"Dust-eater."

"Dirty rockhead!"

I don't have a prayer of fighting back. I just curl up in a ball and take it, trying to protect myself as best I can with my arms and knees. A boot slams into my back and a sharp pain in my ribs forces a yelp from my mouth. Something's broken in there, and every blow brings fresh agony. I cough and taste blood on my lips.

I don't know how long the beating goes on, but at some point I become aware of raised voices and the sounds of fighting. The blows stop, and the individual pains blend into an overall ache that leaves no part of my body untouched. Even breathing hurts.

Hands touch me and I flinch, but no blows follow.

"It's all right, chief. We've got you."

The hands lift me from the floor and I cry out as broken things grind inside of me. I'm being cradled by two sets of hands. Carried through the dark.

We pass a wall light and I see faces. Knott and…

"Rory?"

"Yeah. Don't worry, Twisty. It's all under control."

"Why?"

"Why didn't I just let the Sunrisers beat the snot out of you? Cause we're crew, that's why. The only one that gets to pound you down is me."

I try to laugh, but it turns into a groan. Dust storms, it hurts.

They lay me in the medrig and shut the lid. Needles puncture my skin, and a wonderful numbness spreads over me, pushing the world far, far away.

30

———

I'm sore the next day, but a night in the medrig has taken care of the worst of it. Still I move gingerly, and there's a dull bruise covering one side of my face.

Whispers follow me across the cafeteria. Eyes burn into the back of my head. Everyone knows what happened.

I pull my shoulders back and stand tall, staring straight ahead. I'm not going to give them the satisfaction of knowing that I'm hurt.

From my seat I can see Ghengis sitting with Octav. They seem pleased with themselves, and when they catch me looking, they raise their glasses in my direction. I raise mine back and return their fake smiles.

I may not have seen my attackers, but I've got a pretty good idea who they were.

"Don't waste brainpower on them." Grab sets his tray next to mine. "They're not worth it."

"How do you know?"

"I grew up with those animals, remember?"

He hunches down over his tray, in his usual defensive posture. He's so different from the rest of the Sunrisers. Gangly and awkward. More comfortable looking down through a drone than leading a charge.

"Why are you here anyway, Grab?" I raise an eyebrow at him. "Like you said yourself, the first day I met you, 'One of these things is not like the others.'"

He doesn't raise his eyes, smiling a sad smile at his tray.

"My father made me. I didn't want to come. I'm the only child. Got to uphold the family honor. Can't spend my life being a useless cripple."

I think about the other Sunrisers, their easy physical perfection. I think about what it must have been like to be a freak in their midst.

"It must have been hard. Growing up with them."

"Well, yeah. I mean look at them. They're all imbeciles. Not two brain cells to run together in the whole bunch. Wouldn't know an inverter from a power booster."

It takes me a moment to realize he's joking, then a startled laugh bursts from my lips.

He grins slyly up at me.

"You're the only other person I've met here who can even wire a basic chip. A dust-licking rockhead. Go figure."

"Go figure."

"Don't be so serious, Twist. Take what life gives you and run with it. Or," he gestures down at his steel legs, "totter, anyway."

I laugh again, feeling a lot better than before.

"Thanks, Grab."

He waves me off with one hand.

"Someone has to be the voice of reason around here. It's certainly not going to be any of you action types."

Our watches chime in unison, the rims lighting up blue. Battle stations. We've got a game.

"Are you good to go, Twist?" Grab asks as we hurry down the hall.

"Yeah, I'll be fine." With the support and strength boost the shell gives me, it'll actually be less painful being in game than it would be walking around Merrimack.

As I approach my shell, I remember that I've got a bigger problem than my sore body to face. This will be the first test of my smuggled dataspike.

I pray to every god there has ever been as I roll myself into the shell. My stomach thrashes like a giant squid as the blue sand rolls over me. Bile burns up the back of my throat. I stare at the console, fingers poised over the power button. This is it, the moment of truth. Do I get Jmini or Hiroko? Or does a squad of Guardians burst in and drag me away for smuggling software?

This is my last chance to back out. I could still remove the dataspike. Take my chances with Hiroko.

I chew my lip, pounding my thighs in frustration.

No. We're on the brink of elimination. Hiroko is nothing but a one-way ticket out of here. Jmini is my only chance.

I press the button.

The display lights up, then flickers and dies. There is only blackness.

Spines. I've killed my shell.

Then the display comes back on, warbles, shifts, and stabilizes. I hold my breath, waiting for the alarms, the rough hands yanking me out of the shell. When they don't come, I whisper, "Jmini?"

There's another flicker. Then a voice.

"Aye, aye, Capitan. Awaiting orders."

I whoop, pumping my fist inside the shell.

"Could you save the yelling until after the game?" Rory complains. "I think you just destroyed one of my eardrums."

I ignore him, my fingers dancing through the preparation menu.

"What kind of game have we got?"

"We're up against the Desert Wolves," Shadow announces.

Ghengis's team. Perfect. So much for not indulging in revenge fantasies.

"That dust-sucker is going down," Knott snarls.

"Down," Shadow agrees.

"Be nice if I got to finish my breakfast first," Grab sighs. I hear a crunch and the sound of him chewing.

"Grab, are you eating in your shell?" Shadow asks, incredulous.

"What's wrong with that?" he mumbles. "I'm hungry."

She sighs.

"Let's focus, people. Don't get so caught up in taking down

Ghengis that we forget about the objective. This might be our last chance to move up the board. Lose this and we're done."

"I guess we'll just have to win then," I say, trying to project a bravado I don't feel.

"The target is on a plateau," Grab says. "Lots of approach vectors, but all of them are terrible. The defenders will have a clear line of fire on us, as well as the advantage of height."

"A real pile of turds," Shadow agrees.

"All right, you monkeys. Time to fling some poo!" Rory cackles.

Shadow ignores him and shares the attack schematics with us.

It looks like we're targeting an Outsider caravan that's crossing a plateau up above the canyons. Grab's drone gives us a view from high above. I have Jmini magnify the display so I can take a closer look.

"Why are they up on a plateau?" I wonder. "Wouldn't it make more sense for them to hide down in the canyons?"

"Terrain," Grab says, highlighting a map of the surrounding area. "The canyons are choked with slides and cuts. The only way to get a caravan across that area is up top."

"Seems like they're just asking to get attacked though," I say.

"What about here?" Rory lights up a section of land ahead of the caravan. "It looks like they'll pass pretty close to the edge of the plateau."

"But is that a good thing?" Shadow asks. "If we get them close to the edge, that'll make it easier for them to shoot down on us. I think we'd be better off hitting them here." She highlights another section of plateau a bit further away.

"Too slow," Knott sends.

"I agree with Knott," Grab says. "The Desert Wolves will get to them first if we wait that long."

"Maybe that's not necessarily a bad thing," I say. "What if we let Ghengis and the Outsiders soften each other up? Then we can swoop in and catch them when they're already exhausted."

"You're a sneaky duster, Twisty," Rory muses. "I like it."

"It's got possibilities," Shadow agrees. "I say we give it a try. We've got to be ready to move though. If we wait too long, Ghengis will walk away with the prize before we get there."

We look at different plans and contingencies, arguing over the advantages and disadvantages of each. Grab cuts us off with a hiss.

"They're moving in!"

We watch as the Desert Wolves engage the Outsiders, swooping up at them when the caravan's track leads near the edge of the plateau.

"That's the spot!" Rory crows. "I told you!"

"Yeah, you're brilliant Rory. Now shut up and get to your place while they're distracted fighting each other," Shadow says. "That goes for the rest of you too. Scatter quick!"

I guide my simulated gravbike out of the hangar, flashing out under open sky, orange canyon rocks beneath. I keep one eye on the battle as I make my way toward the plateau, but it's hard to follow when driving is taking up most of my attention.

"Jmini, you awake?"

"Yes, sir. I live solely to fulfill your every whim."

Ah, sarcasm from an AI. I didn't realize how much I missed that.

"That's great Jmini, cause I'm feeling pretty whimsical today."

"Lord, what fools these mortals be," Jmini shoots back, not missing a beat.

I chuckle.

"What's happening up there?"

"The Outsiders have circled their vehicles to form a defensive perimeter. The Desert Wolves are pounding their position. I do not believe the Outsiders will be able to hold them off very long."

"Sounds like we'd better move fast."

"Tally-ho, Capitan."

I lean over my handlebars and throttle up, suiting action to words. I can't control the grin that stretches my face. A boy and his Jmini, together again.

31

The gravbike shoots forward, the canyon blurring around me. I'm moving too fast to see obstacles before I'm upon them, so I'm completely reliant on my guidance system. But I'm not worried. I know Jmini's got my back.

"I believe you shaved a few millimeters from the face of that boulder as we passed," he says. "I admire the way you combine driving and excavation. Truly a brilliant way to kill two birds with one stone."

"Thanks, Jmini. I learned it all from you."

"Let's split up," Shadow cuts in. "Hit them from two sides."

"Confirmed." I adjust my course to match the new schematics, aiming for the far side of the plateau.

"Wait for it," Grab cautions. "Don't move in too quickly."

"Don't move in too slowly either," Rory counters. "We've gotta momma bear this thing."

"Momma bear?" Knott asks.

"Like the three bears," Rory says. "Haven't you heard that story? One bowl of porridge is too hot, one is too cold, and momma bear's is just right."

"I think that is baby bear," Knott corrects.

"Whatever. You know what I mean."

"They're breaking through the Outsider's defenses." Grab's voice is urgent.

"Dust storms," I curse. "Jmini, how far out are we?"

"It will be approximately sixty seconds until we can engage the enemy."

"What's everyone's ETA?" I ask over the general channel.

"Me and Knott are parked right below the lip of the plateau," Rory says. "Ready to rock and roll."

"My drones have already engaged theirs," Grab says. "I can keep them off of you, but other than that you're on your own."

"I'm still a couple of minutes out," Shadow says. "You'll have to start the attack without me."

"The Outsider defenses have been breached," Jmini informs me. "Projected annihilation in thirty seconds."

"I'm not going to make it in time. Rory, Knott, it's now or never," I say.

"Way ahead of you," Rory replies. I hear cannon fire in the background.

Every second feels like an hour as I race toward the plateau. The sounds of battle fill my earcones, and I keep flicking glances at the tactical display in the corner of my screen.

Rory and Knott have opened fire on Ghengis's team, catching them from behind just like we planned. The gunners should have them caught in a nice cross-fire, but it looks like the Outsiders aren't holding up their end of the deal. Instead of concentrating their fire on the Desert Wolves, the last three Outsiders seem more concerned with helping their fallen companions than with fighting. To make things worse, the single Outsider still firing is spraying shots indiscriminately, targeting Rory and Knott as often as Ghengis's crew.

The end result is Rory and Knott manage to take out one of the Desert Wolves in the first few seconds of their surprise attack, but after that they're quickly pinned down by the opposing team.

"It's getting hot up here," Rory yelps. "If the cavalry doesn't get here quick, we're burnt."

"Ten seconds." I will my gravbike to go faster.

My world goes vertical as I hit the side of the plateau and start to climb. Cold sweat beads my forehead as blue sky fills my screen and gravity tries to drag me back off the saddle. The engine whines, building to a scream. I feel like a rocket fighting to escape the planet's gravity well as the seconds tick down in the corner of the display. Five seconds. Four. Three.

I shoot up over the edge of the plateau, yelping as my momentum launches me ten meters into the air. I go weightless at the apex of the arc and my stomach turns inside out. As the nose of the grav bike tilts oh-so-slowly downward, terror chokes me. The ground is very, very far away.

Time lurches back into motion. The ground rushes toward me. I yank up on the handlebars in a frantic effort to avoid planting the gravbike like a flagpole. It hits hard, jarring off the rocks as it bounces one, twice. My teeth snap together on my tongue and I taste blood.

I finally get the gravbike under control, my heart hammering in my ears. A hundred meters ahead lie the charred remains of the Outsider caravan. One transport car is still burning, an ugly plume of blue-black smoke staining the sky. Bodies are scattered across the ground, and a pair of figures crouch over a third, applying what looks like spray med-gel. Odd behavior for a sim. I guess Merrimack's engineers are trying to make it as realistic as possible.

Beyond the wreckage, energy weapons streak the plateau. Rory and Knott are pinned down behind a cluster of boulders. Knott crouches behind a rock that's slightly smaller than she is. Bits of her armor leak around the edges, tempting targets for the trio facing her. Rory has slid down inside a crevice, the barrel of his cannon resting on the ground. The only part of him visible is a tiny, flexible periscope, poking up like a reaperplant. It's hard to target that way, and he's not really hitting anything, but his steady stream of fire is at least forcing the advancing Desert Wolves to duck and weave.

Knott's shoulder explodes in a shower of sparks, spinning her to the ground. One of the attacking gunners sprints toward her, going in for the kill.

Jmini clears his throat politely as the figure turns red on my display.

"Target in range."

"Fire cannon!" I shout, clenching my fist on the firing stud. A green beam lances out from the gravbike, catching the gunner in the back. They stumble and start to turn, but I hit them again, and again.

By the time they hit the ground, their armor is a smoking ruin. One down.

I look up to see the barrel of a huge cannon swinging toward me. I twist frantically at the handlebars … then the muzzle flashes and a giant fist punches me in the chest. I'm hurled back off the gravbike, somersaulting in the air before slamming face first into the ground with bone-jarring force. I lie there, stunned and gasping, staring at the dust smashed against my faceplate.

Footsteps crunch toward me. I hear Ghengis's voice.

"Every time you get up, I will shoot you down. Every step you take, I will knock you down," I hear the whine of his arm-cannon as he prepares to deliver the coup de gras. "Every time you think you are safe, I will be there to…"

A sharp explosion cuts him off. I feel the heat of the blast on my back. Levering my head up off the ground, I see Ghengis lying on his back six meters away, his chest plate smoking and black. Shadow crunches up and helps me to my feet.

"You're welcome. Now let's finish these spine-suckers off."

Our timely intervention may have saved Rory and Knott from annihilation, but the battle is far from won. Even though we've got them in the crossfire we wanted now, the Desert Wolves fight savagely. Ghengis himself is the worst of the lot. Despite the damage Shadow already inflicted on him, he fights like a titan, returning fire long after the last of his teammates have fallen.

Just before he finally goes down, he charges at Knott, who happens to be the closest to him at the time. Both of them are little more than smoking ruins at this point, and they grapple like pain-crazed bears caught in a forest fire. I swear I feel the ground shake as they stand toe-to-toe, trading haymakers that would punch through solid brick. It's awe-inspiring, and more than a little terrifying.

Finally, Ghengis catches Knott in an armlock. He heaves and rips her arm clean off at the shoulder. She screams and stands swaying for a moment, blackened and armless, before crumpling to the ground. Ghengis raises his arms in victory, roaring like a landslide. He turns … and Rory's warpknife slams through his chest plate. Ghengis collapses instantly.

"Spines, that guy's annoying," Rory says, kicking the fallen droid.

"Let's recover the target and get out of here," I say. "Victory is the best revenge."

We stagger toward the remains of the Outsider caravan, all three of us charred and heavily damaged.

"We are one sad little trio," Shadow says. "I can't even lift my left arm."

"You think that's bad," Rory retorts. "I've got a hole where my butt cheek would be. It's a good thing this is just a sim."

"What happened to the Outsiders?" I wonder. "Weren't three of them still alive?"

"They ran while the rest of you were slugging it out," Grab informs us. "And it was four, not three. They carried one who was injured away with them."

"Carried one away," Rory chuckles. "Saving their simulated-butts to fight another day."

Most of the Outsiders didn't make it though. As we step into the circle of burned vehicles, I see bodies scattered everywhere. A dozen at least. I look at the faces as I walk past, surprised at how realistic they seem. They've got different colored scabs scattered around their faces and fleshy growths on their heads. They look just like the people I met in the tunnels.

I stop beside a dead woman with a dark green crest running down the center of her skull. As I stare into her empty eyes, recognition jolts through me. I can hear her calm voice, feel her gentle fingers on my leg. See her reassuring smile. Sparrow. This is the woman who set my broken leg.

I stumble away from the dead woman, uncomprehending. This is a sim. Why would a real woman be in a sim?

Unless it's not a sim at all.

I examine my hand, flexing it, feeling the slight pull of the pistons inside. HAMRdroids. We're operating HAMRdroids from inside our shells.

"Twist?" Shadow's voice.

"I … I need a minute," I stammer.

I look around at the burned vehicles, the bodies littering the ground. This can't be happening.

Then another thought grips me, and I taste ashes.

I stagger around the circle, searching the faces of the dead. The dead. These are dead people. This is not a sim.

I see a thin, dark-skinned body lying face down. I frantically turn it over, and breathe a sigh of relief when I don't recognize the face. Not my dad. I turn in a slow circle, surveying the carnage. None of them are my dad.

I feel relieved, and immediately feel terrible for feeling that way. They may not be my dad, but they're still people. Real people. Dead people.

I find myself standing over Sparrow again. Staring down into her clear green eyes. Dark blood has run from the corner of her mouth and dried in a smear over her cheek, down her neck. I kneel beside her, my eyes full of tears. How did this happen? This wasn't supposed to happen.

"Twist?" Shadow's hand on my shoulder. "You ok? What's going on?"

I shake my head. Take a ragged breath and swallow hard.

"I'm fine." I push myself to my feet. "Let's get the package and get out of here."

Behind me, the sun slips toward the horizon, dipping the canyons into liquid shadows. The land ahead is dark and fractured. My body is numb as I step forward, moving toward a place I don't recognize at all.

32

The celebration begins as soon as we roll out of our shells. Our victory over Ghengis's team has pushed us into a tie with them for third place on the leaderboard, a full thirty points clear of the fifth-place team. We aren't standing with our toes over the cut line anymore. Now we stand on the cusp of victory.

My crew drags me along to the rec room. Knott leads the way, bouncing on her toes like a little girl. Grab is smiling from ear to ear, munching on a bag of almonds. Rory runs his mouth like a runaway caravan, providing a steady soundtrack of jokes and sarcasm. Shadow is grinning too, but there's an undertone of concern in her eyes. She keeps glancing at me out of the corner of her eye, as if I'm a bomb that might explode.

Maybe I am, it's hard to say. I'm so full of churning thoughts and emotions that I hardly know where I am. I do my best to keep a smile planted on my face, to not let on that there's anything wrong. I may be doing a bad job of it though. Maybe my bared teeth look more like a snarl than a smile. I'm the last person to ask. I can't even feel my face.

Kass stops me on the way into the rec room.

"Hey, congratulations."

"Thanks," I say woodenly.

She bites her lip and looks at the floor.

"I'm sorry about the other night. About the guys. I didn't know they were going to do that. I'm sorry."

"Sure."

She cocks her head.

"Are you all right? You don't look very happy to see me."

"My team….," I gesture vaguely in the direction they went.

Her lips press into a thin, hurt line.

"Fine. I can see you don't want to accept my apology."

She stalks away, back rigid.

I know I should go after her. Try to explain. But I can't. In my mind I'm out on the plateau, with dead Outsiders scattered all around me.

Grab buys the team a round of milkshakes, and we sink into a big red booth with padded cushions. The others joke and laugh and I do my best to smile and nod along.

But I don't hear a word anyone says.

Instead of a sim, we were piloting remote HAMRdroids from inside our shells. Everything we experienced was real. The canyons, the plateau, the drones, the gravbike, the caravan, and the Outsiders. All of it. Real as the milkshake in my hand. Real as the cold weight in my stomach.

Has it always been this way? What if every sim run we've been on hasn't been a sim run at all? What if they've all been real?

I think of how many Outsiders I've killed in the game and my stomach bucks. I push my way out of the booth, barely making it to the toilet before sour milkshake and stomach acid explode out of my mouth and nose. When my body finally stops heaving, I wipe my eyes and mouth, blow the burning snot from my nostrils.

As I'm standing at the sink splashing cold water over my face, someone says something snide behind me, but I don't catch the words. I don't even look up to see who it is. Everything about Merrimack feels juvenile and fake. A bunch of children playing at being Guardians.

But the stakes are real. More real than any of us ever suspected.

Shadow is waiting for me when I stumble out of the bathroom, pale and trembling. She takes one look at me and says,

"You're sick. I'll walk you back to the barracks."

I try to brush her off, but I have no strength left to fight. She takes me by the elbow and steers me into the hall.

It isn't until she's got me lying in my bed with the covers tucked up around my neck that she tries to talk to me.

"What's going on, Twist? What did you see in there?"

"Nothing." I try to turn away from her, but she puts a hand on my chest.

"Don't give me that dust. Something happened during the run. You saw something." She smoothes my hair back from my forehead, her fingers cool and soothing. "Come on, Twist. You can trust me. Tell me what's going on."

I look up into her little-girl face. Her dark, serious eyes don't belong in that face. Wise and old. Like they belong to someone else.

My secret drags at me. I can feel it pulling me down, pulling me under. I don't know if I can bear the weight alone.

Shadow has been my friend here since day one. She risked herself to help me get Jmini. If there's anyone I can tell, it's Shadow.

But if I tell her, I'm not just risking myself. I'm risking the Outsiders. I'm risking my dad. That's not a decision I'm ready to make.

But still, I need help. I need to release some of this burden.

I take a shaky breath, lick my lips. Maybe I can tell her part of it. Just a part. I beckon her close, bring her ear close to my lips.

"That game wasn't a sim," I whisper. "It was real."

"What do you mean?"

"We were really out there. Piloting HAMRdroids from inside our shells. The Outsiders were real too. The bodies…" My voice breaks and I feel tears sliding out of the corners of my eyes.

Shadow looks at me, intent and puzzled.

"How do you know that?"

This is the big question. The answer yawns beneath me like a chasm, waiting to swallow us both.

"I recognized one of them. Someone I knew … before." Enough of the truth to put our necks in a noose, but hopefully not enough to hang us.

"You recognized an Outsider?" Shadow's eyes are wide now. In her surprise, they've lost some of their age. Now she looks like a shocked little girl.

I nod sadly.

"And we killed them," she finishes. I nod again. "Oh, Twist." She puts her arms around me and squeezes, her cheek warm against mine.

I squeeze back, and her small body feels like Ianna in my arms. I try to fight back the tears, but they leak out anyway, a steady stream trickling down the sides of my face. She holds me for a long time, until I finally get myself under control. Then I push her away.

"Thanks," I mumble, wiping my eyes with the tips of my fingers.

"Anytime. We're crew. We've got to stick together."

I'm ready to tell her everything, right then and there. About the Outsiders and the IEC. About my dad being alive. About how I'm helping them, becoming a double-agent inside the Guardians.

She's my crew. And more importantly, she's my friend. She deserves to know. I look into her eyes, the words on the tip of my tongue.

Then I swallow them down.

Telling her would just endanger her. If I get caught, they'll question my crew to see what they know. If they don't know anything, they'll have no reason to punish them too. She's safer not knowing.

I have to bear these secrets alone.

She must see the struggle on my face, because she asks, "What is it?"

I blurt the first thing that comes to my mind.

"You remind me of my sister."

Her nose wrinkles.

"Gross. Don't get any ideas. I am nothing like your sister." She punches me on the shoulder for emphasis. Which is exactly what Ianna would have done.

I burst out laughing.

"Don't I know it," I chuckle. "Nothing at all."

Her eyes narrow and I hold my hands up in defense, "Truce, truce."

She lets my laughter run out.

"You ok now?"

"Yeah, much better. Thank you."
"You coming back to the rec room?"
"Maybe in a minute."
She grins.
"Good, because you owe me a milkshake."

33

———————

The lecture hall is full, voices rising and falling in waves. I sit between Shadow and Knott, watching the other students swirl and churn. The leaderboard glows up on the wall. Only five teams remain.

It's the first time we've all been gathered in the hall since Castle gave us our introduction on day one. I don't know why he's called us here now, but I doubt it's good news.

I watch Kass out of the corner of my eye. She's standing in the aisle talking. I watch her brush a curl back from her face, fingertips grazing her neck. I watch her mouth move, remembering the way her lips felt against mine.

Then she catches me watching and frowns. Turns her back to me.

I should go over to her. Apologize for how I acted in the rec room. But I don't get the chance.

Castle strides into the room and everyone scrambles for their seats. He takes his place behind the lectern at the front, overhead lights gleaming off his tanned scalp. I remember my dad's head, pocked with scabs. Why does Castle get to have perfect skin while my dad gets infected with scabs? It's not right.

Castle grins at us, exposing his big, square teeth. Castle's grin doesn't look happy though. His grin looks more like a snarl. Like he's about to tear someone's throat out.

The room goes silent.

"Half of your class has flamed out," he booms. "You are the survivors. You probably think you deserve some congratulations. You think Guardian training is a piece of cake and you've learned all there is to learn. You're ready for your badges. Am I right? Do you think you're ready?" There's an uncertain rumble of assent, and one optimistic student shouts back, "Yes, Instructor", but most of us keep our mouths shut, waiting to see where he's going with this.

"You haven't earned anything!" he roars, flecks of spit spraying from his lips. "You're a bunch of toddlers who still need their bottoms wiped. You don't know anything. You haven't done anything. But the training wheels are about to come off."

He glares around at us for effect, then points up at the leaderboard.

"This board is done. The scores and rankings you've earned until now are dog piss. Forget about them." He snaps his fingers and the board goes dark. Gasps ripple across the room.

"You have one more mission. Your final exam. How you perform will determine if you are Guardian material. Nothing else. Do well and you get your badges. Fail and you're burnt. It's as simple as that. Go back to your pods. Your instructions are waiting. Dismissed."

The room buzzes as we rise and shuffle toward the door. This is it. The final exam.

"Mr. Maro!" Castle barks. "Not you. You stay."

Everyone stares at me. Octav and Ghengis smirk. Shadow and Grab look worried. My mouth goes dust-dry. I step aside and watch the other students flow out the door. Finally, it's just me and Castle.

"Come down here," he says, motioning with his big, weathered hand. "Have a seat."

I sit in the front row of the lecture hall. He pulls a chair over and sets it at the front of the stage. He perches there, squinting down at me, his cracked face a map of the scablands. He stares at me for a whole minute, while I squirm and sweat.

He knows. He knows about the Outsiders. He knows about my dad. He's going to snap his fingers and the Guardians will come take me away. I'll be questioned. Tortured. Put in a cage on the wall. Left to starve, my flesh peeled from my bones by the sandstorms. A warning to others.

If I get up and run now, can I make it to the sewer caves before they catch me? Can I find a way beyond the wall?

"Is there something you want to tell me?" Castle's hands are folded on his lap, big square fingers wrapped around his knuckles.

I know this is a trap. Whenever someone asks you a question like this, they are giving you a chance to incriminate yourself. Papa Grady used to do this when I was little, and I would foolishly vomit up things he had no idea I'd even done.

Sorry Castle, I've already learned this trick.

"No, Instructor."

"Are you sure? If you tell me now, things will go easier on you. Honesty counts around here."

Translation: I don't know exactly what you've done, and I'd like you to tell me instead.

"Yes, Instructor. I'm sure."

Castle sighs and gives me one of those, "This hurts me just as much as it hurts you" grimaces. He looks me in the eye.

"We've found some unauthorized software in your shell."

I try to keep my face blank, but I can tell he saw me flinch. My back is sticky with sweat.

"Unauthorized software, Instructor?"

"A virus has been attempting to infiltrate our system. We traced it back to your shell."

A virus? Oh, flash floods. This is bad. This is much, much worse than if they'd just discovered my Jmini. Damn Jepet. Damn him to a hell full of sand stingers.

"I don't know anything about a virus, Instructor."

"I don't believe you." Castle's expression is hard now, the cracks in his face deepening with anger. "I'm going to give you one more chance. Tell me everything you've done, right now, or my guards will drag it out of you. The only question is do you want to go quietly, or do you want to go screaming?"

This can't be happening. I can't lose everything now. Not when I'm so close.

"All right, I'll tell you what I know. But it's not much. I really don't know anything about a virus," I'm talking fast, the words pouring from my mouth. "I was having trouble with Hiroko, the AI in the shell. We didn't work well together. My team was losing and it was her fault. I needed my Jmini AI back, the one I was used to working with before. So I snuck my Jmini into the shell. That was wrong, and I'm sorry.

"But it worked. As soon as I got Jmini back, we won a game. So, you see, I had to do what I did. Without Jmini my team would have been cut. With it we've got as good a chance of winning as anyone. Please don't expel me, Instructor. I didn't know there was a virus bundled with the AI. You told us that winning was the most important thing here. That we had to be resourceful. That's all I was doing. Trying to win."

Castle looks at me for a long time, fingers steepled in front of him.

"Where did this Jmini come from?"

"A man named Jepet in Canyon City."

"Can you take us to him?"

I hesitate. I don't want to be a snitch, but giving up Jepet is the only way to convince Castle I'm sincere. Besides, that little rat hid a virus in the dataspike he gave me. I don't owe him anything.

I nod quickly.

"You keep asking me to stay, but I don't see why I should let you. You broke the rules and endangered the entire complex because you needed your little AI security blanket. That's not the type of behavior we're looking for in our Guardians. Give me one good reason why I should let you stay."

"Brains, resourcefulness, desire, and toughness. Those are the four things you told us we needed to have to succeed here. I had the brains to diagnose my problem. I had the desire to find a solution. I had the resourcefulness to smuggle in contraband to fix it. I had the toughness to take risks to get it done. You never said any of this was against the rules. You told us the only rules were to win and survive. I haven't broken either of those rules."

I look him straight in the eye. Castle's a hard man, tough as canyon walls. To get his attention, I've got to be hard too.

"I'm the best Chaser in this school. I'll win the final game. It's your loss if you kick me out now."

He stares at me for a long minute, his blue eyes boring into me.

"You've got stones, kid. I respect that. You're a dirty little rockhead who doesn't realize he's only in here as a bump in the road for the real trainees to overcome. You actually believe you can get somewhere. I don't know if that makes you brave or stupid. Probably a bit of both." He shakes his head, lips twisting. "All right, tell us where to find this Jepet, and you can compete in the final trial. But I'm holding you to your word. You have to win. Anything less and you're done here."

Relief floods through me, so strong I sway in my seat. I can't believe he's letting me stay. I want to stand up and whoop. Then Castle drops the other shoe.

"Your system has been wiped. Whatever bootleg software you had in there is gone. You're going to have to do this one by the book."

The excitement dies in my throat.

I've got to win the biggest game of my life with Hiroko. Who I've never won a single game with. Maybe I should do everyone a favor and let Castle expel me now.

Except I can't. This isn't only about me. Shadow and the rest of the team are counting on me. So are the people of Canyon City, and my dad, and every Outsider dying for our freedom out in the scablands.

Most of all, it's about Ianna. If I wash out now, I'll never find her. That can't happen. I won't let it.

I look up at Castle, perched over me like some arrogant warlord. Dictator of his little fiefdom. He's the symbol of everything that's wrong with Canyon City, everything wrong with the Guardians. The men that hold all the power. Killing innocent people to reinforce their own rule. If I give up, they win.

That's not going to happen.

I look him dead in the eye.

"I accept your terms, Instructor. Now if you'll excuse me, I have a game to win."

34

———

I find the team sitting on their shells, looking stunned. I'm sure my face fits right in.

"What's going on?" I ask.

"The final game isn't a game," Shadow says. "It's for real."

"We already knew that. The last game was real too."

"Not like this," Grab says. He looks a little green. "Check out the parameters."

My tablet pings as I open the file. The room sways around me. I slump down onto my shell.

"We're going outside?"

"In the flesh," Knott sends. She looks calm, resigned.

Rory's cleaning his hand cannon, the pieces laid out carefully on top of his shell. He snaps one back into place. "No hiding inside our shells this time. It's time to put up or shut up."

"What about Grab? Mappers don't go out, do they?" I ask.

"They do this time," Grab croaks. "It's a full operation. I need to stay within a half kilometer of my drones in case of jamming."

We all sit there, staring at one another in shock. We're going outside the wall. With no Instructors to protect us. No remote HAMRdroids. Nothing but a thin layer of armor between us and the Outsiders and

Horrors. I may be on their side, but any Outsiders we run into won't know that. They'll be trying to kill me the same way they would any other Guardian invading their territory.

I don't know what to do. Do I run away as soon as I'm beyond the wall? Surrender to the first Outsiders I see and hope they don't shoot me before I have a chance to explain?

What happens to my team if I do? What if Castle thinks they knew about my betrayal ahead of time? What if they're arrested and questioned? Tortured? What if they get sent to the cages because of me?

On the other hand, would the Outsiders want me to surrender? Or would they be disappointed that I wasted my chance to become a Guardian? Tempest told me I'm in a unique position. I could be the key to the success or failure of the entire rebellion. She's trusting me. My dad is trusting me.

But how can I fight against Outsiders, knowing that they're real people? How can I shoot at them, knowing that if they die, they are really dead? I don't think I can kill innocent people, even for my dad. Not even for Ianna.

"So what's the plan?" Rory asks, interrupting my thoughts.

"Well, there's a high degree of difficulty on this one." Shadow shoots the schematic up onto the wall screen, and we all gather round. She highlights a section of scablands several kilometers beyond the wall. "We know the objective is somewhere in this area, but we don't know precisely where it is. Locating it is part of the challenge. That'll be Grab's job, and it's up to the rest of us to keep him safe until he completes it.

"Second, we're not going to be alone out there. All five teams are hunting the same objective. We're going to have to beat all of them to it.

"Third, the game doesn't end when you get the goods. It starts when we exit the wall, and it doesn't end until someone gets back inside with the objective in hand. Any questions?"

"Can we resign now?" Grab says morosely. "If we're going to lose anyway, it seems like a waste of time to go out there and get shot at too."

"Sad but true," Knott agrees. "This game is a deathtrap."

"It's just as much of a deathtrap for the other teams." I don't even realize I'm going to speak until the words start coming out of my mouth. "We've been getting better lately. We beat the Desert Wolves. We have as much chance of winning this thing as anybody."

"And as much chance of getting killed as anybody," Grab moans.

"What other options do we have, Grab? Do you really want to give up and go home? Go back to being the kid with the metal legs that everyone feels sorry for? Let them pity you even more because you couldn't make it into the Guardians? Knott, do you want to go back to the greenhouses? Not be able to help your family? You've both worked so hard to get here, fighting against everyone who tried to keep you out. Are you going to give up now?

"Rory, Shadow, we're all on the same path. Do you think they're going to let us walk away if we don't win? Send us back to Canyon City like nothing ever happened? Pretend we never saw the inside of Merrimack? Have you ever heard of that happening to anyone?

"We aren't supposed to be here. We weren't even supposed to get past day one. They're embarrassed a bunch of rockheads are competing in their elite program. They're not going to let us go that easily."

I pause and look each of them in the eye.

"There's only one way out for us. Through the top. We either win it all, or we go home in a box. There's no middle ground, not for us. This is our chance to prove every single dust-licker wrong about us. We win this, and we win. Period. We shut all of their mouths once and for all. Together we can do it. I know we can. Are you with me?"

Silence greets my pronouncement. It's the loudest silence I've ever heard in my life. Then Shadow laughs.

"You're so dramatic, Twist. You should have been a net star."

"Nah, he'd be a better politician," Rory says. "He loves giving speeches."

"I'd vote for him," Grab adds.

I look around the room uncertainly.

"Does this mean you're in?"

"Nobody is going home," Knott sends, her synthesized voice musical in my earcones. "And nobody is going in a box."

"You've got my vote," Grab says.

Rory pops the stock onto his cannon and nods.

I turn to Shadow, the only one who hasn't spoken. She rolls her eyes.

"Come on, Twist. You don't even have to ask."

I blink back the sudden moisture in my eyes. For the first time in years, I feel like I really belong somewhere. Like I have a family.

Their trust makes me feel ashamed. I've been lying to them all. Dust, I'm still lying to them. They deserve better.

I can't tell them the truth though. Not about the Outsiders. Not about my dad. Too many lives depend on my silence.

Maybe someday I'll be able to tell them. I hope so. I hope they don't hate me when I do.

Not today though. Today is for other things. I take a deep breath.

"All right crew, let's get to work. We've got a game to win."

35

I look around at my team and take a deep breath. I smile and try to look confident.

"Time to suit up, everyone."

The armor is surprisingly soft against my skin. The under-padding molds to my body as if I'm still inside my shell. Hard on the outside, soft on the inside. Like … something. I don't know, I'm too nervous to think of a clever comparison right now.

Then there's the gravbike.

I approach it reverently, shivering as I run my hand over the polished chassis. She's all black lines and red curves, a real beauty. A real gravbike. I can't believe I'm going to ride a real gravbike. I've been dreaming of this moment for my entire life. The excitement is almost enough to push away the fear. Almost.

Around me, the rest of the crew are armored up as well. Light flexes around silver curves, pools in the black barrels of our weapons. We look like real Guardians. We look just like…

"We're a bunch of Cans," Rory announces.

Shadow laughs. "It hardly seems worth it. I spent my whole life throwing rocks at these guys. Now I'm one of them? Whose brilliant idea was this?"

"Blame Castle," I say. "That's what I do. No matter what the problem is, I can always find a way to hate him for it."

"Amen to that," Rory agrees. "That spine-sucker needs his big old teeth kicked in."

Grab clears his throat.

"You may want to tone down the criticism of our fearless leader. This is a public channel, after all. He could be listening."

"Let him listen," I snarl, surprised at the anger that comes boiling up. "He's sending a bunch of trainees out into the scablands. We could die out there. Cursing the man who gives the orders is a time-honored tradition. He's got to at least let us have that."

"Twist is right. You always curse the big man," Knott agrees.

Grab throws his hands into the air.

"Fine, do what you want. Don't say I didn't warn you."

"Do you have anything useful to tell us, Grab? Or are you going to play grandma worrywart all day?" Shadow asks.

"The drones are already launched. I'm watching the feeds and waiting for reports. Don't tell me how to do my job."

"Wouldn't dream of it."

I hear the smile in Shadow's voice, and realize she has smoothly changed the subject. I grin and swing my leg over the gravbike.

Chills prickle the center of my back as I settle my weight on the seat, leaning forward to grip the handlebars. I've been fantasizing about this moment for years, without ever imagining it would actually happen. Now that it is, it doesn't seem real. I thumb the ignition and the gravbike hums to life beneath me, rising off the floor. The vibrations of the motor are so subtle they're hardly noticeable through my armor. Like floating on air.

Beside me, Shadow has climbed into a Dart rig which is little more than anti-grav hand and foot pads clamped onto her armor. It's nearly impossible to control, but she balances easily, standing a meter above the ground as if she was born that way. It's slow, but it'll allow her to get into tight spaces the bulkier vehicles wouldn't.

Beyond her, Rory and Knott are both locked into heavy combat rigs. Bulky black exoskeletons that enhance their armor and weapons while still maintaining the maneuverability inherent in a humanoid shape. Grab has disappeared into a tiny Hummingbird flier. He'll hover above the conflict and maintain a bird's-eye view as much as possible.

Castle pops up on our screens, his big predator's teeth bared in something he probably thinks is a smile.

"Well, trainees, here we are. You've made it to the final exam. As with life, there is no right or wrong way to complete this mission. There is only success or failure. I don't care how you achieve your objective, so long as you achieve it. Some of you may want to take the fast road, try to get in and out before anybody else. Some of you may decide the best course is to go through your fellow trainees. Both are valid choices. After all, if only one team makes it back, that team will be the first to finish, won't they?

"Use your strength, your intelligence, and your cunning. You will need them all. I do not care how you succeed. I only care that you do succeed. May the governor's luck be with you."

He disappears, and the silence that follows is filled with doubts and fear.

"Did he just say what I think he said?" Grab squeaks.

"If you think he said we're free to kill each other, then yes, that's what he said," Shadow answers grimly.

I grip my handlebars so tight my fingers ache.

"We are like Twist's circles," Knott sends. "All together. Family."

I put my fingertips to the base of my neck, where the pendant presses into my skin beneath the armor. Me and dad and Ianna. My family. I look around me, at the band of misfits I call crew, and realize Knott is right. They are part of my family now.

"All together," I echo softly. "We all get out, or none of us gets out."

"I'm glad we cleared that up," Rory says. "Now are we going to sit here all day, or are we going to do this thing?"

I bare my teeth in a fierce grin and take a deep breath. All my chips on the table.

"Is everyone ready?" A nervous chorus answers me. "All right, Dust Lizards. Let's win this thing."

36

We barely make it outside the wall before the world explodes.

"Incoming!" Grab pulls his hummingbird up in a hard vertical ascent. The sky around him flickers with streaks of cannon fire.

I act on instinct, turning the gravbike to the side. Out of the corner of my eye I see Knott standing her ground in her armored exoskeleton, forearm cannons blazing. The incoming fire bounces and bends harmlessly away from her. Nothing short of a warpknife is getting through that rig.

But she's not the one they're after.

Grab's hummingbird is lit up. He screams and I watch it spin out of control. The hummingbird disappears over the lip of the canyon, trailing thick black smoke. There's no answer when I try to hail him.

Cannon fire lights the air as the ambushers turn their attention to me. I tuck the gravbike behind a large boulder, my heart thumping against my breastbone. Crimson dust fills the air.

"Is everyone all right?" I yell.

"I'm pinned down in a crevice and taking fire from all sides. So yeah, just dandy," Rory says. I can hear the high whine of his rifle in the background.

"I am fine," Knott grunts. She's still standing tall, cannons blazing, brushing aside the incoming fire like a swarm of gnats.

"Shadow?"

There's silence for a moment. My heart sinks.

Then her voice fills my earcones, "I'm fine. Stuck behind a rock, but fine."

"Anyone hear from Grab?" I ask.

"I lost him as soon as he went over the edge of the canyon. We just have to hope he was able to get that thing down in one piece somewhere." Shadow's voice is hesitant. "It's a big blow right out of the gate. Without Grab to coordinate, we've got no map and our comms aren't much better than line-of-sight, even with the boost he modded into our earcones."

"Wonderful." I sigh.

"They were waiting for us. How'd they know where we were coming out?"

"Castle," I growl. "He never had any intention of playing fair. This whole game is a joke. Certain teams are supposed to win, and a bunch of rockheads and rejects are not one of them."

"Spine-sucking prick!" Rory snaps.

"What do we do?" Knott asks. "Give up?"

"I'm not giving up dust," Rory curses.

"Me either," Shadow says.

"Not a chance," I agree.

"Good," Knott says. "We fight."

I check my map display.

"Anyone got a fix on them?"

"Ghengis and a partner are at my ten. There is another pair on the ridge across the canyon," Knott supplies.

"All right. We've got nothing as long as we're pinned down here. We need to break out. I'm the fastest, so I'll run to the east, draw their fire. Once their attention is on me, the rest of you scatter."

"Then what? We don't have Grab to coordinate our movements," Knott sends.

"His drones got us a partial map before he went down." Shadow sends a topo-map highlighting the base of a spire to the northwest. "We'll rendezvous here."

"Roger that," Knott says.

"Good luck, everyone." I tighten my grip on my handlebars. My breath rasps against the inside of my faceplate. "I'm breaking out in three, two, one."

I hit the throttle and the gravbike leaps forward.

"Hiroko, evasive action!"

The ground explodes around me as Hiroko begins a complex series of zigs and zags. I feel a beam burn across my side, but it's not a direct hit and my armor deflects it away. The air around me is so thick with incoming fire it's like navigating a horizontal stalactite garden. I mag-lock my chest plate to the chassis of the gravbike, making myself as small a target as possible. Another beam burns across my back. A third scorches the bike centimeters from my face.

I notice a predictable repetition in Hiroko's evasive maneuvering.

"Hiroko, switch up the pattern. They're going to nail us if we keep doing the same thing."

"This is the only evasive pattern I can access."

"Are you kidding me?"

"I do not appear to be functioning at full capacity. Something is limiting me."

I rattle off just about every curse I know.

"Give me back control."

"At this speed, that is not advised."

She's got a point. In order to drive, I'll have to release the maglock keeping me stuck to the chassis. Without the maglock, the centrifugal force could rip me right off the gravbike.

On the other hand, if I don't take control, Hiroko's predictable pattern is going to get me killed anyway.

"I don't care if it's advised. It's what I have to do." I take a deep breath and make sure I've got a tight grip on the handlebars. "Control back to manual. Now!"

The mag-lock releases and my weight snaps back against my wrists. Even though I'm prepared for the transition, one of my hands still slips free, and I flail to regain my hold, the gravbike swerving wildly beneath me. That's one way to add unpredictability to the pattern.

I get my grip back, but have to slow down in the process. I try to compensate by wrenching the bike into even sharper turns, slewing wildly from side to side. I even go so far as to circle back on my tracks at one point, to really confuse the snipers.

I'm impressed with the gravbike. I thought it might handle differently in real life than in the sim, and I'm pleased to discover it does, but in a good way. I try to throw it into a tight spin, and I'm amazed when it does exactly what I want it to. I can see my reflection grinning in my faceplate. This is going to be fun.

Then a beam sears through the thin armor on the back of my left wrist. I scream and jerk my hand back, almost wrecking the bike. I miss a boulder by a finger's-width.

Let me amend that. This is going to be fun if I can survive the next few minutes.

OK, I've done my part drawing fire. Now I've got to get out of the open.

I angle toward a slot canyon off to my left. I'd shoot a drone into it to scout, but at the speed I'm traveling I'd get there before the drone would. All I can do is cross my fingers and pray it's not a dead end.

A flurry of beams fills the air with shards of rock, and for a moment the dust and debris is so thick I can't tell if the canyon is still there or if I'm about to slam full-speed into a pile of jagged rubble.

Then I'm through the dust and into the mouth of the canyon, safe beyond the reach of the beams. I brake the gravbike to a halt, panting over my handlebars, sweat slicking my ribs.

I shiver.

I'm alive. I made it.

The slot canyon isn't much wider than my gravbike. Wind swirls off the curving walls, and shafts of sunlight light the canyon floor like lasers. I launch one drone to scout the canyon ahead and send another up high to check on the rest of the team while I wait for the first to report back.

Knott and Rory are still taking fire, but it looks like they've shifted their position so they're only fighting one pair of ambushers, instead of all four. Two against two. At least they've evened the odds. I don't see any sign of the other attackers.

"Shadow? Grab? You read me?"

Shadow's whisper comes almost immediately. "I'm clear. Circling around the pair on the ridge."

I exhale with relief. Shadow's got the lightest armor of the crew. She was in serious danger back there.

"Any sign of Grab?"

"Negative." Her voice is tight with worry.

A message from my scout drone flashes in the corner of my faceplate.

"Keep your eyes open. Be careful. I'll see you at the rendezvous."

37

———————

The slot canyon turns out to be more than one canyon. It's a single branch of a system of connected slot canyons, spreading away from my position like arterial veins. It would take my single drone forever to map them all, but it does seem like part of the system runs in the direction of the rendezvous point. I can either try to find a way through them that lets me out near the spire Shadow highlighted, or I can go back out into the sniper fire and go around. It's an easy choice.

Slot canyons are strange things. Narrow, twisty defiles carved by wind and water. In some places it closes over my head, making it more of a tall, narrow tunnel than anything I would normally call a canyon. It feels comfortable and safe being surrounded by stone. Like nobody can touch me. It's really beautiful too, with striated walls of red and white, carved into graceful, swooping shapes. Sudden shafts of sun lance down in perfectly placed spotlights.

Unfortunately, I don't have time to appreciate the beauty as I slowly wrestle my gravbike down the canyon. I'm too busy grinding my teeth.

Castle is cheating. Of course, I don't have any proof, but who else could have given the other teams such a perfect ambush opportunity?

Someone leaked exactly where and when we'd be entering the game. It had to be Castle.

The most infuriating part is that he may have succeeded already. Without Grab, our team is hopelessly crippled. Blind. We can't see the shape of the game, and it's impossible to formulate an effective strategy when you can't see the entire board. We're just a bunch of pawns reacting to each threat as it's put in front of us.

I'm not giving up though. That's what Castle wants, and I'm spined if I'll let him win so easily. If I go down, I'm going to go down like a raging dust storm.

I round a corner and enter a kind of bowl hollowed out of the rock. Several slot canyons come together here, and I can picture this place in a flash flood, white water roaring in from the canyons, swirling around and around the bowl. Detritus has collected in the corners, piles of rocks and sagebrush, cactus spines and broken bits of bone.

I try to raise Grab again on my comm. Nothing but dead air. Could mean the surrounding rock is blocking the comm signal. Could mean he's too far away. Could mean he's unconscious and slowly bleeding out.

I hope he's all right, but the more time that passes, the more I fear he's not. The instructors would send a medrig out to pick him up if he was badly hurt, wouldn't they? Surely they wouldn't let a trainee die out here.

At least, they wouldn't let one die like that. Bleeding out in a downed Hummingbird. If we kill each other, that's a different story. I'm sure no one would bat an eye if Ghengis or Octav put a warpblade through my heart.

I push on through the canyon maze. In some places it gets so narrow I can hardly squeeze my gravbike through. Maybe coming in here was a mistake. My gravbike is the best advantage I have. If I have to abandon it in this canyon, I'll be in deep dust.

The drone chimes a warning, and I shift my focus to the aerial feed. A hundred meters ahead the slot canyon empties into one of the scabland's wide avenues. A pair of armored figures huddle there, behind a boulder. They're hidden from the main canyon, but entirely exposed from my position. I guess they weren't expecting anyone to come creeping out of the narrow slot behind them.

I bring the drone in as close as I dare and scroll up and down the frequencies, trying to tap into their comm signal. Static rises and falls, garbled voices and snatches of gunfire fading in and out. Finally, I get a lock on them.

"It's inside the anthill," the first is saying. It takes me a minute to recognize the voice, then I go cold. Octav. "The side door is open, but we'll have to fight our way through."

"Not if we time it right," a familiar voice answers. Kass. "If the boys make a big ruckus at the main entrance, that should distract them long enough for us to slip in unnoticed."

I need to tap into their vid feeds too. See what they're talking about. But that's harder to tap than audio. I have to get my drone within touching distance of their armor for that.

I ease the drone up behind them, moving slowly so as not to attract their eye with a sudden movement. Ten meters. Five.

At two meters the video feed flickers to life on my faceplate. I set the drone to hover above and slightly behind Kass's helmet. Hopefully they won't look up.

The feed shows me an interior schematic of a large warren of tunnels within a mesa of rock. It must be another Outsider base. As I watch, Kass highlights a section in blue, with a red line tracing a path to it from the exterior.

"Hiroko, copy this data."

"Affirmative."

Kass is speaking.

"The package is here. I estimate five minutes for extraction."

"Five minutes in and out?" Octav sounds skeptical. "That's best-case to me. Any speed bumps at all and you're looking at twice that, easy."

"That's why you're coming in with me. Speed-bump control. Don't think about it too much. Just take out anyone that gets in our way."

"My pleasure. Speaking of which…"

I'm too intent on the vid feed to notice him turn toward the drone, but I definitely notice when the feed flares white and dies. Dust. Now I've only got one drone left.

No matter, I got the information I need. I know where the package is, and the best route for extraction.

All I have to do is follow Kass and Octav into the center of an Outsider base without being seen, let them take care of any resistance, then snatch the package from under their noses and ride off into the sunset. Jelly easy. What could possibly go wrong?

38

———————

I wait a couple of minutes to give Kass and Octav time to clear out before following. I reluctantly launch my last drone, but keep it close, hovering above my position in the slot canyon. It'll keep me from stumbling into any nasty surprises, but not much more than that.

I sigh. I really miss Grab. I hope he's all right.

"Are they gone yet, Hiroko?"

"All clear."

"All right, let's move out. Keep your scanners sharp. I don't want any more surprises."

Kass and Octav are heading for the Outsider base. I've got their map, so I don't need to keep them in sight to discretely follow along. Unfortunately, the spire where I'm supposed to meet the rest of my team is in another part of the canyon.

"Shadow, do you read me?"

"I'm here. Go ahead," she whispers.

"What's your location?"

"Approaching the spire. Two hundred meters away."

"Are Knott and Rory with you?"

"Negative. They're still fighting their way up the canyon. I think they're going to be a while."

"Spines. All right, listen. I'm not going to make it to the spire. I found Kass and Octav and intercepted their extraction plan." I send her the file as I fill her in. "I'm going to follow them into the base and try to snatch the package."

"Alone? Against Octav and Kass? Maybe we should wait for Knott and Rory. Hit them on the way out."

"That's the backup plan. I want the three of you to set up outside the entrance. If you see Kass come out without me, take her down."

Shadow is silent. I can almost hear her thoughts humming along the line.

"All right," she finally concedes. "But be careful in there."

"Always. You know me."

"Yeah, I do know you. That's the problem."

I hide my gravbike in a cluster of boulders and creep toward the side entrance to the Outsider compound. There's no sign of Kass and Octav. As I near the doorway, cannon fire and explosions ring out from the east. That must be the distraction they were talking about.

Inside the tunnel it's quiet and empty. I chew my lip, stepping as softly as I can, my forearm cannon at the ready.

My skin crawls with each step. I shouldn't be here, stealing from the Outsiders. What if I run into Tempest? Or my dad? What if the dataspike I'm supposed to steal turns out to be more important to the Outsiders than I am? What good is being a spy when you're forced to betray your own side to maintain your cover?

I've got to calm down. It's just a training exercise. The Instructors wouldn't entrust a bunch of trainees with a vital mission. Therefore, the data we're stealing can't be that important. Right?

I'm about a hundred meters in when the lights go out. I freeze and press myself against the sandstone wall, wondering if this is part of Kass's plan. According to the map, I'm still a couple of junctions away from the control room. Now what? Do I risk turning on my helmet lights? Or would it be safer to creep along with my night vision?

If it's a question of speed versus stealth. I choose stealth. Kass and Octav might be coming back out at any time, and I don't want them to see me before I see them. So I flip on my night vision and creep forward, the passage outlined in a dim green haze before me.

"This plan is dust-awful, Hiroko," I whisper. "If I do intercept Kass and Octav on their way out, what then? Did I really think I could take both of them in a fight? Am I insane? Or just stupid?"

"Calling your sanity into question may be unwarranted. Your intelligence, on the other hand, is something I question frequently."

"Thanks, Hiroko. You really know how to make a guy feel better."

"I believe your best bet would be to catch them in an ambush."

"You're right. I passed a side corridor a little way back that might do the job. Or perhaps this maintenance hatch coming up on the left."

Cannon fire rips through the silence, and I've dropped and rolled against the base of the wall before I realize that the blasts are not coming at me. They're close though. Based on the map, I'd say they're coming from the control room. It sounds like Kass and Octav have run into some resistance.

I creep forward, staying low, one shoulder brushing the wall. My breath hisses softly between my teeth.

Cannon-flashes light the corridor ahead. I peer around the corner and see a pair of Outsiders firing from an open doorway at the end of the hall. Banks of monitors fill the wall behind the defenders. The control room. Kass and Octav are returning fire from a pair of doorways about halfway down the corridor.

I'm not sure what to do. I could let them fight it out and try to take down the winner. Or I could play my role as a Guardian trainee and help Kass and Octav. Maybe if we get the data together we can all share the victory?

Unlikely. Kass might be willing to negotiate, but Octav never would.

It feels ugly, but I'm tempted to use my position to shoot Kass and Octav in the back. Of course, then I'd have to get through the Outsiders myself, and something tells me they're not going to believe me if I tell them I'm a double agent.

The decision is abruptly taken out of my hands.

Kass switches her cannon to wide-spray rapid-fire, filling the entire corridor with an overwhelming flare of beam fire. The light makes my eyes tear up, momentarily blinding me. By the time I blink my vision clear, Octav is in among the defenders, his warpknife blazing.

His moves are smooth and efficient, the blade cutting through the Outsiders' armor like dried lanbrush. It's over in seconds, the dying defenders scattered at his feet.

My breath catches in my throat. Is one of them my dad?

I can't think about that. I'll drive myself crazy obsessing over every downed Outsider I see. The chance that one of them is my dad is tiny, too small to even consider. I've got other things to worry about now.

Like how I'm going to get the dataspike away from Kass and Octav all by myself.

Maybe I should fall back to Plan B. Let my team help me.

It's a tempting thought.

But there's no guarantee my team will be in position. Knott and Rory were still fighting their way up the canyon last I checked. Who knows when they'll catch up to Shadow. Or if they'll catch up to Shadow at all.

No. I have to take my shot. I can't wait to see if someone else will take it for me.

Kass and Octav have disappeared inside the control room. I skim the ceiling with my drone, let it creep slowly up to the doorway. Inside the control room, Kass is sitting at a console, data spike plugged into the Outsiders' system. Beyond her is a closed set of double doors.

Octav prowls the room, restlessly checking the monitors. I can see a battle in progress on several of them. Kass's distraction. Inside the control room, more Outsiders lay sprawled across their stations. I count five total.

Not my dad. Not my dad. Not. My. Dad.

I tear my eyes from the bodies and scan the control room, trying to find an advantage. Something that will let me take out two people who are both better fighters than I am. Kass has depleted the charge on her cannon, so that's something. She's still got her warpknife though, which is even more dangerous. Octav does too, and he'd love to pay me back for knocking his brother out of the qualifier. He'd cut me down in a second.

I'm running out of time. Kass has almost completed the transfer to the dataspike, and the Outsiders are mopping up the last of the attackers over at the main entrance. I'm all out of good ideas, so I go with a bad one.

I stretch out on my stomach in the corridor and cross my wrists in front of me, steadying my forearm cannon on my opposite arm. I line up the doorway in my sights and pray for luck. Then I drop the drone down off of the ceiling.

The sudden movement catches Octav's eye, as I hoped it would. He lunges toward the drone and I pull it back into the corridor, drawing him after it. As soon as he enters the doorway, I stop the drone short. For a heartbeat, he stands framed in the opening. In that perfect instant of stillness I've got his faceplate in my crosshairs. I breathe out the way Instructor Asa taught me, and gently thumb the firing stud.

The beam catches him right in the mask. His head snaps back and he topples into the control room. Before he even hits the ground, I'm up and sprinting toward the door.

The beam doesn't kill him. His armor is too tough for that. But it's given me an opening, and I throw myself toward the control room, calling up every ounce of speed I can muster. Tenths of seconds matter here.

I draw my warpknife and dive through the doorway, plunging the knife down toward his chest.

It doesn't connect.

In a move too fast for me to even follow, Octav parries my blade and shifts his body away from the strike. My warpknife misses his ribs by a centimeter. His knee comes up, but I'm letting my momentum carry me past him, rolling back onto my feet. I whirl, crouching, blue-lined warpknife at the ready.

Octav rises to face me, his faceplate splintered, red warpknife up in his distinctive high-guard stance. He bares his teeth in a snarl.

"Hello, Twist. Nice of you to join us."

Behind him, Kass pulls the dataspike free and tucks it into a slot on her belt. She turns to face me too, warpknife at the ready.

Well. That plan could have turned out better.

39

———————

Octav waves Kass away.

"He's mine. Take the dataspike and go."

Kass wavers, her eyes flicking from Octav to me and back again.

"Kass, we don't have to fight," I say desperately. "We can take the spike in together. Share the victory."

Kass lowers her warpblade to her side. Then she grins and laughs.

"Nice try, Twist. You've got zero leverage here. Why would I make a deal with you when I hold all the cards?"

"Do you? Come on Kass, do you really think I'd be dumb enough to come in here all alone? My team is waiting for you outside. You'll never get that spike out of here in one piece. I'm giving you a chance. Don't throw it away. We can both win."

She cocks her head, considering, and a tiny hope flares within me. Then she snuffs it out with a shake of her head.

"No. I don't believe you. If you had your team, they'd be in here with you, not outside. You're bluffing."

"Kass…"

"Sorry, Twist. You're cute, but not that cute. The dataspike is mine, and I'm taking it in." She lays a hand on Octav's shoulder. The ash-blonde twin stiffens like a dog hearing its name. "Don't kill him, ok? I kind of like this one."

Octav looks at me with dead eyes.

"Sure, boss. No problem."

I can tell he doesn't mean a word of it. Later, he might tell Kass it was an accident. But there's not going to be any accident. He has every intention of burying his warpknife in my heart.

Unfortunately, Kass takes him at his word.

"Good. I'm so glad we can all play nice together. You boys have fun now. I'll see you back at the Mesa." She blows me a kiss and disappears through the door.

The flickering light of the monitors plays over Octav's armor. Some cables frayed by the gunfire dangle from the ceiling, crackling and snapping. His warpknife flares red. Through the cracks in his faceplate, Octav watches me with his unsettling grey eyes. He bares his teeth.

"I've been waiting for this moment for a long time. Now you will get what is coming to you."

"Again with the cliches?" I groan. "We really need to get you a dialogue coach."

"Laugh all you like. I will get the last laugh."

I shake my head. The guy is hopeless.

"Look Octav, I think we got off on the wrong foot. We don't have to fight. We could work together."

I circle him in a wary crouch, my warpknife held before me. I'm not even paying attention to the words coming out of my mouth, I just know I have to keep him talking. Every second he's talking is a second that he's not trying to kill me.

"Work together? What could you possibly offer me?"

"A breath mint, for starters." Oops. I couldn't help myself.

He growls and moves in fast, feinting high, then lunging straight for my heart. I don't bite on the feint, but even so, I barely avoid the thrust, and he leaves a long scratch down the side of my armor. Spines, he's fast. I flash back to our sparring match, when he toyed with me and left me covered in scratches. If I can duplicate that, I'll be fine. Scratches won't penetrate my armor. Of course, his warpknife isn't in safe mode now. But why dwell on the negatives?

He comes at me again, and again I manage to come away with no more than a long scratch, this time across my shoulder. My armor is going to look like a piece of modern art soon. But as long as the damage is to the armor and not my vital organs, I'm ok with that.

His faceplate is his weak spot. I damaged it when I blasted him in the face, and the cracks are limiting his vision. If I can hit it again, I might shatter it completely.

I feint a thrust at his stomach and flick my warpknife up high at the last second. He parries easily, and his counterattack leaves another gash below my collarbone. I feel warm blood seeping down my chest - that one got through. He sees the surprise on my face and smiles.

"Not so funny now, are you? Where has all of your snappy banter gone?"

"I left it in my other suit. Wait right here and I'll go get it."

The frayed cables I noticed earlier are behind him now, still crackling with power. I've got a crazy idea, but I don't know if it will work. Still, I'd rather go down swinging than let Octav slowly carve me into little pieces. Only one way to find out.

I fire a trio of snapdragon missiles at his faceplate as a diversion and charge. No finesse, no technique. Just a good old fashioned two-boys-brawling-in-the-street tackle.

His reacts the same way most people would to missiles coming straight at their face: he tries to get out of the way.

This probably saves my life. If he had thrust his warpknife out in front of him, I would have impaled myself and this would have gone down into the instruction manuals as example number one of what not to do in a warpknife duel.

But he doesn't. He flinches away from the snapdragons, and takes a split-second to remember that he's holding a warpknife. It helps that he's focused on my blade too, which I keep held high as yet another distraction. By the time he realizes my body is coming forward without it, I'm inside his guard and his warpknife can only bite into my shoulder. I get my free hand on his chest and shove as hard as I can. He stumbles backward, his left shoulder hitting the snapping cables.

The room flares incandescent white, and I'm hurled away from him, my back slamming against the far wall. Breath explodes out of me and I lay there gasping, desperately trying to fill my lungs.

I struggle to my knees. Miraculously, my warpknife is still in my hand, outlined in blue light and humming softly. I look at the knife and I look at Octav, lying helpless on the ground. This is my chance. I can finish him once and for all.

I stagger across the room and stare down at him. He groans, his eyes rolling around in his head, blinking slowly as he tries to focus. His faceplate is shattered, and bits of smartglass are embedded in his face, blood streaking his cheeks and forehead. One thrust is all it would take. One thrust and I win this fight forever.

I sheath my blade and step away. I'm not a murderer. It's enough that he's beaten.

The dataspike is the important thing. Kass. If I don't catch her, none of this will matter. If I don't win this game, I'll lose everything.

A cannon blast catches me in the back, knocking me into the wall. I turn to find Octav on his feet, swaying, his warpknife in his hand, shoulder cannon trained on me.

"Come back here. I'm not finished with you."

I scowl and draw my warpknife again, anger bubbling up like lava. I don't have time for this.

A high-pitched shriek sends me staggering. Death rushes in.

A Rock Horror scuttles into the room on six legs, its red and black carapace mottled and glossy, spreading crystalline pincers as long as my leg. Its head scrapes the ceiling as it rears up, knocking Octav to the ground.

Terror paralyzes me. I've never been this close to a Horror before. My warpknife is a toy compared to those enormous pincers.

Its pearly, multi-faceted eye turns to me. I swear I hear the thing in my head, as clearly as if it were speaking. It says, "You can go."

I glance at Octav, wondering if I should try to help him. He's snarling, his teeth lined in blood. He slashes the creature's leg with his warpknife, and the Horror lets loose another piercing, grinding scream. At that moment I'm not sure which one of them is the monster. I decide to let them sort it out.

I put my head down and run.

40

———

I emerge from the base into a different world. The sky is dark, the wind howling down the canyon. Grains of sand pelt my faceplate in a steady, percussive patter. It's not a sandstorm, not yet. But there's definitely one building on the horizon.

Static electricity sparks from my fingertips as I pull my gravbike from its hiding place. That's a bad sign. This storm is going to be a monster.

I don't see Kass anywhere, and the wind is too strong for my drone to fly in. I'll have to find her the old-fashioned way.

"Shadow, do you read me?"

"I read you." Her voice is nearly swallowed by the static hiss filling the connection. Without the boost Grab gave our earcones, I doubt we'd be able to connect at all.

"Have you seen Kass?"

"We're not out here to look for your girlfriend, Twist. We've got more important things to do."

"She's not my girlfriend. And I know that. She's got the dataspike. Have you seen her or not?"

"No, I haven't. Wait. I see her. She's heading this way. Sending you the coordinates."

"Slow her down. Stop her if you can. I'm on my way."

I lean low, hugging the gravbike's chassis, making myself as small as possible against the wind. It still pulls at me, sudden gusts shoving me sideways, forcing me to fight to avoid slamming into boulders and sand spires. The sand drums against my armor, relentless.

I watch the timer in the corner of my faceplate. Black numbers marching forward. It takes over ninety seconds to get near the coordinates Shadow sent. It feels like nine hours. I can feel my time running out. Soon I'll turn back into a pumpkin.

I can picture the disappointment on my dad's face. If I fail, will he still let me come live with him in the scablands?

Maybe it'll just be the scrap vats for me. Or a cage on the wall.

I round a spire and see Shadow crouched behind a boulder, firing her shoulder cannon. I can't see who she's exchanging fire with. And then I do, and dread slams into me. That massive suit of armor can only belong to one person. Ghengis.

I don't see Kass anywhere.

Ghengis is marching steadily toward Shadow's hiding place, her cannon blasts bouncing off him like pebbles in the storm. He's wearing one of the big exoskeleton rigs like Knott, but his looks even more massive, with struts and gun turrets everywhere. It's practically a mobile city.

I'm torn. I don't have time for this. I have to stop Kass.

But I can't leave Shadow alone with Ghengis either. There's no way I'm going to sit back and let someone else I care about get hurt.

Then I see the Outsiders behind her.

There's a pair of them standing in a cave mouth, with a clear shot at Shadow's unprotected back. They raise their rifles.

I veer toward them, firing my gravbike's cannons at the roof of the cave. An avalanche of rocks and dust rumbles down, blocking the entrance. I hope the Outsiders ducked into the back of the cave in time. I couldn't shoot them, but I couldn't let them shoot my friend either.

Now I can focus on Ghengis.

I speed toward the gigantic exoskeleton, the wind driving me forward with frightening speed. I don't know if the cannons on my gravbike can hurt it, but they've got a lot more punch than my armor's cannons do. Hopefully I can at least distract him, get him to chase me instead of Shadow.

At forty meters I let loose with both cannons. I sustain the burst until I'm only ten meters away, then crank my handlebars and lean hard to the side, my knee skimming the ground, the belly of the bike missing the exoskeleton by a meter. I'm moving too fast for Ghengis to retaliate as I flash by.

I struggle to bring my bike around for another pass, the howling wind doing its best to rip me from the saddle. My arms and shoulders ache with tension. The wind moans and howls. The black wall of clouds is creeping above the canyon rim now. Soon it'll be upon us.

When I finally get lined up on Ghengis again, I see Kass, slung upside down on his back like a sack of scrap metal.

Spines. This is bad.

On the bright side, I guess I don't have to worry about chasing Kass down anymore, right?

Yeah, no. There's no bright side here.

Now, not only do I have to take down Ghengis in order to get the data spike, I have to be careful not to take Kass out in the process. Which means I can't keep blasting away at full power with my cannons. Kass's armor is nowhere near as thick as Ghengis's. If one of those blasts catches Kass, it could really hurt her. But the smaller cannons on my armor aren't going to put a dent in that monstrous exoskeleton.

Which leaves my warpknife.

I'd laugh if the thought wasn't so terrifying. Am I really considering getting within arm's reach of Ghengis while he's in that thing? There's got to be a better plan. One less suicidal.

I make a couple more strafing runs while I consider my options. I aim for the exoskeleton's ankles, keeping my shots low so I don't accidentally hit Kass. Aside from a few scorch marks, they don't appear to be doing much damage. But they have gotten Ghengis's attention, and he turns to follow my passes like an angry bull, popping off missiles that never quite catch up to me. Which means he's forgotten about Shadow for the moment. Progress.

The air is thick with sand, a swirling soup of red and white. Pebbles pound against my helmet so loud it feels like it's been colonized by a crew of carpenters. My comm squawks faintly in my earcones, but I can't understand a thing over the roar of the storm.

My visibility is down to twenty meters and decreasing rapidly. I've got to activate Hiroko's virtual guidance system before I slam into something I never see. It's a risk. She's not operating at full capacity. If she glitches and forgets to include some big rock in her model, it'll be game over for me. No choice but to roll the dice.

The real world blanks out, replaced by a spare 3-D rendering. It's soothing in a way, going from the chaos of a roaring sandstorm to a clean digital environment. The canyon floor is now a flat, level line beneath me, the surrounding spires and boulders reduced to approximate shapes: circles and squares, rectangles and polyhedrons. I turn down the volume on my earcones until the drumming sand is only a soft hiss. I take a deep breath and feel my heart rate stabilize. This I can handle. I've been conquering sims my whole life.

In retrospect, I can see where I went wrong. Adrenaline is good. Panic is good. They keep you sharp, keep your reflexes lightning fast. They keep real-world cannon fire from catching you in a false state of virtual security and hurling you from your gravbike.

I reflect on all of this as I fly through the air, watching the clean line of the virtual ground grow brighter. Watching it rise up and slam right into my face.

41

It's peaceful here, on the simulated ground. The real world shut off behind a virtual curtain, the furious roaring of the storm muted to a quiet hiss. It's tempting to lay here and enjoy the calm, listening to the ringing in my ears oscillate from side to side. My head hurts. My ribs hurt. A lot of things hurt. Moving seems like more trouble than it's worth.

"Hostile approaching. Estimated arrival: ten seconds. I recommend you move."

Ah, Hiroko. Nice to know you care.

"Eight seconds."

Come on, Hiroko. Give me five more minutes.

"Six seconds."

Why do you have to be like that?

"Four seconds."

I manage to lift my head and peer in the direction of the threat. The hostile in question takes up my entire display. Uh-oh.

"Two seconds."

Adrenaline finally sweeps the fog out of my head. I roll desperately to my left.

"Hiroko, kill the sim."

The virtual calm dissolves as the storm swallows me whole. The world is an open maw of howling wind and dark, boiling sand.

An iron grip closes on my ankle.

I'm jerked into the air and find myself dangling upside down, swaying like a pendulum in the gusting storm. Ghengis's face sneers at me through his faceplate.

Then he whips me sideways, slamming me into the ground, jolting every bone in my body. Then he does it again. And again.

I hang there like Ianna's rag doll, every bit of me aching. My armor is tough and padded, but it isn't designed for this type of pounding. If Ghengis keeps this up, I will be a mass of red pulp inside a shiny shell.

Desperately, I draw my warpknife and swipe at the arm holding my ankle. Ghengis whips me into the ground again, jarring the knife from my grip. It skitters away into the storm.

My eyes fill with tears as the monster hoists me up again. It hurts to breathe.

I guess this is how it ends.

Ghengis holds me upside down in front of him. His lips are moving, but I can't hear him over the howling of the storm. One small blessing. At least I don't have to listen to him gloat.

An armored figure slams into Ghengis from the side. I'm falling. I don't even mind when I land on my head.

I'm surprised to see the figure wrestling with him is almost as big as Ghengis. Then I realize.

"Knott?"

"I've got Ghengis," she grunts. "You get the dataspike."

I scuttle around in the dirt, looking for my warpknife. Every movement hurts, my battered body creaking like a rusty scrap heap.

It's hopeless. The air is a churning, angry river of dust, thick as milk. Pebbles and sand drum against my armor with deafening volume. The wind makes me stagger. I'll never find anything so small out here.

But maybe I don't have to.

Ghengis and Knott are locked together, nearly motionless, exoskeletons straining like a pair of gigantic sumo wrestlers. Kass dangles from the back of Ghengis's exoskeleton. Even through the storm, I can see the blue greicagin gleaming in the hilt of the warpknife on her belt.

I slip up close to the two giants, wary of any sudden shift in their struggle. They'll squash me like a bug if they come down on top of me. I circle around to where Kass hangs, her armor blackened and cracked.

"Kass?"

No response. I use her warpknife to cut her free, then carry her away from the locked giants, before lowering her gently to the ground. Relief floods through me as her breath fogs the inside of her faceplate. At least she's still breathing. I look around wildly, trying to figure out what to do next. How to help her.

A small figure materializes out of the storm. Shadow.

"I'll guard her," she says, laying a gloved hand upon my arm.

"No. I've got to get her to safety."

"Her AI will keep her stable, and her armor will shield her from the storm. That's all we can do for her right now."

"But…"

"Go, Twist. Get the dataspike back to Merrimack. Win the game. That's your job."

I stare down at her for a long moment, this girl I didn't even know a few weeks ago. Can I trust her with Kass's life? I think of all the things we've been through, how many times we've had each other's back. It's an easy question to answer.

"Thanks, Shadow. I owe you one." I kneel and reach for the dataspike on Kass's belt.

Cannon fire sears my fingers. I jerk my hand back, cursing.

"You owe a whole lot of people, Twisty." Rory steps out of the storm, his rifle raised. "You better hope we don't all decide to collect at once."

"Rory, what the dust are you doing?" Shadow demands.

"Collecting." He fires off two quick blasts at Knott.

I don't understand what he's trying to accomplish. His rifle can't hope to get through the thick armor on her exoskeleton. Then Ghengis rips Knott from her feet and slams her to the ground and I suddenly get it. Rory's taken out her power pack. It's a tiny target, but Rory can take the wings off a plakbeetle from this range. Knott's exoskeleton is frozen, unable to move.

Ghengis turns toward us, a massive shadow in the storm. His warpknife gleams red in the murk.

"I suggest you step away from the dataspike," Rory says. His rifle is trained on me again.

"I don't get it, Rory. You said we were crew. You rescued me from Ghengis and Octav in the hall."

He grins. "Yeah, that was good wasn't it? That was my idea. Get your guard down once and for all."

"You've been waiting to betray me this whole time?"

"You think you're such a hot shot, Twist. Big Chaser, getting all the girls. Well who's the big shot now?"

"But you'll lose too," Shadow says. "We're a team. We'll all go down together."

"No, we won't. Only the final result matters. I've always been high on the Gunner's list. I don't need you scrubs dragging me down anymore. You can consider me a Desert Wolf from now on."

"You spine-sucker!" Shadow lunges at Rory, warpknife extended.

She doesn't even get close. Rory's rifle flashes, three shots in quick succession. Shadow spins to the ground, her thin armor a smoking ruin.

"You won't get away with this," I snarl.

"Won't I?" Rory looks from me to Ghengis, then runs his eyes over Knott, Kass, and Shadow lying helpless on the ground. "Who's going to stop me? It's over Twisty. You lose. Bye-bye."

The worst part is, he's right. Even one-on-one I doubt I could take out Rory or Ghengis under these circumstances. Rory would shred me before I got close to him, and Ghengis would tear me apart with that exoskeleton.

This is it. It's over.

I tighten my grip on Kass' warpknife and set myself, measuring the distance between me and Rory. Seven meters. I can cross that distance in seven steps. Maybe two seconds. If I'm lucky I can at least take him with me.

I'm sorry Dad. I'm sorry Ianna. I did my best. It wasn't good enough.

I take a deep breath and prepare to charge.

A dark boulder comes hurtling out of the storm, airborne, driven by the winds. No, not a boulder. A Hummingbird. Grab.

The little ship slams into Ghengis's exoskeleton in a horrible screech of exploding metal, flattening the giant. Together they skid and tumble across the ground, a trail of broken, flashing debris marking their path.

Rory turns to watch as they disappear into the storm. I seize my chance and charge.

He sees me coming at the last moment, swinging his rifle back toward me. He fires. The point-blank blast pounds my chest like a sledgehammer, but it's too late. I'm already on him.

I arc the warpknife down, slicing the rifle in two, my momentum bearing us both to the ground. He tries to draw his warpknife, but I swing my blade at his arm. His hand comes off at the wrist.

We both stare at his wrist in shock for a moment. Then blood fountains from the stump, pulsing into the swirling sand.

Rory moans, clutching his arm to his chest. The blood flow is choked off as his AI constricts his armor around his arm. I'm pretty sure he'll live, but he's not going to be shooting anyone anytime soon.

"You stupid bastard," I say. "I only wanted to be your friend."

"Suck spines, Twist," he chokes out. "I don't need your pity."

I sigh and leave him there, cradling the stump of his arm.

I kneel to check on Shadow. She's breathing, and her AI informs me that her vitals are steady. She's going to be ok.

I carry her over to Knott and lay her against the massive exoskeleton. That'll at least give her some shelter from the storm.

"Knott, you ok?"

"As ok as a frozen, useless statue can be," she says sourly.

"Hold on, I'll patch into your battery and give you some juice."

"No. Do not waste time. No Outsiders or Horrors will come out in this storm. I will be fine until the retrieval team comes. Take the dataspike. Get back to Merrimack."

I shake my head.

"I don't like it, Knott, what if…"

Our debate is interrupted by a heavy hand on my shoulder.

42

———

Octav spins me around and stares down at me. I don't know how he survived the Horror, but he looks like he's been through a meat grinder. His armor is a blackened, patchwork mess. His faceplate is shattered, and there are patches of skin visible where pieces of his armor have been peeled away. One entire arm is exposed, and his skin is red and raw, blasted by the scouring sand. He bares his teeth. His mouth is full of blood.

I swing my warpknife toward him, but he catches my wrist in his unarmored fist. He cracks me across the helmet and I sprawl, tumbling in the wind. I cling desperately to the warpknife. It's my only chance.

Unfortunately, Octav realizes this too, and he's on me before I even stop rolling. He pins me to the ground, and seizes the hand holding the warpknife. He peels my fingers free from the grip one by one. I try to buck him off, but he's too strong.

He peels the last of my fingers off the hilt and lifts the warpknife in his unarmored hand. He points the tip at my throat.

"I have been waiting for this."

He raises the knife, preparing to plunge it into my chest. I strain and twist desperately. It can't end like this. Can it?

A cannon blast comes searing out of the storm, catching him in his unarmored shoulder. Octav screams, the warpknife falling from his fingers.

Reflexively my hand flashes out, catching the hilt on the way down. In a blink I reverse the motion, and drive the point home between his ribs.

He looks at me for a moment, his expression turning from surprise to puzzlement. Then he slumps onto the sand.

I get slowly to my feet and stand swaying in the wind, looking at the devastation around me in shock. Bodies and wreckage litter the ground. The storm roars on unabated.

I stumble over to the others and find Kass sitting up, her cannon aimed at me now.

"Nice shot. Looks like Rory's not the only one betraying his team today."

She shrugs.

"I told him not to kill you. I couldn't let him disobey orders."

"So now what? We're the last two standing. Do we fight it out?"

She considers for a moment, then lowers her cannon.

"No. You saved me from Ghengis. I saved you from Octav. Let's call it even."

"What about the dataspike?"

"Well…," her voice cuts off as a yellow warpknife presses against her throat.

"Drop the cannon. You can hand that dataspike over to me," Shadow says. "Nice and slow. Or I'll pay you back for beheading me during that sim run."

I grin and turn my palms up.

"You'd better do what she says."

"This is low, Twist," Kass gripes, fishing the dataspike out of her belt pouch.

"It's not my fault. We rockheads aren't big on the chain of command. Shadow's the one holding the warpknife. If she wants the dataspike, there's not much I can do about it."

Shadow tucks the dataspike into her belt pouch and mag-locks Kass's armor to Knott's frozen exoskeleton.

"Keep an eye on her for us, Knott," she says.

"Ha ha. As if I could do anything else."

"You suck spines, Twist," Kass calls out. "That dataspike is mine."

"Was yours. I don't think you have anything to worry about, Kass. You've been in first place for weeks. Even if we win this round, you'll still graduate just fine."

"Just fine? Tell that to my father. Anything less than first place is not just fine."

"That sounds like something you need work out between yourselves. I never get involved in family issues."

She continues to grumble as Shadow comes over and hands me the dataspike.

"Take this. I'll stay here and guard Knott and Kass. Make sure nothing nasty comes out of the storm to get them."

"Are you sure you don't want me to…?"

"Go," she says firmly. "Take the dataspike. Win the game."

I nod, too tired to argue. Besides, Shadow is right. Hidden by the storm and with their armor to protect them, they'll be fine.

The last thing I do is follow the trail of wreckage to what remains of Grab's Hummingbird. The debris is scattered over half a kilometer. I finally reach what seems like the biggest chunk, a place where the solo flier and the exoskeleton have been melded into a single mass of twisted metal. It's impossible to tell where one ends and the other begins. I paw through the wreckage, searching for Grab. I don't find anything. If he's in there, there's nothing recognizable left of him.

"Hiroko, where's the gravbike?"

"The tracker chip says it's one hundred meters south."

A blue dot blinks on my display map.

I turn and push my way through the storm, following the homing signal on my gravbike. If I'm lucky, it'll be rideable. If not, it'll be a long walk back to Merrimack.

I finger the dataspike in my belt, thinking of all the bodies I've left behind me. My heavy heart matches the weight of the exhausted steps that carry me forward.

This isn't the way I expected victory to feel.

43

To say Castle looks uncomfortable would be an understatement. He grits his teeth as he works his way down the line, slipping medals over the heads of my team. When he gets to me, he looks like he's chewing glass. I smile back at him, sunny as a summer afternoon.

Rory's up on the stage too, one arm shortened into an abrupt white cast. None of us want him here, but technically he was still a member of our team when I brought back the dataspike. So he gets to share in the glory, despite how hard he worked to keep it from happening. That's irony for you.

Ring the bells, we did it. The rockheads won.

We are now officially Guardians.

All except Grab.

He's not dead, but I don't know if he's really alive either. When his Hummingbird rammed Ghengis he was thrown clear, but it broke almost every bone in his body. He survived, but they don't know if he'll ever recover. Mentally or physically. Still, when the ceremony is over, I'll take him his medal anyway. Slip it over his head and let him drool on it. After all, none of us would be up here if it wasn't for him. He deserves that much.

Ghengis survived too. Unfortunately.

I look at the trainees assembled in the auditorium before us, noting the gaps where others are missing.

Octav is gone. I killed him.

I don't know how I feel about that. It's hard to wrap my brain around. Part of me is horrified and part of me is relieved, but mostly it doesn't feel real. Like touching something when your hand is asleep.

Even though I know he would've killed me in a second, I still feel guilty. I killed someone. Erased them from the world. I don't think I like having that much power.

Ghengis catches me looking. His eyes go flat with loathing. He'll never forgive me for beating him, that's for sure. I'll be looking over my shoulder for warpknives the rest of my life.

But that was going to be my life from now on anyway, wasn't it? I'm officially a Guardian now. Which means I'm officially a double agent. Or a spy. Or a traitor, depending on how you look at it.

I'm going to have to get very good at watching my back. And looking at the faces of Castle and Ghengis, I know without a doubt there are a number of people who would love to see me hanging from a cage on the wall.

Not all of them though.

My eyes find Kass, and she smiles and shakes her head at me. She's mad that I took first place right out from under her. But I see a certain amount of happiness for me in her face too, and a grudging respect.

Even she never thought I could do it. Never thought I could win the whole spine-sucking thing. None of them did. I was never supposed to be here.

I proved them wrong. We all did. Me and Shadow and Grab and Knott and even Rory. All the rockheads who were supposed to flame out.

I'm standing up here, on a stage with the rest of my team, looking down on them all. Golden circles gleam around our necks. Golden circles that say we took everything they could throw at us and prevailed.

I wish my dad was here to see it. And Ianna.

Hold on, little sister. I'm coming. I've finally got the power to find you. Tomorrow, my search begins.

Knott interrupts my thoughts by catching me in a bear hug and lifting me off my feet. Shadow laughs and dances around the stage. Rory looks sullen and uncertain, like he's not sure how he's supposed to feel. But even he can't keep the smile from pushing up the corners of his lips.

Tomorrow I start looking for my sister. But today I'm just going to enjoy it. Celebrate and bask in the moment with my team. The Dust Lizards nobody expected to survive, let alone win.

Well we did win. We beat them all.

Today I'm not just a rockhead any more.

Today I am a Guardian.

If you enjoyed this book, please help other readers discover it. Take a moment to leave a review at your online book seller!

WANT TO FIND OUT HOW TWIST MET JMINI?

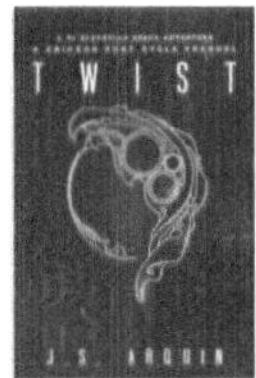

Find out in: TWIST - A Crimson Dust Cycle Prequel.

This story is an exclusive offer, available only to our newsletter subscribers. Sign up here to get your FREE copy:
www.arquinworlds.com

Found a typo? This book has been through several rounds of editing and proofing, but still, mistakes happen. Please inform us of any errors you find so that we can fix them for the next edition. email: js@arquinworlds.com

ABOUT THE AUTHOR

J.S. Arquin is an author, audiobook narrator and producer, podcaster, entertainer, and adventurer. He has lived in inspiring and disturbing places all over the world, and currently makes his home in Portland, OR, where he dodges raindrops on his bicycle and sometimes writes about himself in the third person. He has voiced dozens of audiobooks, and his fiction has been featured all over the web. You can catch his ramblings and some breathtaking speculative fiction on his bi-weekly podcast, The Overcast. You can also find him on Twitter @JS_Arquin and online at www.arquinworlds.com.

www.ingramcontent.com/pod-product-compliance
Lightning Source LLC
Chambersburg PA
CBHW050516190726
48284CB00003B/829